Valerie began her literary career by writing pieces for national magazines and newspapers, including some for *Punch* magazine before its close-down.

On the instruction of a Native American Chief named Medicine Crow, who manifested at the foot of her bed, she wrote a book, *The Magician's Daughter, a Modern Mystic's Journey of Discovery*, under the name of Valerie Gordon. This was a journal of her extraordinary supernatural experiences, precognitive dreams and visions. After having some fascinating past life regressions, she took a year's course in hypnotherapy in order to become a Past Life Regressionist herself.

Valerie has also studied astrology and palmistry and is a Reiki practitioner, master and tutor.

For fifteen years, in the shrine village of Walsingham, Valerie made and sold candles from her own shop into which, to her surprise, many a witch wandered. One day, driving by some pilgrims on foot, who were singing psalms and bearing a huge crucifix, she became overcome with fear and had to stop the car to recover. Believing this to be a past life reaction, she wondered if she had been accused of witchcraft in a previous life. A local woman later told her that there used to be a 'hanging' field in Walsingham… Valerie began to research and discovered that in 1645 the Witch Finder General once lived in nearby King's Lynn when he was hunting down witches, which prompted the seeds of *The Prowl of Unrest* to grow in her mind.

Valerie has always enjoyed animals at her home, having owned many dogs and cats, a telepathic horse, a matriarchal goat and a sheep with ambition, though currently she has only four hens, two parrots and four cats. She has two children and two grandchildren and lives near Sandringham in Norfolk with her partner.

To Kent, Lucinda, Leigh, Tatiana and Zachary

Valerie Anckorn

THE PROWL OF UNREST

AUSTIN MACAULEY PUBLISHERS™

LONDON * CAMBRIDGE * NEW YORK * SHARJAH

A CIP catalogue record for this title is available from the British Library.

ISBN 9781528942638 (Paperback)
ISBN 9781528942645 (ePub e-book)

www.austinmacauley.com

First Published 2023
Austin Macauley Publishers Ltd®
1 Canada Square
Canary Wharf
London
E14 5AA

My thanks to Jo Halpin Jones for her
help with the editing.

Table of Contents

Introduction

The Rectory, Wenham Magna, Suffolk, April 1629

Aged nine years, thin as a rake and with lowered britches, Matthew Hopkins was bent over a stool in his father's study. James Hopkins, a Puritan minister of St John's Church in the village, hit a birch switch hard over the boy's backside causing bleeding weals from the harsh treatment. Not a sound of pain left Matthew's clenched lips as he bore his punishment stoically.

While a few logs flickered dispiritedly within a small fireplace that barely heated the sparsely furnished room, a shivering Matthew, in order to limit the pain, concentrated his mind on the sound of the moaning wind as it forced its way through tiny gaps in the leaded lights of the only window, a noise that alternated with spasmodic rushes of rain against the old warped panes. Every now and again puffs of smoke leaked into the room, forced back down the chimney by the gale that brought with it droplets of icy rain, hissing as they hit the sulking flames. Matthew rehearsed the Lord's Prayer over and over inside his head to stop himself from screaming.

The dark-haired lad knew that after his father had finished the beating—a necessary duty to God—he would have to retreat to his cold attic room and stay there without food until morning. As his thoughts strayed, he hoped that when he eventually fell asleep he wouldn't have that terrifying nightmare of the bear again. In so many of his dreams, the huge creature just stood there on its hind legs, looking at him with small ugly eyes, great claws ready to shred him to pieces and huge yellow teeth ready to gobble him up. Matthew's fear was paralysing, waiting for the beast to move forward and attack. Sometimes he woke up and there the bear would be, right beside his bed, and he unable to move—except he was still asleep and dreaming…then, after what seemed like agonising moments, he would wake up properly, sweating and shaking from fear.

Breaking that train of thought, the switch came down yet again and hit his tender skin, hurting so much and bringing him back to reality. Matthew acknowledged his punishment with fortitude, for he meant to be good, he really did, but learning whole pages of the Bible until he was word perfect was something he found really difficult. He didn't think he would ever be very clever but vowed to himself that he would try harder in future, because otherwise, as well as causing his father's wrath yet again, he would be disappointing the good Lord. Religion—in the 'hell and brimstone' manner—had been drummed into the boy from his early days, so he knew what was expected of him and how important it was to serve God with fervour and humility, otherwise Satan would force himself into his mind and he would have to face the burning flames of hell.

The Rectory was a large, chilly and rambling house with pitched gables and a profusion of exterior beams infilled with wattle and daub, a high roof (leaking in places) that bristled with seldom used chimneys that had been appropriated by a mischief of jackdaws that cawed loudly amongst themselves as they nosily viewed the surrounding countryside and anyone visiting the Rectory. When a person entered the house, a waft of musty odour would assail their nostrils, caused by damp earth beneath the paved floors and even damper walls where the plaster was crumbled in places. In wintertime, the freezing breath that billowed from mouths and nostrils would be just as apparent inside the house as it was outside.

The Hopkinses owned lands and tenements near the castle in Framlingham that brought in a fair revenue, but despite his quiet affluence, John Hopkins was a frugal man, believing that gluttony and material indulgence a crime against his Maker. His wife—a pious woman who said little but took her duties seriously—ran the house efficiently with a rod of iron. Nobody was allowed to shirk any household task, for Mistress Hopkins's sharp nose would soon sniff it out. There were no comforts to be had within the house, other than the smoky fire in her husband's study and a cooking fire in the kitchen. Meals were nourishing, but sparse, though knowing her duty, she made sure that scraps of food were always set aside for the poor of the village, who would line up in their rags beyond the hedge and wait for a bucket of waste to be placed by the gate for them. Mistress Hopkins had no particular empathy for the starving wretches, but as the wife of a minister, she knew that she must provide largesse for unfortunates or she would show herself, and therefore her husband, as lacking in Christian charity.

Whilst John Hopkins was tanning his son's buttocks, Mistress Hopkins stood waiting outside the door with her hands clasped neatly together and her mouth in its usual downturned expression of disapproval. While she had little maternal love for any of her children, she took no pleasure from the knowledge that her youngest child was being beaten, but was curiously impassive. As a good Christian, she recognised the boy had sinned, therefore his punishment was necessary. If he was to become a proper servant to God, he must learn the Lord's book from cover to cover, and if he did not, then her husband was right to beat him.

A sour expression passed over her face as she thought back to the unpleasant conception and birthing of her children. With luck, she would never have to go through that abhorrent business ever again. She had produced four children that had survived and had since informed her husband that her duty was done in that respect—therefore, there would be no need for any further unpleasant carnal behaviour. From henceforth, her bedroom door would be locked. God, she further informed her husband, would be in accord with such a decision.

John Hopkins, wont to visit the worst area of the nearby town in order to save fallen women from sin and corruption, continued with his good works in this direction. However, it has never been documented after the emphatic declaration from his spouse curtailing their spasmodic activities of the flesh, whether or not the clergyman pursued, or indeed enjoyed, any of the dubious favours from those that he wished to save from eternal damnation.

Matthew's ordeal was finally over. He straightened up from the stool, his face devoid of colour. Wincing with pain and sniffing a little, he pulled up his britches, and proffered a small bow to his father, saying at the same time, "I am sad to disappoint you, Father, I will try harder with my learning in future."

His father grunted, nodded, his lips turned down in displeasure and his habitual scowl furrowing his brows.

"Then get up to your room, down on your knees and pray for forgiveness." Thus curtly dismissing his son, he returned the switch to its hook on the wall and sank to his own knees to pray while, with as much dignity as a small boy could muster in the circumstances, Matthew said, "Yes Father. Goodnight," and left the room to encounter his waiting mother in the hallway, who gave him a terse scrutiny but no sympathy or words of love as she watched the boy painfully making his way along the narrow and dark hallway leading to the back stairs that ascended to his attic bedroom.

Once he was alone in his room, already forgetting his father's command to pray, Matthew lowered himself gingerly onto his narrow iron bedstead allowing himself a small sob of loneliness and pain as he sank down into the lumpy straw-filled mattress. Pulling a blanket gingerly over his bruised body, hot tears squeezed from his closed eyes while his hand sought out the only comfort he knew, nestled between his legs. Even at that young age, the lad associated pain with pleasure. As Matthew burrowed down into his uncomfortable bed trying to find warmth, he didn't notice a shadow in the corner of the room that looked very much like the shape of a large bear—his totem, or spirit bear-whose work was to endow the boy with its own strengths and endurances, his aim to aid and assist.

**

That troubled and lonely little boy was never to know that his upbringing and subsequent psychological make-up would warp his mind into sadistic cruelty causing atrocious deeds (committed in the cause of his Lord) that would bring to his name infamy and loathing along the centuries. His story would be taught as grim history in the schools of future generations, causing many a gasp of horror from those school children who were diligent enough to pay attention to their tutors.

Chapter One
King's Lynn, June 1629

A dying log slipped into the warm embers of a fire, causing red sparks to fly up the chimney and out into the night air. Under a star-sprinkled sky that covered Tuesday Market Place in the sleeping town of King's Lynn, a lone owl swept downwards from a high tree to scoop up a careless rodent that ran alongside the fleet—a rank open drain at the side of the cobbles. A short distance away, the River Ouse slapped gently against the wooden pilings of the quayside and where, a little yonder, swirls of mist lingered around the high masts of anchored vessels waiting for the morning tide.

Moonlight illuminated a mark scratched above a doorway where, only nine years previously, the heart of a certain Margaret Read had hit the wall as it burst forth from her burning body. Tied to a stake, she had died in agony, accused of witchcraft.

Inside the bedchamber of Anne Brown, mistress of the house, a large wolfhound hung her head over tangled bed sheets to sniff at the screeching twin babies abandoned momentarily on a huge tester bed hung with gloriously rich brocaded curtains thick enough to keep out the keenest of draughts.

The gentle giant licked gently at the scabby heads of the babes, cleaned up their tight fists, and soothed their cries with her large warm tongue as she lapped up snot and tears. The babies' gazes focussed on the hound, and little gummy grins replaced their previous screams. Nosing the boy baby into a position where she could mouth him up by his stinking swaddling bands, she swung him away from the bed and took the sopping child and carefully dumped him onto her heap of blankets near the warm fire. She lumbered back to fetch the girl child and, in similar manner, carefully put her next to her brother. Settling down, the dog gently licked and cleaned, working with her teeth at the tight swaddling until the bands of both children were gnawed through, then she nosed the swaddling boards away, as well as the offending stinking rags. She then proceeded to gently wash the frightful sore bottoms of the babies until they were sparkling clean, then heaving a sigh, she curled her huge body around the tiny pair, to settle down and doze.

The babies, feeling free at last from their tight confines, wriggled happily against the wolfhound's warm and hairy belly, gurgling with delight at the new sensations of freedom, until by chance they came across her teats, still full as her pups were only that day gone to new homes. The twins, almost starved for the past week or so, soon latched on to their new source of sustenance and gorged until they were completely full, then the little mouths unlatched from the hound's bounteous comfort as the babes fell into the first healthy sleep of their existence.

Shrill screams rang out as the chambermaid, come to remake her mistress's bed, discovered the two babes on the floor with the dog.

"Lawks a-mercy, NURSE, NURSE!" she shrieked urgently, dropping the fresh bedding she was carrying. Hiccupping in-between sobs and cries, she scooped it up untidily, glancing over her shoulder in horror at the placid dog as if it were a rabid beast. "NURSE! Come quickly!"

Having heard the raucous noise, an elderly nurse hobbled in as fast as she could from the nearby nursery, then taking in the situation, she began screaming too, both women helpless to their fears. The babes' pale-faced mother, Anne, wearing a crumpled night shift and richly embroidered slippers, limped through the doorway from her dressing room, holding onto furniture to aid her passage, to see what all the fuss was about. She began to laugh weakly at the endearing sight of her babies so peacefully curled up on the floor with the wolfhound, who now began to growl in warning as the horrified nurse approached.

"Leave Juno be, Nurse, she won't harm them," advised Anne.

"But Mistress, it's roight disgustin'," panted the old nurse, clutching her hands together with horror upon her face. "The dog will kill 'em and look, it's taken off their swaddlin' bands and thay tiny bottoms be bare!"

"Yes, I can see that," smiled the weary mother, "but they look a lot more comfortable, don't you think? It's the first time they haven't screamed since they were born. Look at the state of their buttocks—they are red raw! Perhaps it's not such a good idea binding them in such a way where they can't move and are forced to live in their own filth." She chuckled weakly, "It's good those awful screams have ceased. I'm going to take advantage and get some sleep myself." Nodding at the nurse, she continued, "Dear, please sit in the chair by the fire and keep an eye on them. We all need a rest, and if the dog wants to be nurse, let her—but keep watch, just to be sure."

Turning to the chambermaid, who clearly didn't know what to do next, Anne gently asked, "Will you take those stinking swaddling bands to soak and wash them on the morrow please? Leave the clean sheets too and get yourself off to your own bed, otherwise it will be morning before we know it."

Anne climbed carefully into her own newly straightened sheets in the huge and comfortable bed with its rich hangings and settled herself amongst the goose down pillows for some much needed peace and quiet after so many interrupted nights.

Scandalised, Nurse settled into the wooden rocker by the glowing fire, keeping her beady eyes on the huge hound and her small charges, admittedly quiet and peaceful for the first time since their birth nearly three months ago. Their mother, still weak from the birthing ordeal, nibbled at a biscuit laden with honey for her health and made especially for her by Cook, decided that perhaps tomorrow she might feel like removing herself from her bed at last. The thought of bathing and attiring herself in a gown after so long in bed was appealing, especially as her mercer husband, owning his own ships and trading in expensive cloth, would be home soon from overseas, and she must prepare herself and make herself look beautiful for him.

Nurse smiled tightly at her mistress, and cast her scandalised eyes back to the twins, nestled so cosily with the hound, while the warm, flickering flames of the fire cast moving patterns over the stifling, somewhat odorous room.

"Don't worry so, Nurse," said Anne sleepily. "I've heard that children of the poor are often left with dogs to tend them, and it doesn't seem to do them any harm. As we have not yet found a replacement wet-nurse since the death of the woman two weeks since, this might well be the solution to all our problems before the poor waifs starve to death. The dog will guard them with her life, and no-one could be as gentle as her, so stop worrying, do." She turned onto her side, snuggled down into her bedding, and was soon lost in a dreamless, healing sleep.

Tutting, Nurse poked ferociously at the fire then, taking a slice of bread from her mistress's bedside table, slotted it on to the end of a toasting fork and began to toast the bread in front of the flames. The dog, slowly wagging the tip of her long tail just enough to show the nurse she held no grudge, wrapped herself around the babies and tucked her head under her back legs, the twins' noses just peeking above her fur.

"Whatever next?" muttered the nurse, "The mistress must be sufferin' from ill humours of the head." She had to admit to herself, however, that it was wonderful to have the first peaceful moment for an age and what her mistress had said was indeed the truth, so taking the nicely cooked toast off the fork, she slapped some creamy butter over it, then topped it with some mouth-watering strawberry jam. Taking a deep, satisfying crunch, the old lady savoured each delicious mouthful. Wiping the crumbs off her somewhat whiskery chin with the back of her rather grubby sleeve, she then checked furtively that her mistress was indeed asleep, then slid a small flask from her apron pocket and quickly threw the contents to the back of her throat, 'to calm her nerves'.

"But my babes h'aint slum babes and shouldn't be sucklin' orf a flea-bitten cur," she muttered into her drooping chin. Before long though, despite having been told to keep her eye on the babies, she was also in a deep sleep, getting much needed rest since the arrival of the noisy twins. She had nursed her mistress since her birth twenty-eight years ago, and only admitted to herself that she was getting rather too long in the tooth to be looking after one, let alone two new babies. Before long, the room inside the mercer's house was filled with gentle snuffles and snores as its occupants slept the sleep of the exhausted.

***

Nurse jerked awake as the bedroom door creaked open when the scullery maid crept in to relight the fire. The first streaks of dawn were illuminating the chamber through cracks in the shutters while the dawn chorus of birds loudly announced the day. She heard suckling noises and then, remembering the goings on from the night before, looked down with dislike at the wolfhound, whose placid gaze met hers. The twins were gustily feeding, their bare buttocks as clean as a whistle, their little hands kneading at the soft under-fur of the dugs from which they were feeding.

Nurse felt a flush of anger and resentment at the dog, who, sensing the ill sentiment, growled deeply, slowly moving to release the children, who slid onto the blanket. The nurse shrieked, believing the dog was about to attack, but it merely gazed at her with its all-knowing eyes and lumbered off towards the open door. She could hear its nails clicking down the stairs as it headed off to the garden to relieve itself.

Nurse's scream woke Anne, and Nurse grabbed at the bonnet askew on her head, quickly wiped some dribble from her chin while she eased her aching bones off the hardwood rocking chair to see what harm had become her charges. Her back creaked as she bent to lift the boy to place him on the big bed, where his mother was stretching into wakefulness.

Bending forward, Anne sleepily touched her infant son while Nurse was shuffling back to retrieve the girl. "Look at his lovely little legs," she exclaimed to Nurse, "See how he kicks and how he smiles!" The girl was soon beside her brother and the mother smiled to see her small children enjoying life for the first time, unfettered by swaddling boards and bands as they grasped with their tiny fingers at her own. "Nurse, do open the shutters and let in the daylight, and you go and relieve yourself. You can then see to the babes and dress them, after which I'd like you to order the kitchen staff to heat up some water and bring the tub in here. I need to bathe."

"What?" snapped nurse after assimilating the requests, "you certainly don't need to bathe—bad humours will attack you so soon after childbirth—you will catch a chill and then what will happen?" However, by necessity, she shuffled off to the other room where she could be heard loudly relieving herself into the night bucket with much farting and coughing. On her reappearance, she opened the door to the stairs and yelled down for the tub to be brought up and water to fill it.

Anne Brown felt the first salivary stirrings in her mouth as the smell of kidneys and bacon wafted up from the kitchens below, accompanied by the clattering of pans as breakfast was being prepared. Today, she thought, licking her lips in anticipation, was going to be a good one, her appetite seemed to be returning, and soon her dear husband would be home to see his children for the first time. She must be up and ready for him.

Once returned to the room, Nurse held back the bedding so that her mistress could clamber from the bed in order to also relieve herself, and once the mistress was safely in the antechamber, Nurse, with much moaning and groaning from her aches and pains and locked limbs, bent over to retrieve the swaddling boards from the floor and placed them on the bed near to the kicking and gurgling twins. Her long linen skirts swished along the boarded floor, gathering dog hairs as she tottered over to a chest to take out more bands, and then grumbled her way back to see to her charges.

First she placed the boy on to a board, then pulled his waving arms across his body, crossing them at the wrists and began to tightly bind them. Everybody knew that swaddling bands kept children's backs and limbs straight and true, and no harm ever came from them being left in their own dung. The babe was soon roaring angrily as his newfound freedom was so soon restricted. Once the final band was tied into place and the child bound to the board like a trussed pig, the nurse set him aside and began on the girl, who soon joined her brother in outraged screaming. Both babies were red in the face, their shrill outbursts of anger filling the room.

"Oh no!" exclaimed Anne wearily as she came back into the chamber. "I can't believe that noise. Oh, you've bound them again—well, maybe you ought, but they seemed so happy. You must get them fed properly soon—what are they having?"

"Well," replied nurse holding her hands to her aching back as she slowly eased herself upright, "since that wet-nurse went and died, oi've been givin' them goat's milk, Mistress—Oi've been dippin' a rag into the milk but the children didn't like that one bit and barely a drop went down—though it 'as to be said, for all I know, they have been suckin' away at that darn dog all night and they do look roight filled up."

Anne stared thoughtfully into the old Nurse's rheumy eyes. "Well, surely there's not a lot of difference between goat milk and dog milk, is there, Nurse?"

Nurse humphed and said, "Dog milk hain't pertinent to mercer infants' station in life, Mistress. T'won't do a'tall."

The high indignant wails from the babies grew to a crescendo, so further talk was impossible. The door then crashed open and Juno—almost as large as a donkey—purposefully trotted back into the room heading towards the tester bed where the babies were yelling shrilly. Growling a warning at Nurse, who shrank against the wall, the dog immediately grabbed hold of the nearest baby and took him back to her blankets, then went back to get the other. Nurse ineffectively flapped her apron at the dog, who retaliated with low throaty rumbles, while Anne lay back upon her pillows, with an amused smile upon her face. She knew the hound would not harm her children, and was interested to see what would happen next.

"Nurse, don't worry. You can see Juno is not going to hurt the children. Maybe this is fate—she needs to nurture babies now her own have gone—and you are finding things difficult at the moment—no, don't glare at me, I have noticed how your bones are hurting—just wait and see what the dog does next."

"It's all well and good Mistress, but tain't natural. Look at the size of them teeth. And before we know it, Jupiter'll be up here too and all hell'll be let loose. What if he eats them up for his breakfast then? It's disgustin' it is. Roight disgustin'. And, what will Master say?"

Jupiter must have heard his name, or maybe it was all the noise, for the door was nosed open and an even larger wolfhound ambled into the room to see what all the noise was about. Juno growled a warning to him, so he stopped in his tracks to see what his dam was up to.

By now, the bitch had gnawed away the bands, as she had the night before, and the babies' limbs were once more free and kicking. The shrill cries of the babies had changed to gentle coos and as their gaze focussed on the second dog, standing huge in front of them, smiles lit their little faces. Jupiter moved to the side of his mate, gently sniffing in the baby aromas to his satisfaction, then he lowered himself into on-guard position in front of the small babies. Nurse promptly fainted onto the floor and the chambermaid had to flap her apron to try and revive her. She screamed for Clem, the odd job man, who raced up the stairs to see what was happening, until the bedroom seemed filled with people, large dogs and frantic commotion. He lifted Nurse into her chair, while the chambermaid loosened the buttons at the old lady's neck and shouted, "Burn some feathers! Burn some feathers!" Bemused, Clem scratched his head, then noticing the two dogs, one guarding, the other nurturing the precious twins, said to nobody in particular, "Well, Oi'll be buggered!"

"Thank you Clem," Anne said to her servant, "that will be all. Just bring up the tub now and fill it with water. I need to bathe. The children are fine, but I don't want a word of the matter mentioned outside the house. This situation might be unorthodox, but it has happened, and before this the babies were unhappy, screaming and starving, and now they are replete and comfortable. Nurse has had a shock, but she will get used to the situation, even if she dislikes it. Please go now and attend to my bath."

Clem left, scratching at his sparse hair all the way down the stairs, and entered the kitchen where steam was hissing from a welter of pots with clattering lids hot on the stoves. He tugged out the wooden tub and hoisted it up the stairs, while cook and the chamber and scullery maids bustled up and down, filling the tub for their mistress to bathe, until serenity reigned once more.

Now recovered and muttering to herself, Nurse ignored the dogs and babies on the floor, and took out some clothing for her mistress to wear and lovingly placed them on the bed. She stroked the fine materials and felt pleasure from just touching them.

"Fetch me some lavender oils, Nurse dear, and pour a few drops in the water. Oh, and bring a tablet of the lavender and rosemary soap that I made." Nurse bustled doing as her mistress wished. "That's lovely, thank you," smiled Anne at the old lady, knowing how much she was fretting about the babies. "Don't worry, Nurse. The matter will soon be resolved. The children are safe, they are happy—look at how they are bouncing around waving their dear little arms and legs—our problem is solved for the time being, and we will soon get back to how things should be." As she relaxed in the sweet smelling water, Anne directed a thought to Nurse, "Maybe I could hold the twins in the bath waters for a little while, they might like that?"

"What?" spluttered the nurse, outraged. "Certainly not, mistress. It's bad enough with that beastly great 'ound lickin' their backsides, but to immerse them in the bathwater? It'ood kill 'em!"

Anne, feeling weary from all the to-do and mayhem, as well as all the sleepless nights, and still feeling somewhat poorly, felt that one battle had already been won with her erstwhile nurse, so perhaps it was better not to push the poor woman over the brink. She thought that perhaps later on she might try the babes in an oil scented bath—surely it would do them no harm?…but that would be for another day. She smiled to herself. Bathing was supposed by some to be harmful, and if that were so, why did it feel so delicious?

Muttering to herself, Nurse shuffled off to tidy the nursery and left her mistress to what she believed was a sinful exercise. But she loved her darling mistress and couldn't be annoyed with her for long.

"Nurse, before you go downstairs, please open the window, it's so stuffy in here—I want to smell the summer breezes on the air."

"Certainly not!" snapped the outraged woman, "That's going too far! All of you will be overcome with bad humours and your chest will suffer and the babes will undoubtedly die. Beggin' your pardon, Mistress, but 'ave you gone wrong in the 'ead?"

Anne sighed and slid down in the waters to rub lavender soap onto her body. She washed her greasy hair, to the scandalised looks from Nurse who was slapping things down angrily, hither and thither. After a deliciously long soak and wash, Anne rose from the tub waters feeling refreshed and ready to meet the world. She had gone through much bearing the twins and her body had taken a long time to recover, but she no longer wished to vegetate in a stifling chamber when the sunshine beckoned outside. Glancing over at her babies with a tender smile, she donned her clothing with some help from Nurse, who had already called the maid to tend to her hair. The twins were sound asleep tucked up on Juno's tummy, while the eyes of the two dogs registered everything that was going on in the room, following every movement of both Anne and Nurse—Juno rumbling a warning if Nurse approached too closely.

"Nurse," pronounced Anne, "if Juno is going to look after the babes for the time being, she must have some clean blankets—and make sure she is given raw garlic again to keep her clear of parasites—we don't want them passed on to the babies—oh, I think they need some upper garments now they are not bound, and as I don't know about the properties of dog milk for human babies, I think I would like to see Goodwife Truman—she will probably know if we are doing the right thing—and get someone to sweep up all the dog hairs—the room is awash with them." Anne mused that while she had been languishing in her bed her retainers had become somewhat slack with their duties. Things would have to change!

Nurse, with a face as black as thunder, hobbled off to find someone to deal with all the tasks her mistress was demanding. "No good will come of this," she muttered under her breath, "and what's to become of me, I ask myself, if those wretched dogs are going to take over the runnin' of the 'ouse?"

By the time Anne was dressed in her finery—as a mercer's wife, she had the duty to wear only the best—she noted that the clattering from the hall indicated that breakfast was being put out on the table. Descending the stairs with care, she called back to Nurse, "Do keep your eyes on my babes dear, and let me know at once if anything is amiss. We'll sort the matter out as quickly as can be Nurse, but now I need to get myself into shape, make sure the house is running smoothly for the Master's return, and then we will decide what is to be done about the babes." She heard the "Hmph!" of disgust even from the bottom of the stairs.

As the table had been laid in the hall, Anne sat herself down at the long table, noticing dust everywhere. "Hmmm," she said to herself, running her fingers along the unpolished table, "I've been abed far too long." The food delivered on her platter was delicious and was the first meal that she had enjoyed since the twins had been born. Tucking into kidneys, bacon, chops and eggs and relishing some good bread and butter, she washed the lot down with some small beer. Feeling gastronomically satisfied, Anne mused for a short while making plans and decisions, then rose, taking herself off to the kitchen where her smiling retainers, pleased to see their mistress back on her feet, all dropped her a curtsy, and according to rank stepped back, some twisting their aprons in apprehension, leaving the housekeeper in her position at the fore.

"Now," said Anne smiling gently, "the house seems to have got into some disarray since I have been abed. My indispositions should not have made any difference to the smooth running of the house and I am sad that my absence has caused such a slackness." The housekeeper sniffed, though held her head high, despite her embarrassment.

Anne continued. "My husband will be returning any day now, and what is he going to think if he is confronted with all the dust and untidiness? I want everything swept and polished—the tapestries to be taken outside and beaten, as should be the mats. I want all the old rushes removed from the floor and replaced with fresh ones that I wish strewn with herbs. Oh, and there should be flowers on the table, windows open and fresh air let in."

Anne looked around at the women, all of whom looked suitably chastened. "As to the babies," she continued, "you will all know by now that the unusual situation has occurred with Juno taking over the nursing. This must not be spoken of outside the house, do you understand?" Her servants nodded as she looked at each of them in turn. "I know it is not seemly, but at the moment the hound is keeping the children alive and that is all that matters—but it is not circumspect that others know of the matter. My husband has his position to keep, and our reputation will slide if it is known that his children are sleeping on the floorboards attended to by a dog."

With a small smile Anne nodded and, placing her shawl more firmly around her shoulders, informed her servants, "I'm now going out to get some fresh air in my lungs, enjoy a little sunshine and wander around the herb garden while I wait for Goody Truman to call."

The servants dipped their curtsies to their mistress and guiltily scurried off to their various tasks, knowing they were lucky to have such a gentle lady in charge and not be instantly dismissed without reference.

***

Stepping out into the sunshine at the rear of her home Anne felt like a new woman. As her skirts brushed against a lavender bush, the sweet perfume rose and assailed her senses. Sitting down on a bench in her herb garden, she watched the bees buzzing as they journeyed from flower to flower. Yonder in the yard a cock was crowing from the midden heap that steamed mistily in the sunshine and where she could see happily clucking hens scratching for worms, their colourful feathers gleaming. As she gazed further, she noticed that tethered to a gnarled apple tree was a nanny goat with bulging teats. The goat stared at her with its strange devil eyes and bleated a greeting. "Maybe," mused Anne, "it would be sensible to let the dog have her milk yield—it would do Juno good, and thus the babies."

From the front of the house that faced the town, she could hear the bustle and stir of the market as business was already taking place—the cries of the vendors were already evident; their whistles and laughter; the grating of wheels from handcarts on cobbles, the clink of horses' hoofs. The rumble of drays, the soft neighs and whinnies of greeting, the lowing of cows being herded to their pens, the bleating of sheep and goats and the shriller tones of the kids and lambs. All this Anne heard, as well as the shouting of farmers, the shrill calls of the women—all the usual busy sounds as the town and its market were astir and grinding into action. She smiled as she settled back and stretched her legs, enjoying the sunshine.

Anne basked in the morning sun for a while, letting the sun soak into her pallid skin. It seemed such a long time since she had breathed in the smell of fresh air and felt the elements upon her face. She knew that she had diced with death when bearing the twins and although she still felt poorly, she did feel so much better than before, ready now to face her responsibilities again. She knew she must find another wet-nurse—the last one had died alarmingly of cholera, luckily an isolated case, for the disease had claimed nobody else in the household.

Rising to her feet, Anne broke off a few stems of lavender and rosemary, releasing their pungent aromas, then also plucked some fat roses and sweet smelling honeysuckle and meandered back into the house to find a vase in which to place her posy. Her retainers were now busy with dusters, brooms and buckets and she was pleased to see such a hive of industry, getting the house to rights. After placing her vase of flowers on the central table, she took herself into her day room to await Goody Truman, and didn't have long to wait.

Hearing the rat-a-tat-tat of the knocker on the front door—a heavily carved oak structure with large iron hinges—she decided to open the door herself, and it was indeed Goody Truman standing at the portal with a kind smile on her face. She was a thin individual, wearing a plain linen gown, with her grey hair scragged back into a bun, a few escaped wispy tendrils falling loose. Her nose was quite sharp and she had a rather evident facial mole that sprouted a few hairs on her chin. Anne greeted her with an answering smile.

"Do come in Goody Truman," said Anne, holding out her hand to aid the woman over the portal, "Thank you so much for answering my call of distress. I am in need of your advice. Let us withdraw to my day room—I've asked Cook to bring in some of her famous honey biscuits. Do please follow me." She liked the herby aroma that emanated from the woman, hints of lavender, thyme, fennel and ginger.

Goody Truman noted the deep red sarcenet gown that Mistress Brown wore, with a high lace collar covering her neck almost down to her bosom. Her sleeves were copious and very fully puffed and tied with furbelows. Her long high-waisted skirt rustled as she walked, flowing gracefully behind her. Goody Truman was aware that, despite the political unrest, Anne and her husband had remained loyal to the King, but while still they dressed quite colourfully, were circumspect enough to tone their style to more sombre proportions than previously, in order not to inflame Puritan sensibilities. Oliver Cromwell had many fierce followers who shunned what they considered to be frivolous attire. It was difficult to find the balance.

Anne gestured to a chair for Goody Truman, and they both sat down together. Goody Truman glanced quickly around the room, taking in the rich hangings and carved furniture, mentally assessing the value and wryly comparing it to her own small and sparsely furnished abode.

"Now, Goody Truman, I'm sure you realise I've asked you to visit for a very good reason." The old lady nodded her head. "I've got a dilemma because the wet-nurse hired to feed my two babes died and the children have been starving ever since. Nurse has done her best with goat's milk and rags, but it hasn't been effective, and apart from that the children haven't stopped screaming since their birth…That is, apart from…"

"Apart from what, my lady?" Goody Truman leaned questioningly forward in the seat.

With hesitation, Anne began. "Well, this is difficult to tell you, but the dog—er—decided to take over, dragged the children to her bed on the floor, nibbled off all the swaddling bands, wouldn't let anyone near her or the babes, and then they began suckling from her! They haven't cried since, apart from when Nurse rescued them when the dog went outside for a while. Nurse disapproved greatly and swaddled them again. As soon as the hound re-entered the room, she dragged the babes back to her blankets, bit off the bindings again—and peace has ensued ever since! I feel that perhaps the babies are happier without swaddling bands, but I don't think their place is on the floor with the dog—but, they seem happy. I just don't know what the correct thing is to do. What would you advise?"

Goody Truman chewed on her gums for a while, and said, "The babbies seem happy, you say?"

"Oh yes," replied Anne without hesitation, "they are even smiling, and kicking their little legs happily. If it wasn't for my station in life and my husband coming home soon, I would carry on, just for the peace and quiet—but it just isn't a seemly situation."

"Maybe not, milady," replied Goody Truman earnestly in her broad Norfolk accent, "but I suggest for the moment you let it continue. Animals are very wise and gentle you know, and the dog has the welfare of your babbies at heart. What I think is best is that we continue looking for a wet-nurse—I have in mind a nice healthy young lady who could do with the coins; and yes—keep the babbies out of swaddling—I think they know their own minds on that score. Make sure the dogs get to trust the new wet-nurse, and then allow the dog to continue to interact with the children—it'll do no harm—stranger bonds have been forged you know. Maybe the dog feels Nurse isn't quite competent?"

"Well, I'm not so sure the dog's mind is that keen, Goody, but Nurse is getting old, and I have noticed that she is finding it difficult to walk properly and to hold the babies—her hands are knotted, and her joints so stiff she must be in pain. I know she is terrified that I will throw her out without a penny as if I would! Oh," she added, "if you please, I am sure you realise that this situation is to go no further than this room."

Goody Truman smiled gently and patted Anne's knee with her gnarled hand while nodding her head. "Of course, you can trust me milady. My suggestion is that you put Nurse into a supervisory role. You can maybe give her a new title, and find a younger girl to take on the more physical tasks. Just let nature take its course and let the dog be nanny for a while longer. I'll see about the wet-nurse—

the dog's milk will tide the babbies over for the while and do them no harm. You've given it garlic I presume?" Anne nodded. "And don't worry about what your husband thinks—he is a good man and will know that whatever you feel best *will* be for the best." Goody looked Anne over with shrewd eyes. "I'm going to send along a tonic for you, my girl. You are looking peaky still, and you need something to fortify you. I'd like to see the babbies though, to make sure about them, if that's alright with you?"

"Of course, Goody," Anne smiled, rising carefully from her chair. "Follow me—it's easier for you to go up to my chamber than bring them both down. Nurse is very wobbly on her feet and will insist on carrying them herself and I don't want her struggling down the stairs with them."

Goody Truman followed Anne through the house and up to her chambers where the twins were still kicking in front of the fire and gurgling happily with Juno. Nurse sat rigid, glowering and coughing from her chair, irate that the local wise woman had been brought into her domain, as if she wasn't good enough. At first sight of the babies, Goody Truman clasped her hands together and said with a broad smile on her face, "Ah, what a wonderful sight—what bonny babbies!" Juno thumped her tail on the floor as Goody Truman approached while Jupiter, ever on guard, stood up, stretched, wagged his tail lazily and strolled over to sniff, approve and lick the hands of the wise woman.

Goody gazed at the two infants, but her gaze settled on the little girl, who was staring up at her from the nest on the floor. "Gracious!" Goody uttered, almost to herself. "That's an old soul—look at her eyes!" Turning to Anne, she said, "She do have The Sight you know, I can tell. She's goin' to be special and her life is not going to be like others. If it's alright with you, milady, I'd like to keep an eye on that little'un as she grows." As the old woman tickled the girl's stomach, the tiny infant hiccupped and grinned, which set the boy, busy kicking, into gummy grins as well. The little girl's gaze once more locked on that of the old lady, who realised the acknowledgement of kindred souls was taking place. A picture of faraway places passed momentarily in front of her mind and knew this child had a destiny of travel, excitement and danger ahead.

"They's two happy healthy babbies, mistress, carry on as you are at the moment, and I will send you that girl round as I told you an' all will be well."

Anne wasn't sure what to think of Goody Truman's pronouncement about one of her children having The Sight, but was relieved to have the advice of the old lady and to know that a decent wet-nurse would soon be coming to take over.

Anne led the old lady downstairs and bid her farewell at the doorstep, Goody Truman promising to liaise and send over the new wet-nurse as soon as possible. The wise woman bade her farewells and hobbled out of the door and through the throng in the market, pondering on the aura and knowing eyes of the girl child. Goody knew now who she would be passing onto all her Knowledge and skills, and she looked forward to guiding the child into the old ways as soon as she could. The child was the daughter of a rich merchant but nevertheless, she would one day be a wise woman herself.

Feeling better now that she had spoken to Goody Truman, Anne sallied forth to check on the progress the maids were making at cleaning the house. She didn't know which day her husband would be returning, but she calculated roughly that it wouldn't be long if he had good headwinds. She had sent Clem off to the docks to see if he could find out when her Peter would be returning—there might be some news—and went to the foot of the stairs to listen for any sounds of the babies.

By now, the upstairs room sounded deathly quiet, so Anne took herself carefully up the stairs, avoiding the creaky steps, and peeked around the bedchamber door. Juno was stretched out on clean blankets with the children fast asleep at her side. Nurse was also asleep in her chair, her mouth wide open, emitting snorts. Anne realised that the old lady really did need a replacement. She also knew that she would have to be careful in the approach she took to change the old lady's duties.

A floorboard creaking as Anne entered the room jerked Nurse awake, who immediately tried to show she hadn't been sleeping at all. Anne smiled and said, "Don't worry Nurse—look, the children are fine." As Nurse straightened her apron and cap, Anne looked kindly at her and sat down on a stool so as not to intimidate the old lady. "I have been talking to Goody Truman, who knows a young girl in milk who she is sure will come and feed the children. She says that at the moment, if the babes are fine with Juno, leave them for the time being, and once the young girl comes, she can feed the twins, and then we will take it from there."

Nurse 'humphed' and muttered, "Ta'int roight," but Anne continued, "You know how dear you are to me, Nurse, and I want you to live with us always, but I do feel that these two small babes are too much for you."

"O'im foine, O'im foine mistress," spluttered the nurse, looking frightened.

"No, dear, please don't fret—I'm not sending you away. You will stay here and be in a supervisory position. I'm going to get another young girl in to help you with all the heavy and hard work, and you will train her, telling her the right way to go about things, which is an important role for you to undertake. In the meantime, you have earned your place by the fire when your bones are aching, and you can still watch the babes grow up, without all the worry."

Nurse poked at some stray wisps of hair and shoved them back under her cap and, while still muttering and saying that she didn't need help, secretly she was relieved on both scores—that she wouldn't have so much responsibility and that she would not be losing her home. It was good to think that she would have an important role, while life would be much easier for her. Cogitating, Nurse decided she was very pleased with the idea, and thanked her mistress.

For the next week, the babies thrived in the care of the gentle dog, the house became clean and sparkling once more and Anne felt stronger each day. The new wet-nurse arrived, bringing her own little boy who was nearly two years old and delighted everyone with his large smiles and clear blue eyes, and who seemed to adore the two babies, giving them big fat wet kisses and guarding them almost as keenly as did both Juno and Jupiter.

***

One day, not long afterwards, when Anne was upstairs in her room, there was a sudden commotion from down below and Anne thought she heard her husband's voice. Leaping to her feet, she had no sooner got to the door than her dear Peter, who had leapt up the stairs two at a time, was there in front of her—his face tanned, his eyes looking bluer than ever, and a huge smile on his face. Throwing herself into his arms, she revelled at his touch. Swinging her around, he drew her into the room, where Nurse made a shuffling retreat with a smile on her face and disappeared into her own room. Peter picked Anne up and after giving her a good kiss, asked where his baby was.

Anne, looking shamefaced, gestured with her head, and Peter followed her gaze to see the sleeping twins, all curled up and peaceful alongside Juno's belly. Anne clutched her hands together in anguish. She didn't know how her husband would react, but to her relief, he just barked with laughter and strode, leaving a faint trail of ozone, to Juno's blanket. Juno, by now was wide-awake and madly thumping her tail on the floor, glad to see her master home again. As she rose to greet Peter properly, the babes woke, tumbling off the dog's warmth with loud yells as soon as they felt her absence. They started to kick their legs and wave their arms, but soon stopped screaming when they saw the face of someone new smiling down at them.

"Good Lord!" exclaimed Peter with a grin, "Romulus and Remus eh! Twins, my good wife, how did you manage that?"

Feeling somewhat coy, Anne smiled shyly, "With difficulty Sire, I am afraid—all our lives hung in the balance for a while, but we are well now, thanks to Juno."

Peter bent down and carefully picked up the boy, saying, "Up you come Romi" and then bent down again to pick up 'Remi'. Laughing, he saw the puzzlement on his wife's face—"Romulus and Remus, sweetheart, Legends— twins brought up and suckled by a wolf and who are said to have founded the Roman Empire. Don't worry, it's been done before and perfectly acceptable!" As an afterthought he added, "And who knows, perhaps this pair will found our personal empire for us too!"

Juno was happy for her master to pick up her charges, and stood before him, wagging her long tail, while he inspected his offspring. The babies' sore bottoms were almost healed, both had already put on some weight and were a very handsome pair. Peter's heart swelled with fatherly love and pride.

Settling down together, Anne told her spouse the complete saga of the twins' birth and consequent difficulties, finishing off with how Goody Truman had thought allowing the dog to nurse the twins was the best way forward, and it had all worked out well, for she had found a wet-nurse for them as promised, but the babes would not settle unless they were in close proximity to the hounds.

After more examinations and cuddling of the babies for a while, Peter returned them to soft cushions and the tender devotions of Juno, with Jupiter at her side.

It was now Anne's time to listen to an account of her husband's adventures and how he had returned with an excellent ship's cargo that would make them extremely wealthy when sold. They had much to catch up with each other.

***

Over the next few months the babes, now known as Romi and Remi, though their Christian names had been decided upon as Barnaby and Blythe, grew sturdy and strong. The young wet-nurse was a sensible, smiling woman, bouncing with health and vitality. Juno was quite happy to let the new girl feed and clothe her charges, but as the babies were really only content when curled up with the dog, they spent most of their time with her. Anne and Peter saw no harm in the arrangement and enjoyed the peace and quiet that now reigned. They believed the children would grow out of the habit once they began crawling.

Nurse was pleased to rock in a chair by the kitchen fire, occasionally yelling out orders to the maid and the wet-nurse. They realised that she was only justifying her, by now, easy life and took it all in good grace. As it was, Nurse was not nearly so grumbling as before, so with both her and the twins content, the atmosphere in the house was calm and happy.

Chapter Two

As the children grew, Peter instructed Clem to make a dog cart that could be harnessed to either of the wolfhounds, in which the children could be transported around. As soon as this was accomplished, much giggling and smiling was to be had once the young children were tucked up inside it. The harnessed dog ambled around the garden with them bouncing up and down in their chariot. It wasn't long before they were big enough to be taken out into the market with one of the maids hanging on to the dog's collar, while the twins chortled and grinned at all the vendors in the market while purchases were being made. Smiles were always directed towards the two children who were becoming so bonny and always laughing happily. Gone were the screams now, unless Juno or Jupiter was away from them for any length of time.

The attractive little twins being conveyed in the dog cart was soon a common occurrence in the marketplace and around Lynn—whenever there was an errand to be run, the cart was hitched to one of the wolfhounds, and the babies tucked up inside it. Jupiter, being the strongest, usually pulled the cart, but Juno would always trot alongside to make sure her charges were safe. It wasn't long before the cart was taken down to the quay by one of the maids keen to catch the eyes of a handsome sailor, and the twins seemed to love the sight of water. They looked high into the masts of the tall ships, and adored all the bustle that went on along the docks, with boats being unloaded, barrels being hoisted onto men's shoulders and taken into warehouses; they loved to watch the sheep that were herded by barking dogs onto wherries taking them on to their destinations; they enjoyed seeing ships being caulked, sails mended—lots of nautical noise and action, which kept the twins quiet and contented and gave the maid a lot of scope to flirt to her heart's content.

The children didn't seem to mind the stench of the fish quays, and were fascinated to watch the nets unleashing their slippery captives that were soon boxed and stacked or scaled and degutted by stinking women who constantly quipped at the sailors and fishermen and cackled between themselves. They would smile and wave at the twins who would return the waves with chortles and giggles. Anne was quite happy that the twins' attention was taken up by going out and about in such a somewhat unorthodox manner. The children were inquisitive and alert, and the more their active minds were filled and stimulated, the happier they seemed to be.

***

Remi and Romi soon learned to crawl—being on the floor so often with Juno and Jupiter gave them an edge that other children did not have. They pulled themselves up by hanging onto Juno's long hair, and as she walked slowly along, so did they. Consequently, they were walking far sooner than most children of their age. They were getting more than attractive too. Both had black hair that was fast growing and very thick. Their large intelligent eyes were bright blue and twinkled with curiosity. "That girl has an old soul," said Goody Truman to herself for the umpteenth time when she saw them out and tickled them under their chins. The shoulders of both twins were square and their legs seemed long and straight. Anne was relieved to notice that the lack of swaddling boards did not seem to have made their limbs bow in any way, despite the old nurse's misgivings. How beautiful her babies were, thought Anne, as she gave them both a hug.

Like most wealthy mothers, Anne did not spend a lot of time with her children. So long as they were healthy and cared for, she was content that they were looked after by the maids, and Peter rather liked the idea of his small children being drawn around the town in their dog cart by the large hound—they were fast becoming little celebrities in their own way. He was very busy with his business and Anne was equally occupied making sure the house ran smoothly, as well as entertaining the wives of Peter's business acquaintances, organising supper parties and generally helping her husband rise through the ranks as a wealthy up and coming merchant.

Before long, Romi and Remi were walking, darting everywhere around the house and garden, full of mischief and energy and it really would have been a full time job if someone were to look after them all the time.

Sometimes the twins used to slip out of the door on their own, into the marketplace, always with Juno or Jupiter accompanying them—which perhaps made those in charge of them somewhat lax, as they knew they would be safe with the great hounds protecting them.

At first, the children only explored the territory near to their house, which, of course, was the Tuesday Market Place. The traders got used to them passing by and would shout out greetings, to be met by broad grins from the children. Nobody could tell them apart at this stage, as they both still wore the long gowns of childhood, except that Remi had a small dark mole above her mouth, which her mother called her 'beauty spot'. Their limbs were sturdy and strong, and they seldom walked anywhere, but rushed from pillar to post. Juno usually pulled them towards the slaughterhouses at the Shambles that ran with blood from the meat that was being quartered by the various butchers. Huge carcasses hung from large iron hooks where burly men heaved them around with ease. Flies buzzed everywhere in abundance, laying eggs on the choicest pieces and the inevitable maggots humped their way across what was their succulent meals. There was always a bone flung towards Juno and Jupiter from one of the grinning butchers—the dogs snatched the bones in their soft mouths and carried them home to gnaw.

The twins loved to watch all the bustle of the market, as farmers and their wives came from the nearby countryside with poultry, eggs, vegetables, fruit and milk. Sometimes cattle, sheep, goats and pigs were brought into the market, mostly having been herded along the muddy droves by ruddy faced men who looked dirty and unkempt, having slept in hedges along the way. Once the animals in his care had been penned, the first thing any drover would do was to go to the inn and quaff his fill of ale, and then gnaw greedily on a pork pie. The twins liked to climb onto the bars of the pens and lean down to scratch the backs of any animal whose curiosity was as great as theirs, and who ambled over to see them. The pigs especially liked to have their backs scratched with a stick, and the children usually found one on the ground amongst all the other rubbish, and enjoyed seeing the pig's eyes close in contentment as they scratched at *just* the right spot. The twins were completely inured to the stench of the place.

The local miller had a stall, run by his daughter, with sacks of ground corn for sale as well as deliciously smelling loaves still warm to the touch, baked in the large faggot oven in his bakery attached to the mill.

There was a basket maker, who sat on an upturned barrel, deftly weaving baskets while he kept an eye on the finished ones stacked up for sale. There was a leather maker, with skins from the tannery from which he cut strips for belts and made them while the children watched, and there was also a shoemaker with his iron shapes, skilfully cutting, shaping and hammering shoes. There was a man who whittled clogs and pattens essential for slipping over the shoes of the grand folk when stepping out into the mucky streets. The finished clogs hung on strings from a pole. He had fashioned the twins their own little raised clogs to wear that kept their feet out of all the filth on the ground. The twins loved these, especially as they clattered as they ran.

There was the man who made birch brooms, a barrel maker and then there were the small dark-skinned Fen men who lived amongst the reeds and water, who said little, but fingered the knives in their belts as they sold the seething eels they had caught and kept in high baskets that were made watertight with a mixture of moss and mud.

Hens clucked in wicker cages, live rabbits were crammed into baskets, while skinned rabbits, caught in snares, hung on strings ready for the pot—everything that was needed by housewives and farmers was gathered in the Tuesday Market Place and all the smells and noise were extraordinary. The twins enjoyed their rounds of the stalls and would often stand and watch the crafts people to see how the work was accomplished. More often than not, they were allowed to have a go, their charms being such that they were liked and encouraged wherever they went. Without anyone realising it, they were learning skills, simply by the enjoyment of watching and assimilating.

By the time the twins were five, nobody in their home worried about them at all, and didn't expect them home until the time they returned. Their excursions, more often than not, took them down to the docks where they spent hours watching what went on—the loading and unloading of boats and ships. They spoke to anyone who would give them the time of day, learning, observing, and, when they could, getting some action on the water. There was always someone rowing in a small boat or pinnacle and it wasn't long before their charms had won over a hardened heart who allowed them a chance to try their hands at rowing.

Foreign sailors with dark skins and earrings smiled at the children with teeth that looked whiter than normal because of the colour of their skin and jabbered in strange languages, patted them on their heads and sometimes gave them a small gift, like an animal carved in wood, whittled by themselves in spare moments. They also picked up on the kind of bad language they knew would not be appreciated at home, but between themselves they ripely cussed and swore, exploding into gales of laughter, the coarser they became.

The only place the twins had been instructed not to explore was a dark narrow alleyway running down to the docks where the hovels met across the walkways, leaving the area below dark and dank and where the lowest of dives that sold alcohol were located. All the foreign sailors gravitated to this area as soon as their ships docked and their labours at unloading had been accomplished. Pockets filled with their pay, the sailors were soon rolling drunk at the dirty drinking stalls.

Low life women plied their only commodity there, lifting their skirts against grimy walls, their feet squishing amongst filth and rat-infested ordure whilst grunting tars spent themselves quickly, often slumped down into the mire in a drunken stupor. The previously simpering women quickly rifled through their pockets, divesting their clients of the whole of their wage rolls and tucked it safely into a special pocket in their tatty skirts, then strolled off with swaying hips to find another man sunk low enough in his cups to find them attractive.

Needless to say, Barnaby and Blythe did explore the mucky alley, pushing their way past such coupling creatures without blinking an eyelid, peeping through the windows of the lowly ale houses and scouring the manure-ridden ground for dropped coins. Occasionally they did find some. Sometimes they would stop and watch a fight between sailors, noting how they all seemed to keep a dagger in their boots or belts, which were whipped out as soon as a brawl began. Blood would flow, yellow teeth would snarl, and crowds of rough men would encircle the fighting couple, encouraging their favourite until a victor was proclaimed.

Sometimes a man would not rise at all, and be left dead and bloody on the ground, whereupon the landlord, after having made sure the pockets were emptied, would send his minions to throw the body into the filthy water of the docks where it would soon be crushed by jostling ships and carried off with the tides. The twins soon realised, however, that in the main, sailors were not a dangerous bunch unless they were in their cups, so made the decision that it was probably a good idea to leave that area alone when the ships were newly in harbour, and when too many hot-headed drunks were blundering around.

Only the fact that the wolfhounds always accompanied the children kept them safe—they would growl at any sailors about to take a kick at their charges, but by making excursions into sleazy areas at least made the children 'streetwise' and they acknowledged to each other how privileged they were, living in such a nice home, whereas many thin, white-faced children lived in crowded and horrible conditions around the dock areas. They also realised that while Juno and Jupiter kept them safe, the dogs could easily be knifed to death by an angry sailor, and so learned at a young age the art of responsibility towards the silent creatures who guarded them so well.

Both children yearned to have a dagger down their respective boots, so badgered their father to let them have one each. "For," said Barnaby a little pompously to his papa, "We have a duty to look after Juno and Jupiter, and maybe we should carry a knife in case of attack."

Peter smiled at his unruly children and thought it was a good idea. Life was tough, the town abounded with rough sorts, and while he didn't think the dogs' welfare was his children's main objective in carrying a knife each, he liked the fact that they thought of danger to those other than themselves. He was so used to seeing Blythe dressed as a lad that he didn't think it odd that he was supplying a daughter with weaponry. It would be a good idea that they both carried a knife, he reasoned, for there were plenty of occasions where a weapon came in handy, other than in defence. Therefore, the twins were soon the proud owners of small sharp knives that they kept sheathed and strapped at the side of their boots. They practiced marksmanship often, balancing bits of rubbish on a wall, until they became quite skilled at throwing and striking their targets.

The twins became friends with the gutter children, who looked up to the merry pair, and enjoyed a very free childhood playing and doing exactly what they wanted, unfettered by the normal constraints children of the wealthy were normally bound by.

"Wife," said Peter as he stood one day with his arms around his pale-faced woman, "Our children run wild at the moment, but they are learning much about life—there is time for them to be more constrained and learn what they must in the schoolroom. Barnaby must learn about finance, shipping and the silk industry and Blythe certainly must become a proper young lady, but let us allow them a wonderfully free childhood while it is possible."

Anne leant her head against her husband's shoulder. "I agree, my love. They are so happy and wild, yet not a bad bone amongst them. But I worry that Blythe might not take easily to being restrained in the house."

"Well, dear heart," responded her fond husband, "we will worry about that when the time comes."

Chapter Three

One day, Peter was down on the dockside and heard the deep barks of a hound. On investigation, he saw it was Juno who was worriedly barking by the riverside, then following the hound's gaze, noticed his little hellions, with grime covered faces and hair blown by the wind, pulling at the oars of a small leaky skiff they had found abandoned at the river's edge. Shouting across the waters at them Peter yelled, "Avast there young tars, prithee row to the side and sell me your wares!"

The twins giggled and rowed as fast as they could towards their patient father who was appalled to see the state of the craft they were in, with water slopping in the bottom, and could visualise calamity if they had gone further into the estuary. The boat ran aground with much sloshing and the children hopped nimbly onto the muddy bank, grinning at their father, who tousled their untidy hair. "Look here, my precious two. I'm really pleased that you have become able sailors, but this craft is dangerous!"

"I was baling, father," said Remi earnestly in her clear, high voice, pasting a sweet smile on her face for good measure.

"I've no doubt of that, lass, or the boat would have sunk—but I'll not have you running into such danger again."

The faces of the twins looked glum, wondering if their father was going to stop their activities on the Ouse.

After a moment's thought, Peter continued, "I think the best idea would be for me to get you your own little skiff with oars and a sail, and make sure you can sail it well—one that is big enough to take the dogs as well, and then you can continue your adventures safely. What do you think?"

"Oh, thank you Papa," said Remi, rushing over to clasp her arms around Peter's knees while Romi walked over more like a man, as he had been taught, and shook his father's hand.

Peter wanted his son skilled at sailing in any event—he was destined to cross the oceans in his own ships when he was older, and while there was no need for his daughter to gain such unwomanly skills, he didn't see why not, knowing that she would scream her head off if she were parted from her twin. There would be time enough later for her to learn genteel and ladylike skills.

"Come along you two rapscallions," Peter said as he ruffled their heads, "let's go along and see old Tom and see if he has time to craft you your own skiff."

Taking his children by their grubby hands, with the wolfhound padding alongside, Peter walked, while the twins skipped in excitement, towards the ship building yard, where he had words with Old Tom, and explained that he wanted a good, sound skiff made for his children. "It must be small enough for them to handle easily, but large enough to have the dogs as passengers, as well as roomy enough for them to grow into."

Old Tom nodded, clamped his teeth firmly around his pipe, and speaking through the gap of his mouth, muttered "Aye, aye, Sir," touching a hand to his hat in salute while wondering to himself, how much can I fleece him for?

Remi and Romi jumped up and down gleefully while the craft was being discussed and Old Tom, scratching his greasy hair and waving his pipe, said to the children, "Wot yer gunna call 'er then?" Remi skipped along a line of cobbles chanting "The Cobbles, The Cobbles" while Romi laughed at her, jumped over some coiled ropes and sang out, "The Ropy, The Ropy." Juno barked and barked at their noise and the twins looked at each other and shouted together, "The Bark, The Bark!"

Peter smiled to himself, rather impressed that the children knew that some small sailing boats were called barks (or barques) and asked Tom to paint the name on the side when it was completed. Skipping beside their father, their little clogs clattering on the cobbles and with Juno loping alongside, Peter walked back to the house, surprising Anne who was entertaining in their parlour and not expecting him home for some hours. He could hear one of the ladies boasting that she had met the Princess Pocahontas at Heacham, where she was visiting her husband's family with their small son. "Her name is now Rebecca Rolfe," the woman twittered, "but she is still a native really, isn't she, despite all her court clothes and finery. Her son, Thomas, is rather sweet though and doesn't look like a pagan at all."

"Good morrow ladies," Peter bowed to the simpering ladies as he entered the room. He was a handsome man and the ladies appreciated that. "I've just brought the children home—they were about to sink in a tub full of holes, so I've asked

40

Old Tom to make them their own craft. They might as well become proper sailors than drown before they make adulthood." The ladies tittered behind their fans, and Anne smiled absentmindedly. She was feeling a bit squeamish and rather suspected she was breeding again—a long gap after the twins, and another birth was not something that she looked forward to.

"That's nice dear—I'm sure they will love that," she smiled absentmindedly and passed a plate of small cakes towards her guests. She could hear the clatter of small clogs on the pamment tiles in her hallway and hoped the children wouldn't throw themselves into the room, all dirty and unkempt. They didn't— they knew the rules and the last thing they wanted to do was to be introduced to silly ladies.

Peter slapped them on their grimy rumps and opened the kitchen door. "Cook, here are two starving waifs that need feeding. Give their faces and hands a wash while you are at it."

Cook dipped a little curtsy, and swiped her hands in a mock blow around the children's' heads. "Come 'ere you little varmints." They giggled and dived at the table where sat a jug of frothing milk and some mouth-watering cakes. Peter smiled and left his children to fill their stomachs and could hear them chattering nineteen-to-the-dozen about their new boat to Cook, "Daft, I call it," he heard her say as he shut the door behind himself, smiling as he did so.

***

Old Tom enjoyed the task of building the little skiff for Remi and Romi, who most days would be at his side, 'helping', sweeping up the curls of wood planed from the planks, handing the nails—that they had watched being made at the forge—into his horny hands, handing him his hammer, helping coil ropes, sniff at pots of glue or tar, get in the way, all the time absorbing how their craft was made and watching it form into a wonderful little vessel. They watched as a mast was made, and the canvas cut and sewn to size, and listened to everything Old Tom told them as the boat was caulked and tarred and made watertight. The old boy had even carved a double-headed dog to resemble Juno and Jupiter as a figurehead, which the children just adored! Last of all the words, *The Bark* were painted on the side. Old Tom, not being able to read, had his tongue curled into his cheek in concentration as he copied the words he had been given, but the children, despite their odd upbringing, had been taught the rudiments of reading, and called out the letters as Old Tom carefully painted them on.

Romi and Remi realised that they had to wait for the paint and waterproofing to become dry and set before they could take their boat out, so taking a backwards glance at the boat and waving to Tom as he dabbed at some spots of paint with a rag, they raced from the boat shed, along the quay, grinning at familiar faces, with the ever-faithful dogs loping along at their side. A reeking woman with a grimy face sat on a box scaling fish, and with a toothless grin lobbed a small fish in Juno's direction. Juno deftly caught the offering and swallowed it whole. As the children excitedly wended their way through all the hustle and bustle of the dockside, Romi said to Remi, "Remi, won't it be wonderful when we can sail away along the coast on an adventure?" She smiled back at him, skipped around a crate and jumped over some coiled rope, and nodded back at her sibling. "Yes, and we might meet pirates and find treasure." Their eyes sparkled at the thought.

"Maybe," said Romi, "we will find King John's treasure!" Rumour had it that King John's baggage had been lost years ago in The Wash when the tide had come in on the causeway. Many a hopeful soul had searched the sands to no avail. Remi nodded her head, lost in dreams of glittering jewels, crowns and diamond necklaces.

***

As the twins approached the Market Place they heard hammering coming from a far corner, and looking high over heads and market stalls they could see that a platform was being erected.

"I wonder what that's for, Romi?" queried the girl.

Her brother was curious, so pushed through the throng to join the clusters of curious people who were standing around watching the progress of the work. The twins heard snatches of conversation—enough to realise that a witch was going to be hanged in the square on the morrow.

"Oh, a witch!" Sighed Remi, "I'd like to be a witch."

"Don't be silly, you'd be hanged if you were" replied her brother.

Remi, wondering why, asked, "But why are they hanging her?"

Romi tutted and turning his head said, "Didn't you hear what that man said? She stopped Farmer Flowerdew's cow from bearing milk. He saw her looking at the creature in the field, and a few days later, no milk, which proves she is a witch."

"But," said Remi, "lots of people look at cows and nothing happens, and cows stop their milk anyway when the calves are weaned, so how can they say she is a witch?"

Romi didn't know the answer and just said, "Oh, you are such a girl" and ran off through the crowds towards home. Remi followed him as fast as she could, the dogs loping by her side and keeping her pace.

***

Peter caught hold of his two small children that evening and explained that now *The Bark* was almost ready, they would have the launching of her in two days' time. The twins wailed that they wanted to launch it tomorrow, but their father explained that they would have to curb their excitement a little bit longer. "I have commissioned an old salt to teach you how to sail and use it correctly," he told them with a wink. They stuck their lower lips out simultaneously.

"We know how to row and sail already," they told their father.

"Well, I have no doubt that you can, but I want to make sure that you know all about the tides, the winds, the stars and everything a sailor needs to know—there's more to owning a boat than just rowing, or putting up a sail," Peter explained to his pouting children. They were bright enough to realise that this was so.

"Old Tom's son is going to be your tutor, and I know that he will make it fun for you." Tom's son actually was young, but Peter realised that most adults looked 'old' to his children. He was happy that they were keen to be on the water, but he wanted to ensure that they would be able to deal with the many changes in the elements before he let his children free to their own devices. He knew their natures and that messing around near the quayside would not be enough for them—they would be hitting the coastal areas around Lynn, to Hunstanton, Thornham, Blakeney, Holkham and onwards further to Wells, and he wanted them prepared for any eventuality.

"You will learn to fish as well," he said to the sulky pair, whose eyes lit up immediately. "Yes, I've arranged for some nets to be stowed, and you can provide Cook with as much fish as she can deal with!"

"Oh yes, Papa!" they screamed happily, "We can fish, we can fish, we can fish!" their decibel levels rising until Cook, passing by, threw her apron over her head and exclaimed with a smile, "Tush, whatever next I ask myself."

Once their excitement had died down and it was time for their bed, Romi whispered to Remi, "If we can't take our new boat out tomorrow, then we can go and watch the hanging."

Remi's eyes grew round. "Oh, yes, but we won't tell anyone, or they will tell us we must not." Shoving their nightcaps over their thick curly hair, they grinned at each other and blew out their candle. Tomorrow was going to be good. They hadn't seen a hanging before and looked forward to the excitement.

A small mouse scurried out from the wainscoting, pitter pattering along the wooden floor searching for crumbs—there usually were at this time of the evening.

***

When morning dawned, Nurse hobbled into their room, followed by a maid. Nurse didn't have much to do these days and was really quite bent over with all her aches and pains. She spent most of her days by the fire in the kitchen nowadays, but she had noticed how grubby the pair were looking and had decided it was time they had a wash and a change of clothing. While she felt reasonably sure her Master and Mistress wouldn't throw her out, every now and again, she stirred herself to get the maid to see to the children, otherwise she felt there was no difference between them and the beggar children in the town, all snot and head lice.

"Maid is going to give you a wash today, you young varmints" she snapped at the children, who tried to nip out of the room, but both were thwarted by the two women. A bowl of water and a rag were employed to rub around the grime on their faces and hands, around their necks and arms and down their legs. Both children rebelled when a comb was brought out and applied to their tangled locks.

"What's all this about?" screeched Remi, appalled at such treatment. Romi scowled and felt unmanly and reached for his gown. It was snatched from his hand, and clean garments taken from the chest. By the time Nurse and the maid had finished with the two, they looked almost respectable, but still like two peas in a pod, other than the little mole above Remi's lips.

"That looks better," snapped Nurse with satisfaction. "You must go and say good morning to your mother now. I want her seeing you clean, even if it doesn't last more than five minutes."

Both children scowled…they had things they wanted to do, like get out into the marketplace to get a good view of the hanging, but in the end, they realised it was a good idea to see their mother while they were looking clean, and so they trailed along to her bedroom where she was propped up in her beautiful bed hung with red damask. She looked pale, and held a basin on her lap. She smiled at her healthy offspring and thought how beautiful they looked.

"Hallo my sweet ones," she said. "You are looking mighty fine this morning. I have a tutor coming along today to help you with your letters—I've taught you all that I can. It's time for you both to receive some proper learning."

The twins glanced at each other in horror. "And Remi, it is time for you to learn other things as well. I've asked Goody Truman to teach you about herbs—I don't have enough time or energy to teach you myself. To be a good housewife, you need to stock your stillroom, and know what simples to use for ailments and diseases."

Remi pulled a face, as all she could really think about was The Hanging Today and The Sailing Tomorrow.

"Don't pull a face child—you have run free for long enough. You will be having your sailing lessons often, but life will now be more about learning instead of just having fun. But if you are sensible, you will learn to have fun while you learn!"

Romi bowed to his mother and Remi dipped a curtsy and left the room as mother had begun puking over the bowl. They pulled faces at each other.

"Quick," said Romi as he raced down the stairs, "grab something to eat, and we must get out of the house before the stupid tutor arrives." They skidded around the kitchen door, where a lot of bustling, clattering and delicious aromas were going on, and grabbed some cloths, into which they bundled some cheese, bread and biscuits, with cook turning a blind eye as they did so. Calling to Juno and Jupiter who ambled round the corner at their call, they dodged out of the town house into the milling crowd that was already assembled in the marketplace.

Remi and Romi squeezed their way through the crowds of people—some clean and well dressed, others filthy and stinking—until they were right up against the platform that had been erected the previous day. By now, there was a gibbet standing firm on the deck with some thick rope formed into a noose, and a step beneath it. The children delved into their food cloths and began munching on their bread and cheese and waited in anticipation amongst the growing numbers of excited onlookers who jostled, pushed, spat, urinated and farted. Some were chewing on onions, adding to the general stench.

A vendor handed out earthenware pots of beer. The sun rose and the day became hot. Sweat stained underarms, backs and around hatbands. Luckily for the children, the two dogs kept the crowd at bay around them, else they would have been squashed by the eager people, getting more than excited to see the witch hang. They didn't have too long to wait. There was a rumbling of cart wheels over the cobbles. Romi and Remi jumped up onto the sides of the platform, hanging onto the rope barriers so they could see more clearly, then they saw a small cart being dragged by an emaciated donkey. An old woman with bent back and straggly hair, whiskers on her chin and a glazed, frightened look in her eyes had her hands roped to the front of the cart. People were gleefully throwing old eggs and vegetables at her, and filth and slime covered her hair and trickled down her face. Somebody threw a stone which caught her temple, and vivid red blood gushed down her face and over her eye.

There was nothing the poor woman could do except bow her head to avoid the worst of the missiles. The twins could hear the wailing of a cat, and soon noticed a basket tied to the back of the cart with a frightened cat confined in it that was hissing, spitting and yowling.

"Look!" screeched a woman nearby, "she has her familiar with her!"

"What's a familiar?" asked Remi, but got no reply, just a shrug of Romi's shoulders.

The wretched woman's thin gown was stained, torn and filthy; her face was bruised and it looked like her legs were giving way. The crowd had a field day, booing and hissing and throwing even more filth at her. Soldiers pushed the crowds away so that the cart could make progress towards the platform and when it eventually got there, someone cut the ropes to free the woman's hands and ankles so she could climb onto the platform. However, she didn't move, so men pushed her off the cart, where she sprawled on the ground, barely able to walk.

"She's been tortured, you can tell!" said one of the crowd, with relish.

The poor woman was pushed and shoved up the steps to the platform, and then manhandled onto the steps under the gibbet.

"Get offa there!" someone shouted to the twins, and they quickly jumped down to the ground, only a short distance away from the distressed woman. Remi began to feel sorry for the lady. She didn't look like a wicked witch to her—just a bit like Goody Truman, she thought, who was a nice lady and was going to teach her about herbs.

The struggling cat was pulled out with some string around its neck. It did its best to scratch the fat man extricating it from the basket, leaving bloody weals down his arm. The man angrily pulled the string tightly until the poor creature stopped struggling.

The twins watched in fascination as the noose was placed around the woman's neck, while a priest was saying a prayer beside her from the Bible. He asked her, "Will you confess to God that you are a witch before you are hanged by the neck until dead?"

She shook her head, and only those closest could hear her say, "I h'int no witch." The noose was tightened and secured to the post. In a flash, the steps under the woman's feet were kicked away and there was a crack as her neck broke as she fell the distance. Her eyes bulged out of their sockets and her tongue protruded while her greasy hair hung lank around her humped shoulders. She swung slowly in a half circle and water appeared from under her skirt and dripped to the ground. At the same time, a hefty axe was brought down upon the cat's neck, decapitating it.

As the twins watched, appalled now, Remi noticed what looked like grey smoke drifting from the top of both the lady and the cat's heads that, as it unfurled, looked exactly like a young woman with her cat. Remi felt quite strange as somehow the crowds vanished from her sight, and she just saw the sweet smile of the lady who seemed to look at her directly while the cat was purring contentedly into her arms, and then they just drifted away. Remi just *knew* that what she was seeing was the spirits of the witch and her cat going back 'home' and that the poor dangling body on the rope was just a husk. The real person and the real animal were perfectly all right, though no longer there.

The noisy crowd around them were cheering and booing at the same time. One coarse woman near to them with pockmarks on her face and whiskers on her chin said, "Oi loike to see the men hanged best. You can see their old yards poke up—they seems to loike it at the last!" She and her neighbours cackled coarsely together.

47

The body was being cut down now, and Remi's senses were back to normal, though she was feeling shocked at what she had just seen. Romi wanted to watch the body being bundled back into the cart before leaving, while all around them, people were beginning to shuffle and disperse.

"Did you see that?" Remi asked her brother.

"See what?" he answered distractedly, his darting eyes taking in the scene.

"See the lady and the cat drift out of their bodies?" whispered Remi.

"No, of course not" said Romi. "Don't be daft! And don't say things like that either or people will say you are a witch too!"

Remi tripped on her gown and hung onto Juno as they pushed their way out of the seething crowd. She had a lot to think about. Up until the end when she saw the young lady float out of the old woman's body, she had just been interested in the hanging. She was young, and the young accept what they see—but was she the only one to have seen what she had? In a way, she was pleased the lady was all right and had got away with her cat and seemed happy and had given her such a lovely smile. She had much to think about.

When the children returned home, they didn't tell anyone where they had been, but as they were confronted by their mother trying to placate an irate tutor who had been waiting for them all morning and was not best pleased, they decided to act charmingly and try and win him over to their side. As it happened, once settled in the schoolroom, he found them already able to read quite well and realised that they would be easy children to teach. He asked them what kind of things they liked, and they said boats, adventures, dogs and running, so he decided that if he taught them things around those subjects, he might have some bright children at his hands. After the afternoon listening and learning with the tutor, they were called to their tea, but Romi had come to a decision and wanted to speak to his parents.

When he found his parents together, Romi put all the weight behind his nearly seven-year-old self, demanding, "I'm now old enough to go into breeches." Mama and Papa, "I feel a fool wearing a dress like my sister!"

"And I want breeches too!" said Remi and everyone laughed. She meant it though. She no longer wanted to be hampered by skirts when they were out having adventures.

"Darling, don't be silly. You are old enough, I grant, to have proper gowns now, but girls don't wear breeches! Romi, you are right, you are tall, and while usually you would stay in long skirts until you are eight, you both look older than your age, so yes, we will get you kitted out." Anne noticed that Remi's eyes had filled with unshed tears, so smiled at her daughter, her face pale and gentle, saying to her daughter, "Oh alright dear—you can have some breeches too, ONLY for when you are sailing and where decent folk don't know you!"

Peter patted their heads. "*The Bark* tomorrow," he said, and the children's faces lit up with glee. "Yes, we are going to sail *The Bark* tomorrow!"

***

The next morning the children were out of their beds and dressed at the crack of dawn. They banged on their father's door and asked him if he was ready to come with them to the shipyard. "Yes, I am almost ready" he shouted back, "But we have to wait for the tide, so there is no hurry."

"Yes there is!" called the twins through the shut door…"there will be lots to do first!"

"Be patient," he told them. "All in good time. Go and break your fast in the kitchen and ask Cook to pack you some luncheon."

Hurried along by his children and giving his wife a quick peck on her pale cheek, Peter clasped his cape around him, and walked out onto the cobbled road, stepping clear of all the night waste and rubbish in The Fleet. The day was fine, the sun shining brightly, the Norfolk sky stretching far and high with gulls whirling, diving and screeching.

Both dogs trotted alongside, Juno's belly bulging with pups. The hounds were getting on in years now and grey was beginning to appear around their muzzles, but they were still fit, as well as being the twins' abiding shadows. Romi and Remi raced down Purfleet Lane towards the docks and the shipyard. Merry greetings were shouted out to them and more respectfully to their father walking briskly behind them. Old women cackled and winked their eyes at him, young maids fluttered their eyelashes and flicked back their hair, old salts doffed their caps. The seagulls cried out, flying aloft in great greedy gangs, swooping down every now and again to pick up bits of fish and other snippets of food within their beady gazes. Jupiter and Juno made desultory lunges at nearby birds, not really wanting to chase, but still keen enough to make a little effort. The birds realised there was no real threat, so just hopped and flapped their wings a short distance, opening their large beaks and hissing at the dogs.

Before long, the twins shrill, excited cries reached fever pitch when they spied their little craft ahead of them chocked up with wedges on the slope of a jetty, waiting to be launched. A spry a little boat as ever there was, it was ready to go, with Old Tom and Young Tom waiting to greet them. Both children flung their arms around Old Tom's waist to thank him for building their boat. They had watched practically every inch of it being made, but this was the first time they had seen it outside the shed, and ready to float.

Peter caught up with them and acknowledged the two men's cap doffing, and looking at the water at full tide, nodded at Young Tom, and said, "Let's get going then." He had a small bottle of wine with him, and said to Romi, "Barnaby—you and Blythe are now grown children and are being entrusted with your own boat. First, Barnaby, you can break the bottle over the bow while Blythe, you name her."

With eyes bright with excitement, Romi, or Barnaby now he was grown up, looked at Blythe, and said, "Ready?" She nodded her head, and simultaneously, he smashed the bottle, and she said, "I name thee *The Bark*." And just to make matters even better, both Jupiter and Juno obliged by each barking loudly and everybody laughed and clapped their hands. A few sailors and workers nearby cheered for the occasion and the twins' smiles almost met their ears.

The boat was pushed into the water and the children, dogs and Young Tom climbed aboard. Barnaby and Blythe felt very important, and while they had really wanted to go it alone, they were actually very pleased that Young Tom steered the boat away from the quayside into the middle of the river, raised the sail and steered them away from all the other vessels. Peter waved his hat as they sailed into the distance and smiled to himself. "My, he thought, those children are growing fast—they will be grown up soon!"

***

"Where are we going, Tom?" asked Barnaby, "and when can I have a go?"

"And me too," chipped in Blythe.

"Well," replied Tom in his slow Norfolk accent, "I thought we would go as far as the Dersingham marshes to start with. Mebbe we could get some samphire while we are there – your Cook would be pleased with that and you could have that for your tea."

"Can we do some fishing too, Tom?" asked Blythe

"We can do whatever yew want," replied Tom, tacking the sail as the wind filled it out. "I want yew to watch hard at what I am doing, and I'll let you know when you can take over."

Pulling on the tiller he continued, "If the winds hold, we can go further along to Snettisham, and maybe on to Hunstanton as well. That's pushing it a bit, as I know your father wants yew back for your afternoon lessons, but we do want to know how well this little craft sails, don't we!"

The morning went well, both children excelling at both rowing and dealing with the sail. They absorbed everything Tom told them about the tides and how careful they should be—they noted where the sandbanks were and understood that they shouldn't be sailing over them when the tide was going out, or they would be stuck until it came back in again. They had a few lessons on what kind of clouds were overhead as well. Tom explained the type of cloud to look out for that would show when winds were blowing up and bad weather approaching. He was quite shocked at how the children seemed to take in everything he said so eagerly and quickly. It had taken him ages to learn himself!

Blythe was over-keen to handle the boat, and Tom gently explained to her, "Oi knows you wanna learn Miss Blythe, and your Papa has told me to teach yew—but he says to me that Young Barnaby is more important than you, being a fella loike, and he 'as the first go and the longest go at everythin'. Dew yew unnerstan' young leddie?"

Blythe stared at Tom with gimlet eyes, her lips pursed in displeasure. But she did understand only too well. She knew that she was privileged in being allowed to learn to handle a boat anyway—it wasn't something young ladies did, so she 'buttoned her lip' as she had learned from Cook, and nodded her head. So long as she learned—and she would—she was accepting of being second place with the boat.

The dogs' tongues hung out of their mouths as they panted in the heat of the day, so they lay on the planks of the boat bottom, putting their heads under the wooden seat to gain some shade. Noticing Blythe's gaze, Juno thumped her tail, rocking the boat a little. "Whoa," cried out Barnaby, "don't knock us out, Juno!" which made the dog's tail thump even heavier. Blythe giggled and fondled Juno's ears. Jupiter yawned, his wise eyes boring into Blythe's. A strange feeling ran over her body, and in her mind's eye, she saw that young lady floating out of the old hanged woman's body again and saw her beatific smile. A shiver of presentience ran through her body, that she quickly shrugged away with the excitement of the moment.

They were soon out of the harbour with the oars trimmed and skimming along the estuary towards the coastline of The Wash. They could see the ranks of rattling reeds at the edge of the waters and noticed ducks and other fowl paddling along looking for food. They were going so well past Wolferton that Tom decided to make Hunstanton their first port of call, then they would wend their back to collect the samphire on their return. Tom pointed out the Spire of St Mary the Virgin at Snettisham and told them that when sailors spied that on the horizon, they knew they weren't far from home. The dock was near to the church, and Snettisham was a thriving and large village with a busy port. The twins looked forward to exploring that as soon as they could—it was their first trip to these country parts, and they thought it looked lovely.

They had a wonderful morning, but knew they had to be back for their schooling in the afternoon. They also knew that they would not be allowed out on their own in *The Bark* until Tom had taught them all he knew—so they aimed to learn all they could, as fast as they could!

Framlingham, Suffolk

By now, Matthew Hopkins had reached the age of fourteen. He was quite a stocky lad, with a sallow complexion that was marred by acne, his black hair cut into the severe Puritan style just tipping his shoulders. He was old enough now to wear a hat like his father and proudly strutted his way to the lawyers' establishment where he was learning the trade as a young apprentice clerk. His life so far had been very much tied up in the church, helping clean the brasses, singing in the choir, acting as altar boy, all the while being forced to learn all sections of the Bible and understand the Creed,—his strict father wishing him to become a clergyman like himself. However, it became clear that this would never happen, so James had made arrangements with the local lawyer for Matthew to enter into apprenticeship. The lad had ambition, but alas, he wasn't academic and found that trying to learn about law was just as difficult for him as trying to memorise tracts of the Bible.

However, over his childhood years, Matthew had mastered the art of cunning, was an able liar and had a cruel streak that had blossomed over time. He took great delight in pulling the wings off butterflies and beetles, stamping on anything small that moved, dropping the kittens, that were born in the scullery, from a high attic window to watch them splatter on the stable yard cobbles below. He liked to hear the dog yelp when he kicked it and whenever he saw a small child away from the crowd, he'd corner, bully and hit them. He even pushed an old woman into the pond once to see if she sank or swam in order to determine whether she was a witch or not. Unfortunately for the woman, she drowned so that showed her innocence, but Matthew ran from the scene of his crime, waiting for others to discover her. When his happened, he joined the crowd as she was pulled out of the water, enjoying the sight of the woman's scraggy white legs as her skirt had hitched itself up, and noting her thin drooping breasts outlined by her waterlogged clothing. The crone's death was supposed by all to be an accident, but Matthew's inward excitement knew no bounds, being the perpetrator of her death.

Matthew did suffer some small guilt for his many crimes, for he did not want the wrath of God to fall on his head, but he was adept at excusing his actions. He was sure the old hag had been a witch, so probably something had held her down—reeds around her legs perhaps—so he was therefore right to have pushed her in the water. Witches should be exterminated—that was one thing he was sure of and knew that God would be proud of him.

He hated women. During his life no woman had ever been kind to him, yet he had noticed how his body reacted when they were near. It was Satan, of course, luring him into temptation and that would never do. Those women in the slums where his father had taken him. My God! How they had affected him! Witches all, tempting and beguiling, seducing and tormenting him…he wished that he could kill them, every one of them. To this end he scoured as many laws regarding witches in as many books as possible, gaining some small respect for his seeming diligence. Maybe, Matthew pondered, if he learned the law well, he could enter into the prosecution of witches and watch them burn or hang. Now, that would be a good ambition. Somehow, with that end in mind, his studies became more attractive and he worked hard, earning his father's approval for a change though alas, apart from his witch research, nothing else stuck in his mind and he never rose in the ranks to become a lawyer.

The bear continued to torment Matthew's dreams. He was thoroughly sick of it and ashamed of the terror it caused him. The bear didn't do anything, other than lurk in the peripherals of his dreams, sometimes looming large and menacing until Matthew woke, as usual, panting and perspiring with fear. His room was so dark, with only a little moonlight trickling through his window causing so many shadows, in which the bear seemed to be lurking and hiding just out of view. Sometimes Matthew was sure he could smell a rank and feral odour emanating from a certain dark corner, but once he was properly awake, he realised his imagination was overblown and it was only a nightmare after all.

Chapter Four

The months and years slipped by and the twins' lives were inordinately busy. They had morning tuition in sailing and their father taught them how to use an astrolabe. Both children became extremely interested in the night sky, learning to identify the stars and how they could navigate by them. "If you are ever lost at sea," said Peter to the keen children, "if you know your stars, they can guide you back home." He taught them how to use a sextant too, showing them how it could be used to measure the lunar distance between the moon and a particular star in order to determine time, important in order to calculate longitude, and after they had absorbed that, Peter explained how to find the latitude. He was astonished at his children's ability to learn without much effort, their keen minds absorbing information like sponges.

As their interest in the night sky and the position of the stars and planets was keen, Blythe became interested in the planets from an astrological point of view. By this time, she was around thirteen, and had been learning much of healing and herbs and their uses from Goody Truman, who was teaching her all she knew, and had explained that all plant life was governed by the various astrological signs and planets. She had introduced Blythe to her son Simon, the apothecary's apprentice, who had learned the basics of astrology from the famed William Lilly, whose yearly almanac, *Merlinus Anglicus*, gave information of the planet movements overhead giving those who understood it insight into the planets' varying influences.

Blythe was very interested in Goody Truman's healing too. Goody told her that the healing process had been handed down for generations, and that she should never talk about it, because it was something that couldn't be explained.

"You see, my dear," told Goody Truman to Blythe, bending down to speak quietly, just in case someone was listening. "It's not us that does the healing, it's the gods and goddesses of the natural world, and they use us as a receptor—a kind of channel for the healing to go through."

Blythe was intrigued. "So what do you do, then?" she asked.

"It's quite simple, dear, you just lay your hands on the place that is hurting on your patient, and they might feel heat coming from your hands, or cold—it depends on what needs attending to. It will make them feel very relaxed and cosy too. That's when it is an injury or pain to the body. Aura healing is a bit different. You still place your hands, but not on the body—on the edge of the aura. You will find you won't be able to push your hands onto the body when the healing is happening. Because you are a receptor too, you will be able to help poorly people too."

Blythe was all wide-eyed, but got used to practicing what Goody Truman told her, and while she didn't have any patients yet, she took all her lessons very seriously, for something had told her that she would need them one day.

"That's the *'knowing'* girl—you just *know* sometimes." Goody explained.

Blythe nodded her head. She did know. It didn't happen often, but when it did, it always turned out that her 'knowing' was right.

"Goody Truman tapped Blythe's wrist lightly. There's something else you should know as well, girl. You have 'helpers' with you always that comes from the other-worlds. You might not ever see them. One will be a person, and the other an animal. They will let you know who they are, when the time comes, but whenever you need guidance, you can always call out for it and they will be there for you."

Blythe thought about what the old woman had told her, then raised a question, "I can understand a person helping me, Goody, but how can an animal?"

"The animal will lend you their strength, endurance, wisdom—yes, animals do have wisdom, girl—and give you a different sort of help than a person can."

"Yes, I suppose like Juno and Jupiter? They have helped us since we were babies, haven't they Goody?"

"Exactly," replied Goody Truman with a smile. "You will know your animal spirit when he eventually shows himself to you."

***

By the time the twins were fourteen, although they were still extremely close, they did not spend so much time together as they had previously. Their interests had diversified quite considerably. They felt grateful that their parents had been somewhat eccentric with their upbringing, especially Blythe, who knew that girls were normally considered only fit to learn household accomplishments and certainly not the kind of lessons she was so enjoying.

Barnaby had now found an interest in girls, while Blythe was not particularly interested in boys, finding them all rather silly and unknowledgeable. She would like to marry for love one day, like her parents obviously had, but she did not want to shackle herself to a pompous man just in order to be certain of a home and children. As regards children, she was not so sure she wanted any, because she had seen her mother suffer so much on that score. She had been told how her mother had nearly died after bearing herself and Barnaby, and she had seen her mother lose umpteen babies before their due birth, and how, over time, Anne had become paler and unhealthier. Currently the poor woman was breeding again, into her fifth month now, spending most of her time in her four poster bed, sipping at nourishing soups prepared by Cook, yet throwing it up straight away.

Blythe read through all her papers on plants and their uses and conferred often with Goody Truman, in order to mix tisanes for her mother to sip at that would ease the situation.

Peter, of course, was worried about his dear wife, and knowing that he had a few weeks without the necessity of distant travelling, he wrote to his friend, Nicholas Culpeper, who lived in Spitalfields in London, and with whom he had spent time at Cambridge, both men keeping in touch with the other over the years. Whenever Peter had business in London, he always visited Nicholas, who had informed his old friend that he was currently compiling a book, to be entitled *Culpeper's Complete Herbal* in which he would give a comprehensive description of nearly all herbs with their medicinal properties. It was taking time, he explained, especially as illustration of the herbs also had to be accomplished. He had devoted much of his life to the study of both astrology and medicine and gave free treatment and advice to whomever sought it from him.

Nicholas wrote back to Peter immediately and made arrangements to visit King's Lynn for a few days. In a postscript to his letter, Nicholas had asked Peter for details of both the children's birth—the date and time, which was essential, he wrote. He would like, if Peter were agreeable, to draw up their charts. Knowing Blythe's burgeoning interest in astrology, he knew she would be delighted and he too would be interested to hear what his friend would find out about the planets' influence upon his dear children.

The house was therefore plunged into violent excesses of cleaning, polishing and general panic. Because Anne did not feel at all like overseeing the arrangements for Nicholas's sojourn, she asked Blythe to take over. Blythe was not at all household orientated, but knowing that Culpeper was an expert on the subjects that currently interested her the most (though unaware that he was preparing her astrological details,) she set to with zeal to ensure the wheels of the house were effectively whirring. At this time of her life, Blythe was not particularly interested in feminine falderals, fripperies and fashion, preferring whenever she could, to sneak out of the house in her brother's attire, pretending she were he, and feeling as free as a bird in her outdoor activities, especially on the water. In the meantime, she got by on plain gowns that gave her the maximum of movement, though on her father's insistence in his capacity as an important mercer, that anything she wore was of the best material and design. Because of Parliamentary dictates and Cromwell's influence, the more Puritan designs were simple and covering, and while colours were used, black was preferred as more sombre and pure-minded.

The family politics were for the King, and Cavalier fashions were still worn with flourish, but while Blythe agreed to wear the more colourful and extravagant styles for any social occasion her father wished her to attend, on the whole she preferred the simple styles, purely for comfort and her boyish pursuits, not because of any political or church orientation.

Blythe was looking forward to meeting Nicholas Culpeper, and dearly hoped that she would be able to quiz him on his knowledge of astrology as well as herbal remedies. She had learned so much from old Goody Truman, but knew that she wanted to learn more.

In this instance, Blythe decided to ask her father if she could have a gown made up in some of his better fabrics, and he went down with her to his warehouse on the docks, where he showed her some beautiful samples. She chose thick velvet in a luminous turquoise, with a dull purple sarcenet for her under petticoats, that would be revealed through cuts in her over-petticoat. She was opting for long sleeves that would be straight and point onto her wrists—in direct contrast to the fashion of voluminous puffs tied with plentiful ribbons into flounces. She wanted a gown that was simple, yet beautiful. She wanted to impress Culpeper, not seduce! Peter was taken by his daughter's eye to detail and design and sent the materials off to the local dressmaker, while Blythe followed the boy with the delivery cart, as she knew she had grown recently and the dressmaker would need to take new measurements.

Once in the dressmaker's establishment, she explained her requirements, and said, "I'd be grateful if you could have this made up as soon as possible—I shall need it in two weeks' time for a special occasion, where I need to make an impact!" The dressmaker smiled, and replied, "Don't worry Miss Blythe, it will be done. Will you be needin' anything else to go with it? What about shoes? Do you have any that will blend or match the new attire?" Blythe realised that she hadn't, and thanking the woman for reminding her, said that she would go directly to the cobbler, and get him onto the task. "Just cut me off a snippet of material, so that I can show him the colour." The dressmaker bobbed a curtsey, cut off a small piece and handed it to Blythe.

Constraining herself from running, Blythe walked as fast as she could, taking decorum into consideration (Such a nuisance, she thought to herself) and arrived at the cobbler's establishment. She found him bent over metal lasts, hammering at some leather he was forming into shoes. He straightened up, smiling. Everyone knew the Brown twins and were always pleased to see either of them.

"What can I do for you, Miss Blythe? I imagine it's some new shoes you are after?"

Blythe showed him the piece of turquoise velvet and asked him to make up some pretty pumps in her size, telling him all about the beautiful dress she was having made for Mr Culpeper's arrival. She chatted to the cobbler for a while, interested in the process of shoemaking and asking questions, which pleased the old man. Most of his wealthy patrons were usually curt and while not exactly rude certainly didn't treat him as a person and would certainly never entertain having a conversation with him.

Climbing from his stool and straightening his back, the cobbler said, "Oi think Oi've got some leather to match out in the back room. Do excuse me while Oi go and search through the hides."

"Of course," replied Blythe "It's so interesting in here, I shall have a good look round."

The old man smiled and went off into the dark nether regions of his workshop and Blythe could hear him rummaging around. After a short while, he came back with a big grin on his face.

"Here we are, young leddy, just the colour yew wants!"

In his hands, he held some soft leather, just the right shade for Blythe's shoes. She couldn't help clapping her hands and grinning, and catching her mood, the cobbler did a little dance on the floor, sending up a cloud of dust as his feet disturbed years of bits of leather and curls of wood, left lying where they had fallen and gathered dust. "Oh, how wonderful—I just want plain pumps please—do you need to measure my feet?" The old man nodded, and pulled a rough seat across for Blythe to sit on, then measured her feet length ways and across the width, drawing an outline of both feet onto the back of some old leather.

"Oi'll let you know as soon as they are ready and Oi'll begin them now."

Blythe grinned at the man and waved goodbye as she left the shop, but could not help but let her feet take a few skips as she headed for home. She should be gliding along in a ladylike manner—she did find growing up to be a nuisance.

As Blythe wended her way along narrow streets, avoiding dirt and litter, she pondered on the recent dreams she had been having. She had noticed that the things that she dreamed about came true—like having a dream that Biddie over the road was to have a baby, and she would soon find out that it was true, or that the fat cat in the yard was to have four tabby kittens and one with a ginger patch on its head—and when she did give birth, the kittens were exactly as she had seen them. She had also dreamed that the fish lady in the market would die a sudden and unexpected death, and that too had happened. She had told Goody Truman about these dreams, and Goody told her sharply never to tell anyone else. "You can see into the future Remi," she said, "and these days if people know that, they will call you a witch—and you know what happens to them!"

"But it doesn't seem bad, Goodie" said Blythe, "No, it isn't lass, but you try telling that to the Parson—He'll say you are working with the devil and in no time you will be thrown into the duck pond and if you don't sink and drown, they will say you are a witch. Button your lip, girl, button your lip."

Last night she had had a different type of dream. It had been a short one, but very vivid, where she had seen a dark-haired man with a handsome face. There had been a terrible storm and there was danger and the man had been hit by a spar—and then the dream changed and she saw herself lying naked on a rumpled bed with him, where he, also undressed, was lying next to her bent over and lifting some tresses of damp hair from her face. In this dream, she knew that she loved him. She had woken with strange, satiated feelings in her body, and wondered what all that was about—up until now, she hadn't given a tinker's cuss about men or love and all that went with it, so why on earth would she have such

60

a dream? Maybe, Blythe thought to herself, I am just growing up… but the dream stayed with her.

Thrusting those thoughts away, she found that by returning to her home without running was annoying, but it did give her time to chat to different people on the way back. The flower girl was standing on her usual corner, with a full basket of primroses. "Hallo Dorcas, what lovely blooms—will you bunch up three of those for a nice big posy—my mother is unwell and has been abed for ages, she will love to see those in her room."

Dorcas smiled and wrapped some grasses around the stems and handed them to Blythe, saying "I do 'ope your muvver recovers soon."

"Thank you," said Blythe. "I found a wonderful cowslip patch tucked behind the drove by the South Gates—do you know about it?"

"No Miss, I'd be grateful for directions." Blythe explained how to find the location and Dorcas smiled her appreciation.

Blythe bid her farewell, and picked her way through all the dirt and rubbish on the cobbles of the marketplace. The Fleet bobbed with filth and excrements. She noticed some poor vagrant children scooping the vile liquid into their hands to drink, and rushed to stop them. "Oh, please don't drink from there—it contains bad humours and I am convinced that cholera lurks within its waters."

The scruffy urchins looked at her with astonishment—she could see they thought she was talking nonsense.

"What are we supposed to drink, then?" they asked.

"Well, you could try at the pump, but here," she said, diving into her reticule, "here are a few pennies to buy yourself some elderflower cordial from that vendor over there."

The pennies were grabbed by one of the children who grinned and rushed away with his friends. Blythe didn't think they would take any notice of what she had told them, but hoped her information may have sunk into their heads.

She stepped into the house through the big carved door and thought how lucky they were in her household. They had water brought to the house from a clean spring, through elm piping that only the wealthy in the town could afford. This was a new innovation, and her father was a man with an eye to the future, and had other plans for improving and modernising their home. He had told her of flushing toilets that had been installed in some homes of the wealthy in London and while it was unlikely this was going to happen yet at their house, it was an exciting possibility. At the moment, there were lavish commodes in each bedroom—her mother's, for instance, had one with a soft upholstered seat, and the bowl was beaten copper. Now they had water installed in their home, there was no end to the possibilities!

Blythe ran up the stairs to her mother's room pleased to be able to expend some of her energy and tapped lightly on the door. She stepped into the bedchamber where Anne was lying listlessly, propped up with soft pillows. She smiled wanly as Blythe entered. "Greetings, child," she said through white lips. "What have you been up to?"

Blythe was shocked to see that her mother's colours had shrunk very close to her body, being now a muddy brown. Having seen colours around people since she could remember, she seldom talked about them because she had assumed everybody could see them. She had once asked Goody Truman why her colours had gone dull one day. Goody Truman had looked sharply at her and said, "You see auras, child? Not many people do."

"Oh, I didn't know the colours are called auras," Blythe had said. "I thought everybody saw them."

"No child," Goody said with an enigmatic look on her face. "Only special people do. Auras are vibrations around people, which show their energy and feelings. If my aura looks different today, it is because I have got quite a lot of pain in my legs and hips. I'm getting old now, and this is what happens. When the weather gets warmer, I feel better, and when you see my aura then, it will be bigger and bouncier." Blythe had taken Goody Truman's advice not to talk about auras to anyone else.

"Child, we live in uncertain times, and we don't want people saying you are a witch, and having you hanged in the marketplace." Blythe's memory went back to the hanging she had witnessed when she had seen the lady and the cat coming out of the bodies like smoke.

"Oh Goody, do you think I am a witch then?"

"No," said Goody, "you are just an exceptional little girl with special gifts—make sure you use them wisely and only for good. And keep anything like that under your bonnet, or people will talk."

Remembering Goody Truman's explanation, Blythe was worried that her mother's aura showed how low she had become, and thought maybe by telling her all about her exploits this morning the story might perk her up. She explained to her mother about the material, her description so colourful and enthusiastic, that her mother's eyes twinkled, pleased that her boyish daughter was at last gaining some interest in feminine matters. She listened to Blythe's anecdote about the urchins and the water, and nodded, her own thoughts too were that unclean waters could harbour ill humours.

"Mother, will you be able to leave your bed and join in the feast we are preparing for Master Culpeper? It would be such a pity if you were on your own, feeling miserable, up here? Surely it could only do you good, and you would not be expending energy, apart from the journey down the stairs—well, and up again!"

Anne smiled weakly and grasped Blythe's hand. "Yes, I shall do my best. I want to see you in your new gown anyway, and it will be good to hear your father and his old friend talk about their interests."

Blythe noticed that Mother's aura was wider now and vibrating and while still brown, looked perkier. She eventually left her mother's side, pleased that she was taking an interest in something other than feeling poorly, and kissing her mother, she left the room, hitched up her skirts and bounded down the stairs two at a time.

***

The day of Nicholas Culpeper's arrival eventually dawned. The house was gleaming, at its best. Blythe had made sure that flowers were placed all over the house, and that all the ingredients for their meal were at the cook's disposal. Cook was in a frightful state of nerves, her face as red as the slab of meat she was dressing, and shouting at all the maids to do this, that and the other. Everything was going according to plan, but that didn't stop her distress. She slammed pots down on surfaces, made sure the fires were roaring and shouted at everyone until they all raced around like demented ants.

Peter had arranged to meet Nicholas at the local hostelry on his arrival, where his carriage and horses would be safely looked after. The family had their own stabling behind their home, but it wasn't large enough for visitors' steeds or transport. He and Nicholas greeted each other warmly and proceeded to have a few tankards of ale and a pie, after which they strolled through the town and down to the Purfleet mooring to view Peter's ship, the *Morning Star,* and a recent purchase that he had named the *Evening Star*. They bumped into *Evening Star's* new Captain, Ambrose Bonnesby, and being in a jovial mood, Peter thumped the young man on his shoulder saying, "Come along for a meal this evening—we are dining at eight—it's time you met the family."

Ambrose was busy checking out the ship and didn't really want to waste his time but felt it prudent that he accepted the invitation with grace—after all, he was dependant on Peter for his livelihood at the moment and didn't want to give him any reason to dismiss him from his captaincy. He was the fourth son of an impoverished Earl who had lost most of the family fortune through gambling. Ambrose was an ambitious man, keen to earn his own living and make his own fortune. Ambrose had done well to gain such a position but had plans to rise further and own his own ship eventually. On consideration, he realised the more he listened to his employer's business talk, the better, as he knew that one could never gain too much knowledge, and the more you learned, the more advantages you could glean from life, so bowing to Peter, he said, "That's extremely kind of you, sir. I'll finish off what I am doing, spruce myself up and be there on the dot."

"Good man." Peter slapped Ambrose on the shoulders once more and acknowledging Ambrose's bow, they parted company.

A boy had been given a few coins to take Nicholas's travelling bags to the house, where they had been taken up to the chamber allocated for him, and a maid was sent to empty the bags and place his clothes on the rail, and put out what she felt he would want to wear for the evening's meal.

Eventually, after some hours at the inn, with much jollity and many guffaws, the somewhat inebriated men returned to get themselves ready for the evening's repast.

Blythe had spent considerable time getting herself ready, and felt she looked very good in her new gown and shoes. She brushed her hair and let it fall naturally—children and young girls did not have their hair put up—and then she went into her mother's chamber. As she opened the door, she found Anne had managed to gather herself together and was dressed and ready to go downstairs. She was still very pale, but the thought of having an interesting person to dine had rejuvenated her to a certain extent.

"Oh Blythe, you look beautiful!" exclaimed Anne, clasping her hands together in delight.

Blythe smiled somewhat bashfully, replying, "Oh thank you mother. I'm just not used to wearing lovely robes, but I have to say I do rather care for this one. Look, I have pumps to match."

Blythe pushed the toe of one of her pumps out of the folds of the beautiful gown.

"Oh yes," exclaimed her mother in delight, "hasn't the cobbler done a good job? You are going to be a really beautiful woman my dear—if only you would stop your boyish ways."

Anne kissed her daughter on the top of her head, and allowed Blythe to carefully help her down the stairs, where they both were keen to greet Nicholas Culpeper.

Tempting aromas were drifting from the kitchens where Cook could be heard screeching out on occasion. There was much clattering of kitchen paraphernalia, and Anne smiled at her daughter, knowing that Cook would present a perfectly wonderful feast for them. Anne greeted Nicholas cordially, and Blythe, feeling a little awed by her father's friend, bobbed him a curtsey and smiled shyly. Her shyness didn't last for long, especially when Culpeper informed her that he had drawn up both Barnaby's chart and her own. All shyness forgotten, Blythe couldn't wait to get through the meal in order to find out her astrological details.

Just before they were ready to seat themselves around the table, there was a knocking at the door. "Oh, that will be Bonnesby," exclaimed Peter, who then realised he had not informed anyone of the extra guest.

"Quick, get the maid to lay another place at the table and inform Cook, Blythe—Oh, and where's Barnaby—I haven't seen him yet."

"He's upstairs getting ready Father, and will be down shortly."

Blythe had actually seen Barnaby arrive home with hay in his hair and glowing cheeks. She didn't realise it, but Barnaby had been having an extremely pleasant encounter with a dairymaid in the hayloft above the stables. She had been passionately keen to acquaint Barnaby in all matters carnal, and he had been as equally keen to learn. Now feeling like a true man, he bounded up the stairs to execute a quick toilet and throw himself into his evening attire. He now felt somewhat superior to his sister, whose general knowledge seemed to surpass his in many matters, but now he felt he held an upper hand over her, and things were more equal in their sibling rivalry, which did flare up from time to time these days. The new Juno and Jupiter were waiting for him in his chamber, and he gave their ears a quick scratch. Their long tails thumped on the floor loudly.

Gazing at the pups, Barnaby recollected the awful time when the original Juno and Jupiter had died quite near in time to each other. Juno had gone first, and badly. She had suffered some kind of fit, and had lain on the floor, making the most awful noise all night—a dreadful kind of groaning gasping noise. Both the twins had lain with her, with Jupiter keeping guard, and eventually the old lady had heaved her last. The dog weighed in mighty heavily at around fifteen stone. They had to roll her body onto some thick canvas and hoist her out into the garden, where a large hole was dug to contain her huge body. The twins were completely devastated, for they had nursed at her teats, and learned to walk and run with her. She and Jupiter had been by their sides for all of their lives.

Jupiter mourned Juno's departure, howling at the moon and refusing to eat or drink, and soon followed her to the grave. Both children had wept until there were no tears left and went into a decline of despondency, only alleviated by the pups that Juno had left behind, who licked at all the tears, threw themselves at the mourning pair, until their joyful antics brought Barnaby and Blythe out of their misery. Peter, in his wisdom, had advised the children to keep the puppies of their choice, realising that their wolfhound, wet-nurse and guardian and her sire were getting very elderly and their days numbered.

Barnaby flung on his knee breeches and fine lawn shirt with its voluminous sleeves and lace collar. He knew himself to be a handsome lad, and with his recent newfound conquest in the hayloft, left his room with a new swagger and ran down the stairs, with the dogs following, to find his father greeting a stranger at the door. He was quickly introduced to the sea captain, who was in charge of his father's new ship, and began asking keen questions about the vessel, saying how he looked forward to soon joining as crew on either the *Morning* or *Evening Star*. Captain Bonnesby hoped that it would be the *Morning Star* captained by another man upon which the young whippersnapper was placed—he had no need of the spoiled brat with his airs and graces of a wealthy merchant upsetting the wheels in motion aboard his ship.

Anne drifted into the reception room to greet her new guests formally, and invited them to partake of a glass of wine before they went into the hall to dine. Peter thought she looked very beautiful, but it was clear to see that while she looked stimulated by company and the thoughts of an entertaining evening, she was far from well. She smiled sweetly at him, and he raised his glass to his dear-heart wife.

Blythe came into the room at that moment and saw Captain Bonnesby for the first time, and felt her heart miss a beat. Her faced flushed, her heart palpitated and her legs trembled. She found herself completely tongue-tied for this was the very man she had seen naked in her dream! For some reason she felt like there

66

was a rope binding them together—which was a ridiculous thought, but that's how it felt—whilst at the same time, with a panicked feeling, thinking that eventually ropes would fray.

What an odd thought.

She was pleased that her father introduced them only briefly, but as she crossed the room, she was aware of his every movement, his every expression, his voice, his laugh and even when her back was turned, she knew exactly where he was in the room. She tried to compose herself, but could not take her eyes from his face. He had black hair like her own, that was long and tied back away from his face. Unlike her own, his hair was straight. His eyes were a smouldering, deep brown that looked almost black, and his face and hands were weathered to a deep tan. He was a tall man—unusual to see in Norfolk—and taller than she and Barnaby. She didn't think of her own height too much as it didn't bother her, but she had often thought when the time came that she had to have a husband, he would probably he shorter than her!

The captain's name was Ambrose, she thought, *ambrosia, wasn't that the food or drink of the gods that gave immortality to those who partook of it?* To Blythe, this man looked like a god, and while she tried to act normally, it was difficult. Luckily, in one way, Ambrose took absolutely no notice of her at all, except politeness on greeting, and Blythe realised she was far too young to attract his attention, even in her beautiful gown. "*However*," she thought to herself, "*I shall become an adult soon and I will meet him again, and I shall find a way to his heart.*"

Nicholas Culpeper had noticed Blythe's attraction to the sea captain. Having prepared the young girl's chart, he smiled to himself, as he knew that her fate was going to be unusual—she was spirited and passionate and so very near to an age where her unusual upbringing would allow her to seek adventure in unethical ways, unusual for young women of those times. His gaze then followed that of Ambrose, who was in animated conversation with Peter, about the countries he wished to visit and the kind of cargo he would like to transport home to make his fortune. Nicholas decided he would ask Ambrose for his birth details before he left. He was sure that somehow the fates would draw together Ambrose and Blythe, but felt that sparks would fly, one way or the other.

Peter queried Nicholas about his astrological work. "What exactly do you do, Nick? I know about the planets of course for navigational purposes but I know little about how you apply the art to humans."

"It's fascinating, you know. I've found that the planets seem to influence each one of us in a different way. For instance, the Moon, which as you know, governs our tides and makes dogs howl when it is full. It has been found to also govern our emotions—how we feel at any given time, how we react to emotional events and so on. So, wherever the Moon falls in a natal chart, I know how that person is going to react in emotional circumstances."

Blythe, by now, had temporarily forgotten all about Ambrose, and all her attention was riveted on Nicholas and to what he was saying. Her interest was so acute she could almost feel the cogs in her head whirring into action. She fleetingly thought of what she had to tell Simon, the apothecary's son, when she saw him next.

"I thought the Sun was the important planet in astrology?" she questioned, and Nicholas turned to her smiling, "Yes, it is Blythe, the Sun is looked upon as 'self' or 'ego', so whatever zodiac sign it falls in, then you are influenced strongly by your Sun sign. However, wherever the other planets fall also brings strong influences." He looked into Blythe's intelligent, questing eyes.

"You and your brother," he continued, are born under the sign of the Ram, which means that both of you will hold strong passions and drive and will fight for what you believe in. "You will be forceful but with Fire as your element, you will also both be warm hearted and generous, but prone to 'flaring up' at times and letting your element run away with you, as a fire out of control. You both have Sagittarius on the horizon, another fire sign, but symbolised by the Archer, half man, half horse. You will have a yen for travel and adventure which," Nicholas turned to Blythe, "will not be an easy seat for a young woman whose place is in the home."

Blythe looked up at Culpeper, her keen gaze searching his. "I don't have to stay in my home at all times," she said with a stubborn look. "I want to sail the seas with my brother and discover new lands. I seek not to have a boring husband and make sure the tapestries are free of dust."

Culpeper laughed and said, "Indeed. I will speak with you on the morrow, and explain the other aspects of your chart. I had realised you would not be keen to stay in one place all the time, but it is not usual for women to be adventurous away from their home. But, my dear, you have your life in your own hands and I don't think your parents are as strict as many. Also, maybe you might find a husband who will take you along on his own adventures, though that would be a rare thing indeed."

Blythe smiled at him, her eyes ablaze, then could not help her gaze return to the Captain, chatting seriously with her father. Maybe he felt her gaze unconsciously, for he turned for a brief moment and their eyes met, but his glance did not linger as he turned back to Peter and continued with their discussion.

The meal continued with general talk, mainly about Peter's business, his vessels and cargos, and about Nicholas's work with the poor and unhealthy, how he felt that various herbs helped cure many ailments, and how he, like Blythe, was sure that water should be boiled before being drunk, as his observations had shown that unless this was adhered to, people became ill after partaking of water containing effluence.

Turning to Anne, seated beside him, he quietly spoke to her under the general hubbub of conversation.

"Forgive me for being presumptuous, Mistress Anne, but your husband has acquainted me with your travails in certain delicate matters."

Anne worriedly clutched at her skirt, but admitted that she did have problems and would be pleased at his advice. "Well, if you have some Quinces stored, they are excellent to strengthen the child within, but you should abstain from sharp meats, bitter or salty food, and avoid things such as garlic, onions, mustard, fennel and pepper."

"Well, currently I eat very little, as I can't contain it. What should I take?" Anne questioned.

"Cinnamon is good and a moderate clear wine is also. Keep exercise to a minimum, don't dance nor ride out in a coach that shakes you." Advised Nicholas.

As Anne had been keeping to her bed, this advice wasn't particularly helpful, but she supposed that she was actually doing what was best, and he had confirmed that for her.

"If you place a clout upon your belly," he further advised, "that has been dipped in oil of sweet almonds, jasmine and oil of lilies, this will keep the skin loose and free of stretches, and," continued with a kind smile, "drink wine boiled with water containing cinnamon and bathe in a concoction of lily roots, mugwort, agrimony—oh my dear, I can see I am tiring you. I shall give the ingredients to Blythe on the morrow, and she can prepare them for you—and to close the womb after birthing—polypodium of oak or vervain gathered in May or June will do the trick."

Anne thanked him weakly and rather wished he hadn't raised the subject, as for a short while she had forgotten about the horrors of the impending birthing. She would make her apologies soon and retire—her guests would understand.

The men were left to their port for a while—Barnaby was included—he appeared older than his years, and was keen to soak up the men-talk, especially asking Captain Ambrose about his sea adventures, who, while not exactly fobbing him off, made it clear that his interest was in his father, his business acumen and what could be gained for himself out of any conversation. Barnaby, used to not being listened to seriously, found his mind back in the hayloft with Betty the buxom dairymaid. My, how exciting it had been, he mused, when she lured him up the loft-ladder and into the hay. She had not been backward in coming forward, and had lifted her skirts to show him what was underneath. He might have fumbled a bit, but with Betty's giggling guidance, his excitement had known no bounds, and her squeals of delight had got the horses stamping their feet and their brasses a-jingling in the stable below until they heard an ostler clumping over the cobbles to look over the stable doors and find out what was bothering the steeds.

Blythe whispered to her brother, "Wake up Romi, you are dribbling with a most stupid expression on your face. I must retire anyway now mother has, and leave you men folk to get stupid in your cups!"

After the evening ended, Blythe mounted the staircase to her bed. She couldn't sleep after such excitement—first she couldn't get over the fact that Ambrose Bonnesby was the very embodiment of the dream she'd had recently. Was it just coincidence, or did the dream mean something portentous? In her dream she had felt the oddest and wonderful sensations that were not re-enacted on meeting him this evening. She had found him so handsome, but he was dismissive of her and had barely acknowledged her. She knew she was only fourteen years, but she felt she had looked rather stunning tonight, and really had deserved a little more from him! Maybe when she was somewhat older he might notice her. In the meantime, she could dream…

Blythe's thoughts wandered on to Nicholas Culpeper. He had told her he would go through her natal chart with her on the morrow—that would be interesting, and she so hoped that he would tell her the way to understanding astrology more than she did. She was very keen to learn. His knowledge on herbs, too, was extraordinary—how she would love to learn more about those too.

Goody Truman had taught her a lot, but Blythe felt that one could never learn enough about subjects one was interested in.

Eventually, she fell asleep. Small scuffles came from within the wainscoting where the family of mice rose to wend their way down to the kitchen to see what was on the menu. One of them rolled a small piece of mortar that had dropped off the wall, and another joined in, both playing as they scurried down the walls and onto the flooring squares. There was plenty of food dropped on the floor after the meal. The scullery maid snored in her corner of the kitchen while the mice ate their fill around her. She would have screamed her head off, had she known a few had run across her sleeping body.

***

Dawn was announced by a cock a-doodle-doing outside Blythe's window. Stretching her arms above her head, she yawned and decided she might as well get up and get ready to converse with Master Culpeper, and she didn't want to waste a moment. By the time she had performed her ablutions—by now she took more care of herself than when a child—she could hear other people were rising around her in the house. Delightful breakfast aromas were wafting up the stairs, so she skipped down them and rushed into the hall, where Nicholas and her father were already seated and eating their food. Jupiter and Juno II were lying hopefully by the fireside, waiting for stray food to come their way. Even as pups they were too large to linger under the table but the handsome pair usually got some good snippets thrown their way.

Nicholas beckoned to Blythe to sit next to him. He patted at his pockets, and told her that as soon as they had broken their fast, he would explain her chart. As there was yet no sign of Barnaby, he told her she would have to explain the planet dynamics to her brother herself. She nodded with keen anticipation.

As soon as the meal was completed, Nicholas beckoned Blythe over to a corner chair, where he drew out a rolled paper and flattened it on an occasional table. Blythe could see a circle drawn within a circle, segments like pieces of tart, and astrological symbols drawn, with lines going from one to the other.

Pointing to some symbols, Nicholas said, "See here, Blythe, these are the symbols, or glyphs, of the zodiac signs." Blythe nodded. Goody Truman had taught her these, and she was able to express her knowledge to Nicholas. "And these are the glyphs of the planets," said Nicholas. You will need to recognise all these symbols otherwise you will never understand a chart.

"Yes, I think I know most of them, Master Culpeper—Goody Truman taught me some, and her son, Simon taught them to me as well. He learned from Master William Lilly."

"Oh, did he now!" exclaimed Nicholas—"He is a lucky lad then, William Lilly is master to none in the expertise of astrology. It would be good if you could meet him."

Culpeper pointed to a middle line on the left hand side of the chart. "Now, as I told you last night, your Ascendant sign is Sagittarius—the Ascendant sign is just as important as your Sun sign, so as an Aries, to have another fire sign makes you doubly a Fire elemental."

"What does that mean?" queried Blythe.

"What does fire mean to you child?" parried Nicholas.

Blythe answered, "Well, hot, with red and yellow flames, it burns bright, but even when it burns down to an ember, can still be dangerous and burn."

"That's right, and anyone with a lot of Fire in their chart, will be a warm and passionate person, sometimes burning strong, but ready to reignite enthusiastically at the whim of the wind." Culpeper smiled, pleased with Blythe's enthusiasm, "Do you know what Sagittarius brings to a person?" he asked.

"Not really," said Blythe, "though I do remember he is the Archer, half man half horse, so maybe he brings strength and activity to a person? Maybe he brings a person a good seat on a horse?" She smiled as she said this, and Culpeper joined her, saying, "Well, yes, in many ways you are correct. Do you enjoy horse riding?" Blythe nodded her head. "This is the sign of the athlete and traveller— a jovial soul whom people cannot but help liking." Blythe nodded, knowing herself, even for a girl, a tough strong person with such a yen for travel.

Culpeper swiftly ran through Blythe's chart, explaining what he thought she would understand, and was very impressed by her quick understanding of what he was telling her.

"Because you were born at a different time to Barnaby, my dear, your chart differs slightly to his, even a few minutes can make a vast difference, but it is clear from your charts that you were both born to be adventurers. I hesitate to say, however, that I don't really know in what way you might be an adventurer...I know that your father has allowed you a great deal of freedom in your life, but while I can see your brother sailing off on the seven seas and having many a fine adventure, I don't see how that can happen to you. As you know, women do have to stay at home with the babies, but maybe you can adventure in your mind!" "You do both have planets—look, see here—in Pisces, the two fishes, whose influence is a love of water and dreams…I shall be interested to see how your life spans out in the end, and you also have aspects that show you could be a healer too."

This all sounded fine to Blythe, though she didn't like the thought that she might not be able to travel. "Master Culpeper, I know you can't teach me astrology in a few short moments, but I am keen to learn. How can I do so? What books would I need to learn?"

"I can send you some my dear, and maybe you can ask the apothecary's son to aid you in your studies more than he has? As he studied with William Lilly, he would be a good tutor for you! Is there any possibility that you could meet the man and ask him to be your tutor?" Blythe resolved to ask her father if she could do this and in the meantime she would ask Simon to help her more. Questioning Culpeper on various other points, he was glad to answer, pleased at her eagerness and quick thinking.

Blythe pondered. Master Culpeper had said she was born to be an adventurer and sail the seas—that was if she had been a boy—that she was passionate and of warm temperament. He'd said she was a dreamer and a lover of the waters, and that the Moon gave her a caring, loving nature. He had also told her to quell her sometimes questioning nature, as that could get her into trouble…He had said she was intelligent (not a particularly encouraging occupation for a female) and that she had healing abilities and could be interested in divine arts, but should be wary that she was not discovered…He hadn't told her whether she would get married and have children, but that was not something she was concerned about at the moment—other than getting to know the Captain, and more importantly, getting him to notice her.

Juno sauntered over and leaned her large body against Blythe. Absentmindedly she put her hand on the hound's back—level with her own waist—and gently stroked the fine long hair.

Eventually it was time for Nicholas to pick up his bags and leave. Peter walked with him to the livery stables, where Nicholas's chaise was being readied, though he had decided to ride his horse for the beginning of the journey. The two men clapped each other on the shoulder.

"Do keep in touch," Peter said to Nicholas.

"I certainly will," his friend replied with a smile, putting his booted foot into the stirrup and alighting his horse—"and that Blythe of yours—I feel she has a curious and perhaps dangerous future ahead of her. I think if you want to keep her safe, you must curtail her more wayward instincts and keep an eye on her! However, she is very keen to learn more of astrology and if you could manage some tutoring with William Lilly, I know she would learn well. If she is bent on study, that might keep her out of harm's way!"

Peter laughed, and said, "I will think about it!" and waved his hat to Nicholas as his friend clattered over the cobbles towards the South Gate and his road to London. He had a couple of outriders with him in case of any attack on the journey, and waved a final farewell as he disappeared around the corner.

When Peter returned home, an anxious maid was waiting for him. "Mistress Blythe asked you to immediately go the milady's bed chamber, as she has taken a turn for the worse."

Peter raced up the stairs to find his wife in agony in her bed, with Blythe mopping her brow with a damp cloth.

"Father, I do believe she is losing the baby—again. Please call for Goody Truman, as poor mother seems to be in a fever as well—she is mighty hot and sweating."

White faced, Peter ran down the stairs, calling for Clem, who in turn, raced out of the house as fast as his arthritic legs could take him to find the Goodwife. Peter paced anxiously up and down waiting for Goody Truman, who soon came puffing and panting through the door, with her bag of herbs and other midwifery items clutched in her arms. Briefly telling the story, Peter gestured the woman to go to Anne's chamber, and took himself off to his warehouse to do some work to take his mind off the matter. There was nothing like work to sooth a troubled mind.

Blythe worked together with Goody Truman for many hours, until finally a small bloody and lifeless baby was drawn from her mother's body. There was no way Blythe ever wanted to have a child—she had seen her mother suffer so much, miscarrying over the years. There seemed to be a great loss of blood, and Goody Truman called for some moss to be taken from her bag, which she packed around the birth channel, to ease the flow of blood. Anne's face was deathly white and her eyes seemed glazed. She didn't seem to know what was going on, and Blythe feared her mother was dying. She could see that her mother's aura was so tight to her body and almost transparent. Goody Truman asked for some brandy, which she thought might help, and once it was to hand, Blythe tried to trickle some into her mother's lax mouth, but it just trickled out again.

Both Blythe and Goody Truman stared at Anne in anguish. They had done all that they could do, and all they could hope was that she would rally round and come through. She lasted only a short while, with the two women doing all that they could, to no avail. Anne shuddered out one final weak breath and lay still. Blythe saw her floating out of her body, just like the woman and the cat, so long ago in the marketplace. Through her sorrow, she saw that her mother was smiling and was cradling a small baby with tufts of black hair as they disappeared from her view. Blythe felt a small comfort knowing that her mother was 'alright' but now she had a pale, stiffening corpse in place of her smiling, kind and lackadaisical mother, and she also had to let her father know.

Goody Truman put her arms around the girl giving her a tight, comforting hug. "I'll do the laying out—that is part of what I do, child. You must go and find your father and give him the bad news. I'll do all that is necessary and your mother will be looking pretty by the time you return."

Blythe nodded, and left the room, when Goody Truman picked up the tiny blood smeared baby, cleaned him up and wrapped him in some cloth and placed him carefully by his mother, ready for the coffin, once it arrived. She then cleansed Anne's body, and with a maid helping her, dressed her in one of her fine gowns. She brushed her hair and let it fall over her shoulders, and eventually Anne was ready on clean bedding for her final journey. Goody Truman sniffed and wiped away the tears from her eyes. Women died so often in childbirth, but she never failed to grieve the loss of beautiful lives.

Goody Truman had a precognition that times of change were not far away, and not for the good, and were about to descend on the household. She hoped she was wrong.

Manningtree, Essex, September 1644

Eyes glittering, he tested the needle-sharp tip of his retractable blade with a well-manicured finger. "Yes!" he told himself with relish, the snarl of a smile crossing his sallow face. "This will find me witches a-plenty…"

Outside, an angry wind whipped trees into a frenzy, throwing leaves at the leaded windows through which cold draughts moaned and sighed in equal measure, somehow adding to the excited anticipation in Matthew's chilly heart. He was about to embark upon a journey to King's Lynn in Norfolk, commissioned by Parliament to unearth witches throughout the country. Obsessed with those cohorts of the devil—succubae, crones, tempting young women with salacious smiles, each and every one with a wart *somewhere* on their body for his defining witch test.

If a wart were to be pricked hard and not bleed with his specialist knife, this would prove a woman's guilt. That he had the knife made to ensure women's warts didn't bleed when the blade retracted into the handle was neither here nor there. It was his fail-safe way to gain his witches *as well as* plump purses of gold into the bargain. That his method was grossly unfair was not part of the equation. Matthew needed to purge the land of its cesspit of witches in order to rid unnatural and forbidden desires—desires that he suffered himself that were sent directly from Satan. The special knife was his solution in order to serve God.

Gazing at his image in a small, speckled mirror, for a moment he thought he saw the burning red eyes of the bear looking back at him. He had dreamed of it again last night—the great beast with rancid breath, forever pursuing him. He had awoken hot and sweating, panting with fear. He shook his head to erase the memory, then adjusted his pristine white collar, slapped his hat on his head, drew a thick felted cape around his shoulders and then checked his travelling bags one last time. After pulling on his long boots and picking up his bags, he strode through his chamber to clatter down the stairs and out of the house—a neat, if sombre, Puritan figure in black he set off for the stables. At his approach, the waiting horse laid ears flat to her head and rolled her eyes in dislike. A nervous stable boy scurried, keen to avoid his master's displeasure, and quickly saddled up the mare, hastening to buckle on the bulging travel bags.

Clipping spurs around his boots, Matthew took his whip down from its hook, impatiently slapping it against his gloved hand while following the steed as it was led out into the untidy yard. Using the lad's cupped hands cruelly, he stepped into them to hoist himself into the saddle. Once the reins were adjusted to his pleasure, he gouged his spurs into the sides of the mare and whipped her rump hard as she reared, skittered and slid before clattering out of the yard, leaves and small twigs swirling behind them.

With a saturnine smile, Matthew dug the spurs further into the horse's flanks. Raising his hat in a salute as he looked up at the heavy sky, he yelled out to his

God in the face of the gale, "Matthew Hopkins, my Lord—Witch Finder General—at your service and on my way to Glorious Duty!"

Branches lashed, leaves flew, rain began to pour and the frightened mare's nostrils flared as she attempted to flee from her pain.

Chapter Five

Three years had passed since her beloved mother had died. Blythe was sat in the front parlour, fiercely jabbing a needle into embroidery that her stepmother was forcing her to do. Blythe hated embroidery and hated that woman. She thought back to the funeral of her mother, at how her father had nearly gone out of his mind, how she and Barnaby, trying so bravely to keep back the tears, had watched the coffin being placed into the brown soil. How quiet the house had been, how their father had disappeared on his ship and sailed away from his despair. How they had not bothered to comport themselves, but had taken out *Bark Two*—a larger skiff—and tried to forget their sadness in a busy time of 'adventuring'.

Barnaby got into a gang of ne'er-do-wells and came home drunk half the time and stank of cheap perfume the other. Blythe, when not out on the waters, poured over the astrological books that Culpeper had sent her, called on Simon to discuss Trines, Squares, Sextiles and other planetary angles, and whenever Simon could get away from work, he helped her with her studies.

Blythe had finally met the famed William Lilly who had sent her many papers for her to learn, and they corresponded regularly. However, her stepmother had put a stop to it, once she had discovered Blythe's 'unladylike' pursuits.

The house had seemed empty without her mother, and the household staff got lackadaisical and dust gathered in corners. Nurse had turned up her toes and died too, and Cook, getting older and with no-one to encourage her culinary prowess, just sat in her chair in front of the kitchen stove, and left the day to day cooking to the undermaids. All was in disarray, until one day, when Blythe and Barnaby were just seventeen, their father returned. *With a new Bride.*

Both Barnaby and Blythe were in their old clothes, having just come back from sailing, with armfuls of samphire for the cooking pot. Blythe was in breeches and a jacket belonging to her brother that she had commandeered for her sailing exploits, and both were grimy and grubby. When the front door opened and their father entered, the twins exclaimed in delight and ran towards him, but as he stepped aside, a very beautiful woman stood behind him, with her daughter at her side. Both were garbed in the height of fashion, their hair expertly coiled and coiffed, their hats dripping with feathers and bows, and both with tight mouths and horrified expressions at the dirty vision of the twins who stood, mouths agape in front of them.

Holding a pristine handkerchief to her nose, the beautiful woman said, "Gracious, Peter, tell me these are not your children?"

Peter, somewhat embarrassed, replied, "Well, yes, they are, but clearly not dressed to receive you, my love." He frowned at the untidy pair, and continued, "I'd like you to go upstairs and wash and get yourselves dressed correctly, and then come down again to greet your new mother and sister."

The twins were too aghast at the vision of the somewhat sneering woman and her offspring, not believing that their father had remarried without telling them, and both wondering how this was going to change their lives—for change it she certainly would. They both turned and clattered up the stairs and once out of sight stopped and looked at each other with appalled faces. "What's going to happen now, Barnaby?" whispered Blythe.

"Goodness only knows, but I don't think it is going to be good" replied her twin. They went into their respective rooms. Blythe stripped off her boys' clothing, but instead of throwing them into the back of her wardrobe, wrapped them up carefully, and stowed them under a loose plank in a cupboard by the fireplace. She had a premonition that she would be in a life or death position and that she would need her 'disguise'. With a shudder, she also packed an old bag with a couple of gowns, some warm clothes, extra serviceable shoes and some coins, and placed with them a few items that she thought ought to be with them, including a knife, a tinderbox and flints and some clouts that were necessary monthly. She didn't know why, but knew she had to do this. Once they were hidden away, she poured water from the jug into the wash bowl, and gave herself a good wash, brushed and pinned her hair into an orderly bun, drew out a sober dress from her closet, and got dressed as quickly as possible. She was not keen to meet that woman. She knew already that she would be trouble and would not be kind to Barnaby and herself.

Once ready, she left her room and knocked on Barnaby's door. He was ready too, with a glum face, and they both took themselves downstairs and into the best parlour, where their father was waiting with their new mother, who looked up and down the lengths of the twins with disdain, but made sure that her husband did not see her face, which when turned towards him was wreathed in the loveliest of smiles.

"My dear children, this must come as a surprise, but I wish to introduce you to your new mother, who will love you as much as Anne did. Her name is Arabella, but of course, you will call her Mother." Pointing towards the daughter, who looked around sixteen years, he carried on, saying, "And this is Arabella's daughter Dimity, your new sister, whom I am sure you will welcome into our family, put at her ease and help her in every way you can."

Dimity stared at both Blythe and Barnaby, and curtseyed low, though the look in her eyes was calculating, the same as her mother's, and her lips turned down and seemed as if they seldom smiled.

"I am such a lucky man to have found such a beautiful bride," Peter continued, smiling at everyone. Arabella twinkled back at him, making "Tush" sounds, "and I know that once we are all settled into a new regime, we will once again be a happy family." Blythe stared at her father. Why couldn't he see that this woman had a cold heart and was only pretending to love him to gain a rich husband and a lovely home?

"Well," said Arabella with a false smile, "Are you going to show me to our rooms?" Looking around her she continued, "Judging from the state of things here, there is a lot to do. You do have staff, Blythe? Do you have enough?" Blythe mumbled, "Yes, we do have retainers, but since mother died, things have gone downhill a bit." Arabella raised her eyebrows, looked at Peter, and said, "Well, just a tad—Darling Peter, maybe you should show me around your home, and then I can decide which staff to turn away, and how many we need to employ."

With a smile, Peter proffered his arm to Arabella and the other to Dimity, and proceeded to show them his home. The twins, who remained where they were, listened to the silly simpering of Arabella, as she drifted off through the hallway with Peter,

"Oh darling, all this dust and disarray. Don't worry Peter dear, I will get everything organised in next to no time."

Blythe whispered an aside to Barnaby, "She's no doubt calculating all the silks and satins Father will be able to provide her with. Barnaby, this is not good. That is one scheming woman—why can't Father see it?"

Barnaby hissed back, "Blythe, I've told you before, men's brains are in their breeches, and a pretty smile and a pert bottom make sense go out of the window!"

Blythe smiled..."Huh, and you should know, pock face, judging by that ghastly girl I saw you with the other evening!"

Barnaby grinned. "That's just practice, sister. She isn't the type I shall eventually marry."

"And I know what that woman is going to do, Barnaby," grimaced Blythe. "She is going to try and get rid of us as quickly as possible. She is going to do her best to find an ancient husband for me, and get you off to Cambridge, or on a boat before you can turn round and see your shadow! At least you are too young for the parson's mousetrap yet!"

Barnaby wrinkled his nose—"Yes, well I won't mind the first two, but I certainly don't want a bride yet—I want to live first!"

"And so do I!" retorted Blythe. "What are we going to do?"

"Well, we will just have to go with the flow for the time being," said Barnaby, pulling a face, "and maybe they won't be as bad as we anticipate, but there is no point antagonising that woman—we must be on the look-out and make sure we mind our p's and q's."

"I'd better go and warn Cook, and tell her to think of something good for this evening's meal. Luckily we have all that samphire, so that gives her a head start!"

Blythe ran off down the corridor to the kitchen, to find Cook with her feet up against the wall by the fire.

"'allo moi lovely," said Cook, her face cracking into a hearty smile, "Wot yew been op to then? Why's yew all togged up in your besties?"

Blythe pulled a face. "Cook, you have got to look lively. Father has come back with the most awful woman who he says is our new Mother. She looks a right devious bitch, but with the smile of an angel. She is going to be trouble. You must get cracking straight away—sort out the kitchen and scratch together a decent meal for this evening. No doubt she will be in here soon. She's looking to get rid of some of the staff and get in new, so make sure you curtsey and give her your best shot!"

Cook's face paled and she straightened in her chair and stood up, shaking out her rather crumpled skirt and apron, then tucking her hair into her bonnet, she screeched out to both the scullery maid and the under housemaid and started issuing orders, called for Clem to go out into the hen roost and grab a couple of chickens for the pot, turned around a few times in panic, then after collecting herself together, she became their 'Old Cook' again, looking to prepare a decent meal for the evening. Luckily for her, by the time she had got organised, Peter brought Arabella in to introduce her, and when Cook was asked what was on the menu this evening, she was able to tell her new mistress in detail without fluster. Arabella asked to see the housekeeper, who was nowhere to be found, and Blythe knew that poor Mrs Hutchings was going to be the first to go.

The meal served up that night was actually very delicious, but there was a strained atmosphere that Peter really didn't seem to notice. Arabella treated the serving maid very coldly, and Dimity ignored the servants altogether. Half way through the first course, Arabella placed her cutlery at the side of her plate, smiled sweetly at Peter, and then gazed at both Blythe and Barnaby. Dabbing at her lips with a less than perfectly ironed napkin, she said sweetly enough.

"Now, Barnaby and Blythe, your father has told me all about you two, and it seems to me—and he agrees—that you have had too much free time on your hands and are running somewhat wildly."

Blythe rolled her eyes at Barnaby.

"Your father has agreed that it is time that both of you are brought to heel, and Barnaby, he feels that it is time that you went to Cambridge and completed your education, and that you Blythe, need to Come Out and find a husband. You are almost on the shelf as it is." She tittered coyly when saying this. "We need to get your wardrobe up to date, and then your father and I will begin to entertain, have a ball which will be lovely, and ensure that suitable gentlemen with good prospects are invited, who I am sure will all be falling over themselves to vie for your hand."

"I don't want to get married yet," said Blythe grimly, and looking at her smiling father, pleaded with him, "Not yet Father—I wanted to go on some journeys with you on *Morning Star*."

"Don't be ridiculous!" snapped Arabella, forgetting her sugary persona for a moment, then more kindly, "It just isn't suitable that you go adventuring. Maybe one of your suitors will have his own ship and will agree to take you, but you really cannot carry on as you have been doing. It is just so unseemly and you will lose any chance of finding a suitable suitor carrying on in the fashion you have been."

Blythe's stomach tightened. She knew that what her stepmother was saying was actually true. She had been lucky to get away with such a carefree existence for so long, but she didn't trust this woman, and didn't feel that the woman would have her best interests at heart when it came to husband hunting. She just wanted both her and Barnaby out of the equation and have the house to herself and her daughter. She sighed, thinking of what her life undoubtedly would be turning into shortly. She would be sat indoors doing embroidery or painting landscapes, waiting for simpering fools to ask for her hand, and stifling, just stifling for the rest of her life. No doubt her stepmother would opt for some rich but ugly old man to be her spouse, and there probably would be nothing she could do about it. It was different for Barnaby, he would probably enjoy himself at Cambridge and make lots of nice friends, and he could carry on adventuring, working for their father in the business, going overseas seas for new cargoes and enjoying his life to the full—but she could see her own life bleakly stretching into a dreadful future.

***

True to the twins' beliefs, Arabella began to rule the house with strict efficiency. The housekeeper was disposed of, and suitable candidates knocked on the door in the hopes of being taken on. Eventually a gimlet eyed, poker backed woman called Emily Fuller, dressed entirely in black, was taken on by Arabella. Blythe suspected that the two were actually hand in glove and had known each other previously by the way they whispered together when they thought nobody else was around. The house, however, was soon looking absolutely sparkling, but lacked the homely, loving feel that had always been there with their mother.

Father had given Arabella carte blanche to choose fabrics from their warehouse and a French seamstress from London, a Madame Extier, was hired to live-in and make up gowns for the two girls and Arabella. While Blythe did not want fancy clothing, she had to admit to herself that Arabella had impeccable taste when it came to clothing, and she did secretly get rather excited at the beautiful gowns that were soon hanging in her closet. All sorts of fancy gloves and shoes, fans and furbelows were added to match and Peter was very pleased to see Blythe looking like a proper young woman for a change. Arabella had also hired a lady's maid to tend to all the clothing, and who fashioned her hair, and that of Dimity and Blythe when necessary. All the women that Arabella had hired were extremely suspect to Blythe. They came from London, they said, but were reluctant to talk about themselves, but while Arabella didn't outwardly show any familiarity with any of them, Blythe felt they knew each other well. She wondered why, and if there was a suspicious background that her father ought to know about. But Blythe could see he was completely besotted by the woman who used her feminine wiles and guiles to the utmost. She acted out the helpless woman who adored her husband, hanging on to his every word, laughing at his jokes, telling him how handsome, how clever he was, and Blythe could see his confidence and ego puffing by the minute. She realised that her father would never listen to her if she viewed her disturbing thoughts to him, though she did air them with Barnaby. "The woman's a harlot," declared the young man—"I can see it a mile off. She saw Father coming and played him for an idiot." Blythe had a sudden vision of a smiling Arabella greeting clients in a bordello, with 'Madame Extier' seeing to the girls' clothing and Emily Fuller the housekeeper…crystal chandeliers dripped from the ceiling and velvet chaise lounges were placed next to statues of satyrs…then the vision faded. Was that my imagination, she wondered, or a reality? Had her new stepmother been a prostitute in a well-run bordello? She really hoped her imagination had been playing tricks on her.

Arabella had made sure that Peter introduced her to all the affluent and important people of King's Lynn, and those to whom she hadn't had an introduction, she left her calling card at their homes, inviting them to call for afternoon tea, when she then befriended the wives and bewitched the husbands. She was organising a grand ball at home, planning to turn the hall into a ballroom and had all sorts of decorators and designers in, turning the house upside down and changing it irredeemably.

With a sigh, Blythe threw her 'stupid embroidery' onto her footstool, tried to forget about all that was wrong in their house, and walked to the window to stare out over the rooftops where she could see the top masts of ships waiting in the quay. How she yearned to get out in the fresh air and be out on the water.

Chapter Six
King's Lynn, September 1644

Matthew Hopkins had journeyed via Norwich, where he had an audience with the Bishop, outlining his plans to rid Norfolk of its witches. On the last leg to King's Lynn, he had stayed overnight at The Ffolkes Arms coaching inn at Hillington, which was around seven miles from the town. He especially wanted to check out the attic rooms that he understood were used as overnight gaols for the occupants of prison carriages on their way to Norwich. Any witches that he denounced would have to first go to trial in Norwich, and he needed to ensure that they would be secure if a stop was necessary. He mused upon his acquaintance, John Stearne, a staunch Puritan as well as a witch finder, who lived not far from Matthew's home in Manningtree, and had the same fervent determination to seek out witches. Matthew wanted to trounce John in the witch stakes by becoming established at King's Lynn as 'The General' of Witch Finders and denouncing a few witches before summonsing John to aide with their fight against Satan. He would require help in his search—after all, there were many witches reputed to live in the area, and he could not cover the entire county on his own—so long as John ceded that Matthew was in charge, despite him being the younger by around fifteen years.

As he had become soaked from his ride the previous day, he had requested of the landlord that his clothing was dried and spruced up before he left in the morning. He wanted to freshen up before meeting the Dean of Lynn and to create a Godly and pure appearance. While he was a fervent servant of the religious Cromwell, he preferred to woo as many people as possible who would boost his new career as the Witch Finder General—a self-imposed title of which he was most proud—and wanted his first appearance in King's Lynn to bear some weight. Although vanity was a sin, of course, he nevertheless took pride in his appearance, for in his opinion, to be dilatory in one's cleanliness and attire was ungodly.

Matthew was, despite his fanaticism regarding evil and witches in particular, a young man in his early twenties. He had thought, when a child, to follow his clergyman father and join the Church, then decided to be a lawyer, but early on into his training decided, after failing some exams, it was not for him. Due to his childhood experiences of a fire and brimstone education from his father, he knew what was right and what was wrong, but because of his fevered imagination, especially the nightmares and sexual fantasies that beset him, he blamed these problems onto wicked, sinful women, believing them all to be vessels of debauchery with beguiling cesspit female parts—so to save his own spirituality, would denounce as a witch any woman that lewdly attracted him. He did not blame his heightened sexuality on himself, but on the vile, flaunting harpies.

Matthew's face was pale, with spots of bright pink on his cheeks. He was plagued by a cough that sometimes drew flecks of blood in his sputum. In later years, his condition would be understood as tuberculosis, but of course he thought it was little other than a condition, named by his doctor as phthisis, that would eventually pass. Sober minded to the letter, Matthew had no sense of humour whatsoever—frivolity was a sin in his mind and he was set on a path of duty to God. Luckily, he didn't lack for funds—he had inherited well—but he nevertheless looked for ways to add to his fortune, and he had found that witch hunting was remunerative.

While eating at the inn, Hopkins had been repelled by the serving wench, who was garbed in the lowest cut gown imaginable and who made certain that he received eye-to-wobbling-bosom treatment whenever she placed either platter or tankard upon his table.

"What is wrong with you, woman?" he hissed at the girl, finding it difficult to take his eyes from her warm, heaving breasts, the dark nipples of which were displayed when she bent low, and he hated her for the effect it was having on him. He could not help but imagine the forbidden delights under her skirts.

"Why sir, I don't know what you mean?" replied the hussy, batting her eyelashes and hoping for some entertainment later together with some coins in her garter. She had noticed the rise in the gentleman's britches.

"Your disgraceful attire! Luring men into sin. Cover up girl, or Satan will surely get you! Get out of my sight!"

Giggling, the girl sashayed off, the hip pads inside her skirt causing a sensual sway of hips. "Satan can have me Sir, iffen 'e pays! Would you like a little sample, eh? You look as if you would, even with your sour countenance!" She blew him a bawdy kiss, waggling her tongue suggestively as she disappeared back into the kitchens.

Matthew drew out his black book and noted her details down within. She was a siren-witch sent out to lure the Godly, using witchcraft to increase a man's desire. Women who caused a good man's parts to rise in an unseemly manner and who made him think lewd and ungodly thoughts, were witches sent straight from Hell, and should be sent back there immediately.

Hopkins thought of how he struggled daily with temptations of the flesh, that he believed were sent directly from the Devil and knew he did his best to keep them at bay, with little success. Damn the woman. Damn all women, especially those phantoms who came to him in the night and writhed around his body while he slept with their throbbing sexual parts, forcing him to have sex with them in his dreams. They *must* be needled out to allow decent people like himself to live their lives pure and without lustful thoughts of sin.

Hopkins's worst nightmare, however, was nothing to do with sexual thoughts. It was that of a great shaggy bear who pursued him through the nights, especially at the full of moon. This bear had chased him from his childhood, through puberty, and still did so. Matthew had no idea why such nightmares occurred, but they thoroughly frightened him and always left him in a sweating, panting state of fear when he eventually awoke. Casting all thoughts of the bear aside, he patted his pockets to find his money.

Calling over the landlord to pay his bill, Hopkins asked, "Are my clothes ready for me? For I am soon to continue my journey?"

"All in your room, and will be brought down shortly Sire, and a pleasure to do business with you," grovelled the landlord obsequiously.

Hopkins stared at the man, nodding his head with distaste at the girl across the room, "You must get rid of that fornicating wench. She's an enticer, a siren—a witch, and it's my work as The Witch Finder General to denounce all witches in this county!"

The landlord laughed, perceiving this statement as wit, so replied in jocular manner, "That's my daughter Meg—she's no bad wench, just a bit saucy—it's what our customers like and it brings in more coinage if the men like her. Maybe you might like to delay your journey for a little while longer and enjoy her?"

Hopkins stared back at the landlord, his face grim and snapped, "It's no joke, and you heed what I say my man. I will be back, I promise you and she will be denounced."

Scratching his head, and letting out a loud belch, the landlord went back to his customers, muttering, "A queer cove, that'n."

Once he had gathered his bags and got himself spruced up for the last leg of his journey, Matthew left the inn without further ado and found an ostler to saddle up his mare, who as usual showed a skittish nature upon the sight of her master. However, she realised a whipping would be in order if she did not behave, so remained docile while he used the stepping-stone to mount. As he rode out of the establishment, Meg, who had just come out to empty a slop-bucket onto the midden, turned around and flicked up her skirts at Matthew, revealing a very pert and naked backside. As a jolt of lust shot through his body, he vowed to himself he would return and make sure the harlot was hanged. He made the sign of the cross at her, and giggling, she watched him ride away thinking, what a weird man.

Letting the mare go at her own pace today, Matthew looked around him as she picked her way along the muddy road. Flat ground surrounded him with elder trees and hawthorn alongside the drainage ditches and plenty of willow too. In the distance some of the fields were cultivated, while the others held sheep. A new drainage system had been started, but there were still plenty of wet and rank reed beds. Matthew thought of the waterlogged Fen areas that were avoided by travellers because of the small dark men who hid in boggy areas that held much fever and disease. Dykes seethed with eels that the taciturn Fen men caught from their narrow flat-bottomed boats. Strangers who ventured onto their land seldom emerged alive. He wondered if the dykes here held eels.

As he meandered towards King's Lynn, Matthew pondered over this and that. He knew there were some rich and landed farmers in this area, with large estates, and Matthew hoped many would be Puritans, though he had heard that Lynn was strong for the King, despite the siege of the town the previous year. If so, in time, he hoped he could show them the error of their ways. Charles had to go, if there was to be any sense in the land—his flippancy and lack of religion showed him to be nothing more than a whoremonger and his garish manner of dress a disgrace—all that flapping lace, feathers, colours and jewels—not a way of life that God wanted his subjects to follow at all. Everyone should show modesty in all things, wearing simple clothing devoid of colour in respect and honour of The Lord God.

Matthew was aware that the port of Lynn was a very busy one, shipping out fleeces in the main, and bringing in tanned leather from Sweden amongst other items. It was a busy and rich town and he hoped that with his new work of hunting down witches, he would be welcome and consequently rise in status in the world. He believed his work to be Godly and necessary and didn't see his fanaticism or cruelty as anything other than doing what was necessary.

The North Gates were in sight, and Matthew straightened his spine and clattered across the cobbles, asking the gatekeeper the way to the Dean's residence so he could announce his presence, and once duly arrived, he was warmly received. After some pastries and small beer, during which time Matthew outlined his plans for the ousting of witches, the Dean arranged for a cleric to take him to the lodgings that had been made ready for him at the Old Exorcist's House, which had just been newly rebuilt after a fire had gutted it. It was built at the side of the graveyard at St Nicholas's Church, not far from the Tuesday Market Place. The house, under the new law of no thatched roofs, had been designed with a Dutch gable on the north side that flanked the tombstones, yet, even new, it seemed somewhat sombre, which pleased Matthew. He was also satisfied that his new lodging was so close to the Church. Feeling rather important as he gazed at his new home, he dug into his pocket, reached out a coin and tossed it to the cleric as the key was handed over. The man touched his hat in acknowledgement and left Matthew to get acquainted with his new home.

Entering through the heavy and studded oak door, Matthew gazed around the stark entrance hall. It was furnished sparsely, with a heavily polished console table, holding a Bible. He stroked his clipped beard and inspected all the rooms, all new and smelling of polish, freshly sawn wood and lavender. All met his approval.

Only a short while later, he heard a polite knock at the door, and upon opening it, Matthew discovered a neat, plain-faced Puritan woman standing on the doorstep, who bobbed her head respectfully, and in a soft voice said,

"I am so happy to meet you, Sire," she said, bobbing Matthew a curtsey. "My name is Mary Phillips."

Matthew's brows creased as he stared at her. "Yes?" he snapped, irritated to be so quickly disturbed in his new abode.

Proffering him her basket, the woman explained, "I've bought you some sustenance—you'll find bread, cheese and other simple fare, and some ale. This will tide you over until you have found your way around the town and had your larder stocked. I hope you don't find this impertinent, but I wanted you to feel welcomed."

Matthew merely grunted. Mary looked up at him with a tentative smile. "I would be happy to find you a housekeeper and other servants suitable for you if you wish. We are all so thankful that you are here to expose the witches—there is so much evil in our world and you must be some kind of saint to be on such a mission!"

Flattered by the woman's humble yet pleasing address, a faint smile of satisfaction crossed Matthew's face. "Thank you, Mistress Phillips, that is very kind of you. You seem like a good God-fearing woman?"

"Oh yes," she replied earnestly, the smile wiped from her thin face, "I am devoted to God and good works, and if you require any help with your own work of witch-finding, I would be very happy to offer my services to do so—these dreadful women should be needled out as soon as possible. Hanging, in my opinion, is too good for them. I think it's a shame that the burnings have been banned. Evil creatures, they deserve it. My mother was there at the burning of Ann Read in Tuesday Market Place. She said the whole town smelt like roast pork, and the witch sizzled in her own fat and juices—her screams could be heard for miles. That was the burning where the witch's heart popped out of her burning body and hit the wall of one of the houses—the mark's still there, I'll show you, if you'd like."

Matthew nodded and stared back. He liked the look of this woman. She could never be called beautiful—she was very plain, her eyes were very close to her long thin nose, making her look a little cross eyed, and she had absolutely no sexual allure whatsoever. She could never lure him into cardinal sin, thank the Lord. He felt this was an excellent beginning to his stay in King's Lynn.

***

Mary Phillips quickly made herself indispensable to Matthew, finding him servants, showing him around the town, giving him the names of the important people that she felt he should know, as well as the poorer folk who she felt would probably denounce any suspected witches in their area. Being a pious woman, she ingratiated herself into Matthew's confidence, and she had a natural ability to inflate his ego by praising everything he did or said.

Matthew Hopkins gave himself an air of importance. Though he dressed in plain Puritan clothing, his black fabrics were of the best. His white lawn shirts were of the finest linen, his jacket and breeches of costly velvet. His stockings were of the smoothest knit. He sported a tall hat on his head of the best and most expensive beaver skin. His hair was clubbed just beneath his ears and was oiled to the utmost shine. Mary Phillips soon guided him to the best laundry women, and told him of the finest tailors and hatters, so that he would always look his best.

Matthew appeared to be a paragon of neatness and well-groomed severity, though at times his brown eyes glowed dark with fanaticism. He soon drew in many of the wealthy, for he possessed a dark charisma, which seemed to attract people to him. He was soon wining and dining with the upper echelons of King's Lynn society, constantly asking questions about women who were, or might be witches. He wanted to know who dealt in herbs and medicines, who were interested in astrology and other 'dark arts', who were the midwives, the healers, and most importantly the women who had prominent moles upon their person— "For," he told anyone who would listen, "women who have a mole upon their body allow succubae to feed from them. They are harbingers of the devil, feed the devil's soul, their familiars suckle from them and *must* be found and despatched quickly before they cause destruction to us all." Heads would nod in agreement, his constant fervour inspiring all who listened to him.

People of the town were put into a panic, not wanting to be accused of witchcraft, so to save themselves, were soon lining up to tell Matthew Hopkins who they thought to be a witch. The gaol was filled with the wailing of innocent women waiting for trial.

Hopkins would arrive at the gaol, attended by a Mary Phillips, by now his devoted assistant, and they would take the so-called witches down into the dungeon and torture them until they extracted a 'confession'. Physical torture such as the rack had been banned by Parliament (to Matthew's annoyance) but nevertheless there were still plenty of ways that would make people talk. Sleep deprivation was one of them—it was surprising what the women would confess to after a few days and nights without sleep.

Matthew had his special knife made with the retractable blade, that only he knew about, and with this, he would prick any moles that a woman might have in front of witnesses. The blade would disappear into the handle, not coming into contact with any mole at all, but it would look as if the knife had penetrated. When there was no blood from the piercing—it seemed miraculous—then Matthew would declare that was because the woman was a witch, and off she was thrust into a cell, shackled to a wall, until the time came for her trial and subsequent hanging. Needless to say, Hopkins would do the knife trick in front of witnesses, but the torturing he would do on his own. He found it very sexually satisfying to see a woman in pain and would go to endless lengths to torture slowly, to intensify his own pleasure. He devised all sorts of atrocities, within the new laws, that the wretched women had to undertake, that satisfied his warped pleasure and eventually bagged a parcel of witches—all in the name of the Lord, of course. Mary Phillips attended whenever he allowed, and she too received her own pleasures.

Sometimes in the dark, unpleasant cells, lit only by a tallow candle within a lantern, Mary noted in the dim glow the bulge in Matthew's trousers, so she would then 'accidentally' brush past him, or perhaps fall against him, and between themselves they found inordinate shivers of pleasures as they tortured the poor women tied down in the dark cellar. Eventually, the women, deprived of sleep, and hurt by so many ways and in excruciating pain, would confess to witchcraft and moan out the names of their familiars, just in order for the tormenting to cease.

On one occasion, when 'stumbling' in the dark as she passed Matthew, her hand came in contact with the bulge in his trousers. "Oh, I do beg your forgiveness, my Lord, I mean no disrespect." Matthew, embarrassed that his condition had been discovered, just grunted. Mary brushed him down gently, making sure her fingers slid gently across the bulge. "I am aware, Sir, that these harlots of the devil arouse you against your will, and indeed they make me feel wickedly and similarly inclined. It is all part of their enticing devil ways."

"Maybe," she said, brushing gently at his man parts, "if I just carried on as I am doing, in the name of God, it would rid you of the lust engendered by these wicked women? Would you not feel better with the relief that it would afford you?"

Matthew grunted and unconsciously stroked the whip handle as if it were his own member. He considered what Mary had just said, and felt it was a moot point. He lashed the whip painfully across the woman currently tied naked to the table while he considered.

"You are right, Mary," Matthew pompously agreed. "I should not contain the evil lust that this dreadful harpy has engendered within me. I will allow you to rid me, purge me of my sin, knowing that neither of us will receive pleasure from it. You have my permission to exorcise me of the sin."

Later, as Matthew quickly buttoned up his trouser flaps, Mary gazed at the woman's bleeding welts almost lovingly. "Did you notice, Sir, that while the Devil was being expunged from your body, the familiar of that woman materialised and clawed at her body until it was shredded and bled? Why would that be, I wonder? Why would the Devil claw at his own? I think we should pray, sir. Pray that you have been safely delivered of Satan's frightful lust and are back in the glory of God. Let us kneel Sir, and I think as you are Godlier than my poor self, that you should lead the prayer." Mary was using hallowed tones and continued, "I assure you, Sir, we had to do what was done, or your suffering would have been intense, and all was only done in God's name. It wasn't as if you nor I took pleasure in it."

Appeased, and cleansed of any guilt, Matthew coughed and they both knelt on the cold stone floor. "Dear Lord," intoned Matthew, "As you are aware, I am dealing with the matter of discovering and expelling the Devil's Minions, in your name, in order to bring your Godliness closer. Mistress Phillips has volunteered assistance in this distasteful manner to exorcise the evil from my body caused by vile witches. This good woman is as keen as I to rid the country of witches, those cohorts of Satan, thus bringing order from the chaos they cause. We both serve only you, my Lord. Amen."

Mary muttered her Amen, after which they dutifully left the cellar and its broken occupant, Matthew striding from the building with confidence and Mary scurrying behind him filled with secret euphoria. Thereafter, this procedure became an unspoken yet much enjoyed secret between the two—Matthew could indulge himself in the carnal manner to completion, because as he told himself, he did not desire Mary in the slightest and did not see that what she was doing to him was any other than helping him rid himself of ungodly 'humours'; in the meantime both were delightfully satiated, with God's supposed sanction, to the screams of various poor women being whipped and brainwashed in the dark, dank cellar, to be denounced as witches and ordered by the Norwich magistrate to be hanged.

Chapter Seven

Simon Truman hammered on the door of the Brown residence and luckily, eighteen-years-old Blythe was the one who let him in. She noticed his face was as white as a sheet and asked, "Oh Simon, what on earth is troubling you?"

"It's my mother, Blythe, she has been imprisoned as a witch by the Witch Finder General!"

"Oh, that's dreadful, Simon, what can we do?" cried Blythe, her hands clasped to her face in horror.

"I don't think we can do anything, but Blythe, Mother managed to whisper to me before she was carted away. She told me to get rid of all my astrological books, and to tell you to do the same. They will incriminate us if they are found and we too could be accused of witchcraft."

Blythe paled, and asked, "What, straight away?"

"Yes, I think so Blythe, as people are pointing fingers to save their own souls, and nobody is safe. Make sure you have nothing around that can be used against you. No books on herbs either, for Mother was accused because of her knowledge of herbs. It won't be long before somebody tells the authority that she used to teach you—oh, and she said to try and cover your mole!"

"This is terrible, Simon. Your mother is no more a witch than I am! I will go and see her at once." Blythe immediately reached over to take her cape from its hook.

"No, Blythe, mother said not to," replied Simon earnestly. "She knew that is what you would want to do and she told me to make it clear that is the last thing you should do. She doesn't want anyone to notice you, especially with your skills and knowledge." They clasped each other's hands in anguish.

Blythe heard the whisper of silk behind her and turned quickly, to see the housekeeper, Emily Fuller, backing quickly and turning to walk along the hall. How long had she been standing there? How much had she heard?

"Can you trust her?" Simon asked, as the woman almost glided through a distant doorway.

With a pale face, Blythe answered, "I don't think so—but that is by the by. What can I do for your mother? Shall I get cook to send along some food—she won't get fed in the goal."

"It's alright at the moment, Blythe," said Simon, "I can cover that—I will ask you if I need anything. In the meantime, keep a low profile—don't get noticed, and get rid of those books." Kissing Blythe on the cheek, Simon left at a run and Blythe went straight up to her room, tears in her eyes, and locked the door. She wondered what she should do with her books—if anyone searched for them, they would look in all the likely hiding places. After some thought, she bundled them up and tied them together and opened the window. For the time being, she would thrust them out of sight by the eaves of the house, and later under darkness she would find a better hiding place for them. Leaning far out of the window, she pushed them out of sight. No sooner than she had done this, the latch on her door was rattled.

"Why are you locking yourself in, Blythe?" came the voice of her stepmother. "Open up at once!"

Blythe unlocked the door and said, "Yes, what is it you want, Stepmother? Sorry, I often lock the door against Barnaby—he's such a sneak." Her stepmother nodded, unconvinced and glanced around the room and seeing nothing untoward, stepped towards Blythe.

"We are all dining out tonight, Blythe, and I want you to look your best. We are going to Clifton House—the marvellous one with the towers, which is an experience—who would think, the highest building in the town, and built by the wealthiest man of all! I want you on your best behaviour, and in your finest gown." Wrenching open the closet door as if she would find secrets within, she went through the gowns, drawing out a beautiful creation that shimmered in the light coming in from the window. Arabella patted around the closet with her hand *("What is she looking for,"* thought Blythe) and found some shoes that matched, a fan and shawl and laid them out on Blythe's bed. "Wear these," she said to Blythe, and with a sly smile mentioned, "You never know who will be there tonight. Maybe you will meet your husband-to-be, that would be lovely, wouldn't it, dear?"

Blythe noticed Dimity standing in the doorway with a pouty leer on her face. What on earth were they up to, she wondered.

As Arabella departed downstairs, Dimity came in Blythe's room and sat on the edge of the bed. "Mother says you will soon be gone and out of the way. I can have your room then, which is much nicer than mine."

"That's as may be," retorted Blythe. "I'm not ready to be married yet, if that's what you mean, and will only marry for love. What's wrong with your room anyway? You managed to get poor Barnaby out of his and up into the attic so you could have it—not that he cares—and that was unkind."

Dimity smirked and jumped down from the bed. She wandered around the room, touching things, looking at the few books that Blythe had on her table-top, and generally, Blythe thought, searching for something incriminating. Surely she and her stepmother were not going to accuse her of witchcraft? She must be careful what she said and did from now on.

***

Later on that evening, Blythe sighed as she began to ready herself for the evening ahead. It was the last thing she wanted to do—sitting there uncomfortably in her new gown, listening to unutterably boring old people exaggerating about their wealth, as well as saying unkind words about their less moneyed neighbours. To think there might be an ugly old man looking for a wife who might decide she was 'the one'—to think of having to climb into bed and go through what wives have to do with someone she didn't love…

A vision of Ambrose played in front of her eyes—his dark hair flopping over his face as he bent over her with his shirt flung to the floor—she felt herself flush and wondered where on earth that image had come from! She hadn't seen Ambrose since he had been invited to dine so long ago. She had thought of him with yearning quite often, but how odd to think of him now. *Well*, she mused, *it would be wonderful to have a handsome man like that to marry, but life,* she thought, *didn't turn out like that.* If only she could have a happy marriage like that of her father and mother…but now, he was married to that, that *harpy*! Yes, Blythe thought, *that is just what she is like… Sweet as pie, but like a vulture underneath.* She thought of the woman pecking out her father's entrails with the gold coins flying from his pockets… "Stop it!" she said out loud to herself.

The gown she was climbing into was made of some of her father's finest fabrics. Her underskirts were of a pale blue, with darker blue overskirts. Fashionable, with a high waistline, the satiny material flowed like a river, gathered at the back and also under her bosom. Despite Blythe not wanting a low décolletage, Arabella had insisted that her neck, shoulders and bosom were on display, saying that she didn't want her stepdaughter thought by the town to be out-of-mode. Blythe felt really uncomfortable displaying so much, and found a shawl that she would place around her neck to offer a more circumspect look.

Madame Extier knocked at her door and entered without waiting for a response. "Just checking to make sure all is well with you Miss Blythe—oh my, the gown looks très ravishing, doesn't it? Now, what about your 'air? Shall I get going on it? What about an oiseau or deux?"

"No!" Blythe glowered at the woman, "I'm not having dead birds on my head!"

Madame Extier smiled, and said, "Well, let's see what else we might have to finish the look. You must have *something* in your hair."

"How about a galleon then?" said Blythe with a laugh, knowing that some women did ridiculous things with their wigs, but she was having none of that. "Look," she said, picking up some gauze butterflies on wires, "These will do, and they match the fabric—I don't want anything bizarre."

"As you wish, mademoiselle," said the woman with heavily exaggerated accent, and expertly swished Blythe's hair up and arranged it 'just so', popping the butterflies at just the right angle to gain perfection.

"Oh, I rather fancy a tress or two to dangle down my cheek near my mouth," said Blythe casually, remembering about her mole. Not knowing who was going to report such things, she would prefer to hide her mole as much as possible. "Oh no," said the French woman with horror, "It will make you look très untidy."

"It will make me look as if I have a little originality," replied Blythe firmly, so reluctantly Madame readjusted the hair style so a few tresses coiled down.

Juno, who had been asleep in a dark corner of the room, stood and stretched and the woman gave a shriek "Oh, that 'orrible 'ound! It frights me so!"

Blythe, watching through the mirror noticed how spiteful the woman appeared when looking at the dog, and felt that anyone disliking animals so much could not be a pleasant person. She wondered why her stepmother kept a retinue of unpleasant women around her.

Once she was ready, Blythe picked up her reticule, her fan and her gloves, with the shawl folded across her arm—she knew that Arabella would take it away from her if she wore it now, and had decided to don it at the last moment as they entered Clifton House. Peter was waiting downstairs, Barnaby was elsewhere and not attending the meal that evening, so it was just Arabella and Dimity that were awaited. It was only a few moments before Arabella swept down the stairs, looking completely ravishing. Blythe could understand her father's lust for the woman, but wished he could see into her heart and realise what she really was like. Dimity followed her mother and wore a dress just that much richer than Blythe's, and she looked very well, except she had a sulky, spiteful face—Blythe thought that the girl needed to learn her mother's skill of hiding her sly feelings.

The clopping of hooves sounded on the cobbles outside, announcing that their chaise had arrived at the door, so Peter ushered them out, and held the carriage door open for them. Arabella climbed in first, Dimity pushed Blythe out of the way to follow her mother, then Blythe stepped in, followed by her father. There was much arranging of skirts and patting of hairdos, to ensure that nothing of their ensembles was marred.

The distance wasn't too far to Clifton House in Queen Street with its famed tower and the barley-twist pillars by the door, but their way was impeded by crowds milling around in Tuesday Market place. "What are they doing, Father?" asked Blythe.

"Getting ready for the witch hanging tomorrow," said Dimity with a gleeful smile on her face, "Your friend Goody Truman will soon be dangling at the end of a rope!" Blythe felt the blood drain from her face and turned to face her father, who instead of answering her, stared out of the chaise window. Blythe bit her tongue to stop herself from speaking, for she felt that Arabella and Dimity were waiting for her to say something that would denounce herself as an intimate of Goody Truman and thereby a witch herself. She swallowed fiercely and looked out of the window without seeing anything.

What could she do to save her friend? Blythe noticed that the marketplace was bristling with soldiers from the local garrison. Recalling the hanging that she and Barnaby had attended so long ago, she only remembered a couple of soldiers being there—the crowds at that time were relatively orderly, but maybe the troops were patrolling this evening as people were already getting too excitable. A number of drunks were shouting and gesticulating, but the military poked them with the sharp ends of their bayonets and that stopped them for a while.

Swaying, drink-sodden tars caused a hold up too, as they weaved their way out of a nearby inn, shouting, singing and cursing as one of them fell over in a stupor. The horses blew nervously out of their nostrils, stepping high, their heads tossing back and forth, their manes flying. Eventually they arrived at their destination, where the atmosphere was calmer, and once the chaise step had been pulled down by the postilion, they all clambered out, the ladies pulling and shaking their gowns free in order to let the natural flow of their fashion ensue. Peter and Arabella went first, with the girls following. Blythe ignored Dimity's whispered and gleeful remarks about her friend being hanged on the morrow. Blythe tried to keep decorum uppermost but really wanted to slap the cruel girl around the face. She actually felt faint from horror at the thought of what dear Goody Truman must be going through.

Many well-dressed guests mingled in the large vestibule, where a lady was skilfully playing a spinet that was placed in an alcove. Blythe was intrigued to notice that a stuffed bear was displayed in a corner and wondered if there was a story attached to it. A butler was serving glasses filled with expensive wine and when Blythe was offered one, she downed it as fast as possible. She needed something to give her strength as she was so upset about the thought of Goody Truman's imminent hanging. Eventually they were all called by their host to climb the stairs to the topmost tower room where they were to eat. A series of high windows overlooked the harbour as well as the important buildings of Lynn and one could see for miles over the town and estuary. It was indeed a wonderful sight. A glorious red, pink and purple sunset was lighting up the evening sky, that reflected in the water, and Blythe absentmindedly noted some grebes gracefully paddling their way amongst the various moored vessels, picking amongst the flotsam to find snippets of food.

Just as they were being seated, there was a commotion at the door, and Blythe felt prickles of discomfort course down her neck, like the hackles of a dog when sensing trouble. She looked around and noticed a dark man entering the room, who had jumped in shock when he noticed the taxidermist's bear. Blythe saw him turn white and begin to shake, but he pulled himself together when the Usher enquired and called out his name as, "Master Matthew Hopkins." The man gave a light bow, and as he was being shown to his place, he apologised for his tardiness, due to the crowds in the Market Place. He was seated in the only available place, almost opposite Blythe and next to Arabella. She gazed at the Witch Finder General, shuddering inwardly, twiddling with the locks of hair deliberately unfurled down her face, and hoped that it would hide her mole. So *this* was the man accountable for Goody Truman's hanging on the morrow.

Blythe noted the odious man was of medium height, neither good-looking nor ugly, though he had a somewhat bulbous nose. His eyes were deep-set and dark, and he had a way of seeing all, thought Blythe, as those eyes flickered and took in the details of everyone around the table. He was garbed in a finely cut Puritan outfit with a white lace collar and wore buckled leather shoes. To Blythe he emanated evil, yet he pronounced that his work was to fight evil and banish those who worked with the Devil. Blythe noticed his aura, which was wide and active, but as black as tar. She had never seen a black aura before, and she shivered though the evening was warm. Blythe didn't taste any of the food on her plate, though she managed to swallow a few mouthfuls.

Arabella was in her element, laughing and joking to the men seated beside her, bending over to reveal her cleavage, touching them on their arm, or their thigh, flirting outrageously but not enough to be dismissed as a harlot. Little do they know, thought Blythe.

Leaning towards Hopkins, Arabella looked him straight in the eye, and asked him in a loud voice, "What, dear Mr Hopkins, do you look for in a witch? I am vastly interested to hear. Tell us how you know, and is it something that we can all look out for?"

Matthew Hopkins coughed importantly, and said in a deep, penetrating voice, "Well, Madam, it is not always obvious—these witches are clever and don't want us to know who they are. They can be old crones living in tumbledown hovels, like my first witch, Old Mother Clark, a toothless one-legged old crone. Then there was 'respectable' Anne West and her fifteen-year-old daughter Rebecca. They were all held in Colchester castle for four months. Rebecca was acquitted, but the other two women were condemned and hanged. Most witches are hanged," he continued, as he gazed around at his by now silent audience, "Except Mary Lakeland. As well as being charged for being a witch, she had killed her husband and had conspired to kill a man who had broken off his courtship to her granddaughter. She was burnt at the stake." His dark eyes boring into those of Arabella. "But not all are old hags, madam, some are fashionable women like yourself, living in a life of luxury."

Arabella momentarily flinched, then tossing her head back flirtatiously retorted, "Gracious, Master Hopkins, don't tell me you suspect me!" fluttering her eyelashes at the unresponsive man.

"No, madam, I don't suspect you, but there might be something that hints that you might be a witch. Do you have any moles upon your body?"

Arabella laughed nervously, pulling up her fichu a tad, saying, "La, Sire, doesn't everybody have a few moles upon their person?"

"Most probably, my lady, but the moles of a witch do not bleed when pricked with a blade—that is the proof I need to denounce a witch!"

"Oh," laughed Arabella, "that would rule out most, I imagine, but how do you tell? Does it have to be a facial mole—for instance, like that of my dear stepdaughter Blythe over there?"

Shocked, Blythe gasped, Peter scowled and Dimity giggled, while Arabella tinkled out laughter as if her own suggestion was absurd. Hopkins gazed unblinkingly at Blythe, who made sure her hair was covering that side of her face, while Hopkins continued his remarks by saying,

"And all witches have familiars, an animal—usually a dog or a cat, into which they can magically be absorbed while they go around in the dark of the night to perform their evil deeds. During other days they suckle the familiar in a disgusting manner. Sometimes when we are interrogating witches, we see imps attempting to sneak into the cell where a witch is being watched. Once I saw a whitish thing, not quite as large as a cat, on another occasion, there was something like a dog with sandy spots, and on another occasion, we witnessed a creature similar to a greyhound with long legs."

"Oh," said Arabella innocently, "you should see the huge hound that constantly trails alongside my stepdaughter and would you believe it, she and her twin suckled off the ghastly creature when they were babies!" Turning to Blythe, she smiled sweetly and said, "Darling, did you hear what Master Hopkins is saying? That great dog of yours could be your familiar! How droll! Oh, how I'd love to see *you* suckle *her*!"

Shocked guests around the table had stopped talking to each other, as they listened and watched the dreadful scenario taking place in front of their eyes. Was Arabella Brown being dim-witted, or was she virtually handing her stepdaughter on a plate to the Witch Finder General?

Blythe felt she could faint at any moment, but held her back stiff and firm and managed to breathe deeply, despite her corset. She even managed to shrug and smile at Matthew Hopkins, in a manner to suggest that what her stepmother was saying was preposterous.

"Many witches," continued Hopkins, glancing at Arabella and resting on Blythe, "are keen herbalists—do you have a still room, Mistress Brown, where you distil brews from plants both poisonous and benign?"

Blythe could not open her mouth to reply, for Arabella instantly tinkled out the sweetest of laughter, saying, "Oh, yes, of course Master Hopkins, as most households do. You should see her stillroom—I mean to sweep it clean of course—she is always collecting strange vegetation and brewing it into bottles—taught by her mother's friend, a Goody Truman I believe." Bending forward, revealing a great deal of her generous bosoms, Arabella, pealing with darling laughter, coyly remarking to Peter, a few guests up from her, "Dear heart, I think you must have spawned a witch—oh how droll!" then turning back to Hopkins, she asked, "Is there any other sign perhaps, Sir, to denote a witch?"

Hopkins, his brow covered in the sweat of excitement, glanced at the girl and at the stepmother. If anyone were the witch, he felt, it was the stepmother, but he had one more 'sign' to deliver. "Astrology," he said. "Anyone who understands and dabbles in the magical art of astrology is bound to be in league with the Devil and my work is to rid the lands of all Devil worshipers and hang every one of them from the neck until they are dead!" His face was puce by now and his hands were shaking, as if in a fever. He coughed, and grabbing a kerchief from his pocket wiped away some smears of blood from his mouth.

Arabella tinkled her seductive laugh once more and said prettily, "Oh la! Indeed, she has been tutored by both Nicholas Culpepper and William Lilly—her brother has too—would that make the lad a warlock, I wonder?" As she said this, Arabella tapped her fan across Hopkins's arms, as if it were all a huge jest.

It was clear that Arabella was about to utter further damning revelations, but Peter barked across the table at her, "Enough Arabella! This is beyond a joke. Master Hopkins has a serious job to attend to, and it is not amusing that you jest with him about our daughter and son." Saying this, he noticed the flickering unpleasant emotions upon his new wife's face and wondered what he had missed before. Was she deliberately placing Blythe directly into the wolf's mouth, or was this just a joke gone too far?

Blythe felt terrified. Loud embarrassed talk suddenly resumed, everyone was attempting to defuse the situation, all secretly wondering if Arabella Brown's cogitations regarding Blythe were correct, or was she just a hen brain?

Matthew Hopkins' gaze continued to rest upon Blythe, who, in order to avoid his worryingly hypnotic eyes, spoke avidly to an old gentleman by her side, who was actually in the market for a new bride, and believed his luck was in—witch or no witch! He imagined she would definitely be a saucy little strumpet in his bed! Clutching Blythe's knee under the table he let his podgy fingers slide upwards. Blythe, stifling a scream, let her glass of wine 'accidentally' fall upon the gentleman's jacket, and made a loud fuss about it.

"Oh Sire, do forgive me, I am so sorry," but inwardly thinking, what a ghastly old goat, as a male servant hastily brought over a serviette in order to dab down the coat, thus averting more unwanted attention to Blythe. Never had an evening been so long, never had she so much wanted to be elsewhere.

After the meal, Peter drew his womenfolk to his side and said they must be going. "Oh must we?" tinkled Arabella. "We haven't even danced at the ball yet, and I am having such a wonderful time and so is my Dimity—I noticed a handsome young man taking quite some attention to her, and it would be good that she got some marriage offers, even at her young age, don't you think, darling?"

"No, we are going home now," said Peter, dragging them outside and looking out for their carriage. As soon as it was out of the ranks of waiting horses and carriages, he bundled his family inside, his lips tight pressed, his brow creased into a frown.

"Whatever," he addressed his wife, "did you think you were doing, giving that man cause to be interested in Blythe?"

"Oh darling, I meant no harm—it was just a joke—he would never have taken me seriously!" said Arabella, fluttering her eyelashes at him in innocent concern.

"I think not wife. Blythe is now in a dangerous situation, all due to you. I have to think now, for I believe it will not be long before Matthew Hopkins will be hammering at our door, issuing a warrant for Blythe's arrest, and with all the evidence you have thrown him, we will be hard pressed to find a way out of this."

The occupants of the chaise spoke no more as the chaise clattered over the cobbles towards their home. Once the carriage had drawn up outside the door and Peter had ushered them into the hall, he said tersely to his wife, "Madam, wait for me in the withdrawing room. Dimity, go with your mother. Blythe, follow me into the library."

Blythe almost had to run to keep up with her father as he strode into his room. A room that she had so loved, the walls lined with shelves bearing many leather-bound books. She adored being with him in this room while he wrote letters—she'd select and read one of his books, curled up in a chair while he was working, or when he was not, sometimes watching for him out of the window…now it was a very different situation. Peter grabbed hold of the heavy velvet drapes and pulled them across the window so eyes from outside could not see in.

"Blythe, you must go from this house as quickly as possible. I don't know when he will strike, but that Witch Finder General is going to pounce on you as soon as he can. You will be tortured with hot steels, pricked and cut, and possibly even raped for all I know, and all in the Name of God... I just can't let this happen to you. Dear Goody Truman is to hang tomorrow, and she did nothing but good for the local people...I have been thinking what to do on the way back from Clifton House and this is my plan. The *Morning Star* and the *Evening Star* are waiting for the midnight tide. The *Morning Star*'s first port of call is in France, and the other vessel is sailing to Constantinople. I shall pen a quick note to the *Morning Star*'s captain, and I want you to quickly don Barnaby's clothing (yes, I know you of old!) as they will serve you better, gather up some of your own clothing and go to him quickly—he will see you safely delivered to friends of mine in France, who will look after and protect you until the danger is over. Danger and death is certain for you in King's Lynn at the moment. I will visit you as soon as I can."

Blythe nodded her head and gulped—though she was quickly realising that she was now in the midst of an adventure that, though frightening, was at the same time thrilling.

As Peter swiftly penned a note to his captain, Blythe bit her lip, and they both jumped when a loud pounding started at the front door. Peeping through a small gap in the drapes, Blythe said, "It's him!"

"Quickly daughter, go to your room and out of the window—I know you have done it enough times in the past!" Pressing the paper into her hand together with a purse of money, he quickly hugged her and pushed her out of the door. Blythe ran along the corridor and up the stairs while Peter made a great thing of rattling keys and took his time drawing back the bolts. As she reached her room, locking the door behind her, Blythe could hear the tones of Hopkins' voice below. She tore off her clothing, dived to retrieve the ready packed bag that she previously had the premonition to pack, as well as pulling out the boys' clothing from beneath the boarding in her closet, threw on the trousers and jacket, rammed a cap onto her head, bundling her hair inside it, pulled on her high boots, grabbed her bag, threw up the window and climbed out. She retrieved the astrological books and niftily ran across the roof top, jumped down onto the stable roof, ran quickly into the stable to shove the books behind some loose planking in one of the stalls, then raced through the back stable door and out into the night. She heard the clicking of Juno's claws and realised the hound was following her. Blythe gasped, "Back home, Juno!" but the dog took no notice and ran alongside her. Her 'familiar', her dearest Juno. Maybe it was best the beast came with her, for that dreadful man might kill her dog, believing that he was slaying her at the same time.

A sea fret was rolling in fast from the estuary, which she felt was lucky, for it would delay her pursuers who would inevitably go to the quay and search the ships for her. Knowing the way like the back of her hand, she ran through the thickening fog, avoiding crates and coiled ropes and the occasional drunk laid flat out on the cobbles. She surprised rats scavenging for food, but they quickly scurried out of her way until she had run by, to then continue with their suppers. By the time she came to the mooring where the two ships should be anchored, she realised there was only one. The other must have already set sail. She could hear the rattling of chains and the muted shouts of sailors getting ready to cast off, though she could only see ghostly shapes. Suddenly looming in front of her, she saw the outline of the gangplank and leapt on it with Juno fast on her heels, hoping she was on the *Morning Star* and on her way to France and safety.

A sailor yelled out hoarsely, "Where d'ew think yew be goin'?"

"Don't worry," shouted back Blythe, "the captain knows." Well, he didn't yet, but she felt it best that no delay was caused, wanting the assurance that the ship was sailing out of the harbour and into the estuary to ensure her safety. If it was the wrong ship, it didn't really matter—at least she was out of the clutches of the horrible Witch Finder General and would be on to an adventure to far Constantinople where silk fabrics would be waiting after their long journey on camelback along the Silk Route. She actually felt very excited, especially as she had outrun her pursuers.

Not wanting to be in the way while the captain and crew were busy negotiating the water ways and hoisting the sails as well as the many jobs necessary, all made more difficult by the thick fog, Blythe, clicking her fingers to Juno, decided to take cover in a nearby stored skiff hanging at the side of the deck in order to lie low while so much was going on. She clambered inside, with Juno following and burrowed down under some tarred canvas to keep herself dry and warm. Sticking her nose out, she couldn't see a thing, though hearing all the familiar sounds of a ship setting sail, she felt very secure. She stuck her duffle bag under her head and despite all the fright of the night, quickly fell asleep, lulled by the movement of the water under the boat, the muffled cries of the men, the rattling and thudding noise of sails being raised, all the sounds of activity that she loved. Juno snuggled close to her, giving her warmth, and surprisingly she slept like a log.

***

Whilst Blythe had been racing through King's Lynn docks to safety on the *Evening Star*, Peter had been dealing with the thunder-faced Matthew Hopkins who was accompanied by several heavy men. Arabella and Dimity had come out of the withdrawing room, Arabella smiling seductively at the man in black. She said as if receiving a guest, "Oh please enter, Master Hopkins, do follow me, at this late hour you must be ready for a brandy." They walked down the hall with Hopkins following Arabella and the others trailing behind. Arabella poised nicely by Peter's chair, beckoned for the Witch Finder to take a seat. She gracefully went over to the cupboard where Peter kept his brandy and glasses, and offering Matthew Hopkins a filled glass. She also poured for one for Peter, who sat down in the opposite chair.

"I'm presuming I made a fool of myself earlier this evening and gave you reason to suspect my stepdaughter is a witch. I was merely joking, I assure you, she is no more witch than I am!" Arabella trilled merrily, while Peter watched her over the rim of her glass.

"As it happens, I do want to question your daughter," said Hopkins, directly to Peter. "I had already had some reports about her in any event, and your remarks were certainly interesting, madam, and seeing the girl myself, merely accelerated the situation in my mind. As you say, after examination, we might find her innocent, but if not…I have to do my duty. Where is she now? I would like to speak with her."

"Blythe is in her room," Peter said. "Dimity, go and fetch her please." Dimity ran off with a flushed face, excited to be able to see the downfall of her despised stepsister. Once out of sight, she raced up the stairs two at a time, and ran along to Blythe's room and pushed at the door but of course, it was locked from the inside. She rattled the doorknob and shouted out, "Blythe! You must come downstairs at once! Hurry!" There was no answer, so she shouted and banged on the door. Blythe was not answering her. Surely if she had been asleep, the noise would have awakened her?

Dimity ran down the stairs to report the situation, so Hopkins rose to his feet and said to Peter, "Show me the way to her room. I'll soon have her out!"

Peter led the way and tapped on Blythe's door. He reasoned that she was long gone, but had to go along with the charade. Arabella was standing by, her hands clasped to her bosom, looking worried and afraid. Peter thought maybe he had got her wrong, and it was just a silly mistake she had made. Or was she an excellent actress? He didn't notice Dimity stifling giggles behind him.

Hopkins pushed Peter aside, and said, "Leave this to me!" He beckoned to his heavy men, and gestured towards the door. Before Peter had time to realise they were going to break the door down, the lock gave as huge shoulders thudded against it, and the door swung open. Blythe's evening clothes lay strewn on the bed, the window was swinging on its latch and the sea mist was pouring into the room.

"The bitch has fled!" exclaimed Hopkins,

"And so has her hound," gasped Arabella, still clasping her hands. Peter glanced quickly at her, thinking whether she really had to point that out—could she really be so stupid?

"Ah, she has disappeared with her familiar then," said Hopkins with a somewhat satisfied expression on his face. "They have flown out of the window to serve their master, the evil one. She must be found." Arabella pretended to stifle a loud sob. Again, Peter wondered if she really was an excellent actress, while Dimity's satisfied grin spoke volumes. As they all trooped down the stairs, the housekeeper and the French seamstress were keeping an eye on proceedings with keen interest.

Cook was listening at the door with her mouth wide open. "Dear God," she gasped, "Our wonderful Blythe a witch? It don't make no sense? She is no more a witch than the goat in the garden! Oh my!" and flung her apron over her head to try and make the nonsense disappear.

"Where has she gone, man?" The Witch Finder asked Peter.

"I don't know, Sir, and that's a fact. She was in her room, and now she isn't."

"Clearly she has flown off on a broomstick," Hopkins commented.

"Don't be a fool, man," snapped Peter, "she has but climbed out—she has been doing that since she was a child."

Hopkins frowned at the interruption and continued, saying to his men, "We will keep an eye open for her. She can't have gone far. Gather to, men, split up and start the search for her—she can't be far—and try the docks first. I shall take my leave now." The two men bowed to each other and as Hopkins strode out of the house with his men, leaving muddy footmarks throughout the house behind them, Peter shut the door with a sigh.

"Where has your daughter gone, Peter?" Arabella questioned her husband. "I demand to know."

Peter raised his eyes to hers and sighed again. "As I told Hopkins, I don't know." As he told the lie, he realised he really didn't know, for his ships might have missed the tide in the fog, and even if they had sailed, had Blythe managed to get on board? The fog was still thick, and anything could have happened to her.

Telling his wife to go to bed, he sat in his library for a while after which he slipped out of the back door and strode along to the harbour. Peering through the fret, he noted with relief that both the ships had gone from their moorings and some of Hopkins' men were milling around, shouting and searching the many moored vessels, causing a lot of annoyance. Curses abounded, curs yapped as they were kicked, and curled their lips back on yellow teeth to growl and bark at their assailants.

Just in case anyone had noticed him, Peter didn't want them to put two and two together and realise that he had sent Blythe onto one of his ships, so he carried on walking until he reached his warehouse, where a channel of water led right inside for goods to be unloaded. He unlocked the door and went inside, and turned the key behind him. Once inside, he climbed the steps to his small office, lit the fire that was already set, and sat back in the comfortable chair at his desk, deep in thought. He eventually dozed until the morning and when he awoke, he fervently hoped his darling daughter had got away and was by now in France.

***

Arabella, believing Peter was still in his library, went along to her housekeeper's room, beckoning her French maid to accompany her. Once enclosed in the rather gloomy room, Arabella hissed, "Tarnation! The girl is at least gone, but not hanged! It was so near, so very near! I could weep!"

Emily and Ethel, who was no more French than the beggar in the gutter outside, commiserated with their mistress. "But at least she is gone. If she comes back, it won't take a second to inform the Witch Finder," Emily consoled.

"True. My theory is that the bitch ran off onto one of Peter's ships—they were due to sail at midnight and he seemed remarkably calm about her absence. No doubt he told her to jump on board. Hopefully they will sink."

"But then that just leaves Barnaby and Peter to dispose of, doesn't it?" said Ethel.

These two women had been Arabella's maids when she was a courtesan. Peter of course knew nothing of her old life, her old *hard* life, almost climbing out of the gutter and selling her body to keep alive until she struck lucky with a rich man. She had gone from one wealthy man to another, amounting riches as she went. The odd amount of poison administered in a late night brandy had helped. Her plan was to eventually dispose of Peter to gain his wealth, home and ships and she could then settle back into a free and unfettered life, until she bagged her ultimate prize—that of a Duke. "You are doing a good job, girls, you are fine actresses—we shall all soon be free, and Dimity will become a proper young lady. And, as soon as Barnaby returns home, I think he is going to have a very bad stomach indeed…"

As it happened, Barnaby was snoring his head off in the ship bound for France together with Simon. They had been roistering in the town most of the night to alleviate Simon's pain of his mother's hanging in the morning and were well in their cups. For some drunken reason, that had seemed an inordinately splendid idea at the time. They had decided to sneak on board the vessel, aided and abetted by one of the equally inebriated crew. While in their cups, the thought of a sneaked trip to France seemed like great fun, so with much guffawing and 'shhhhing', fingers to lips and falling over, they tipped into a dark corner in drunken oblivion, while their erstwhile aider and abettor weaved his way off to his hammock, feeling 'he had done them nobs a good turn' and fingered the silver in his pocket they had given him. He knew when the lads awoke they would have very sore heads and stomachs too, as well as some explaining to do, but the boss's son could get away with it.

Barnaby did not even feel the swell of the waters as the *Morning Star* cast off her moorings and sailed out of the harbour, her masts hazily silhouetted and looking like a ghost ship in the fog. Neither Barnaby nor Simon realised how fortuitous their bosky prank was to them both. Matthew Hopkins also had them both on his list to arrest as suspect warlocks. Barnaby, as the girl's twin, was naturally under suspicion and also had a huge hound as his familiar, and Simon, as Goody Truman's son and with an interest in herbs and astrology, was under the finger of suspicion too.

While Hopkins had tortured and hanged mainly women as witches, he was not averse to apprehending and sentencing a few men too, that he named warlocks. He was a self-imposed 'expert' on the subject of witchcraft, mainly inventing most of their so-called attributes as witches, and the various means of 'discovering' them. He liked to incorporate the ducking method as well as interrogation and torture, as it gave the crowds something to get excited about and it was another fool proof way to find out if a woman was a witch or not. He had invented a cruel way of tying their limbs in an unnatural and contorted fashion, with their thumbs tied to their toes, putting them in a very painful position, then throw them into a deep pond, and if they sank and drowned, they were innocent and if they floated and survived they were guilty—in which case they were retrieved from the water, tortured and interrogated some more to gain 'confessions', then hanged, or burned at the stake. The crowds loved a good ducking and would roar and shout at the wretched woman as she was thrown into the filthy green duck pond.

When Hopkins realised that both the Brown twins had disappeared into thin air with their familiars, he was red faced and apoplectic with anger.

That night, he dreamed of the bear again. He was running on leaden legs to the safety of the gaol and slammed the door behind him, but he heard it crash open as the bear followed him along dark corridors and even darker slimy and slippery steps to the dungeons below. He could hear the click, click, click of the bear's claws on the cold dank flooring slabs. Matthew ran as fast as he could and threw himself into the furthest cell and tried to slam and bolt the door fast. He could smell the stench of excrement and urine of past prisoners in the filthy straw and feel the cold condensation dripping down the slimy iron door. But the bear was pushing it open, despite all his efforts to close it. Matthew was panting with fear, he could smell the rank breath of the bear and see its red eyes as its face appeared around the door, yellow fangs dripping with saliva. The bear's powerful arm shot out and his claws raked across Matthew's face. He screamed in pain and fear, waking sweating, panting, hot and terrified.

Mary was there, shaking him gently, "Shh, shh, whatever is the matter?"

"It's the bear, that awful bear!" screamed Matthew, "Get it away from me!"

"There, there," soothed Mary, patting the man's shoulders, "there's no bear here, t'was but a nightmare." Mary lit the candle at Matthew's bedside and watched him as he sat, trembling, in his bed, the sheets all tangled and twisted around him.

"Oh, you poor man!" "Look, you have scratched your face and you are bleeding. Let me get a cloth to stop the blood." She went out of the room to get a basin and rag, while Matthew with trembling hands gingerly touched the side of his face where he could feel great gouges raked down his left cheek. No, he hadn't scratched his own face—it was the bear, and it was getting nearer and nearer in time to destroying him completely. He shivered and shook, desperately frightened, while Mary returned to fuss over him, dabbing his cheek with the cloth, giving him a warm drink to sip and smoothing down his bedding. He never even thought to wonder what she was doing in his house in the middle of the night, nor did either of them ever mention it.

***

So, the fates had engineered that both twins sailed away from the dangers of a sadistic madman—as anyone who could read the progress of the planets on their astrological natal charts would have foretold.

Chapter Eight

Blythe woke up feeling disorientated and wondered for a moment where she was. Then she remembered. She had run away from Matthew Hopkins and his accusation of witchcraft. Maybe the man was correct about her in any event. She did seem to know certain things were going to happen in advance, she had premonitions, saw auras and visions, knew about herbs, had practiced healing and understood a bit about astrology, but surely none of those things made her a minion of the Devil? She didn't feel wicked and she only ever wanted to help people.

Anyway, she had other things to think about now. Here she was, curled up in the bottom of a skiff on board her father's galleon, in the wrong one as it happened. She felt through her pockets to find her father's letter, only to pull out a soggy mess. The ink had smudged and the words were indecipherable. Oh well, she thought, it's the wrong captain anyway, the wrong destination—where is this one sailing for—oh yes, Constantinople. She felt a frisson of excitement knowing that she was going to enjoy every aspect of the sea journey: here she was adventuring like a man as she had always wished she could, and if she kept up her disguise as a young fellow, she would have no restrictions to her activities. It would be easier if the captain didn't realise she was a girl—he wouldn't be under so much pressure, especially as women on ships were thought to bring nothing but trouble, so she would stick to her disguise and hope nobody saw through it. She would like to work on board in any event, not just sit around watching the waves and certainly wasn't afraid of any hard labour involved.

She could hear sailors stirring and moving around on the vessel. Some would have been on watch during the night, steering by the stars, but the main crew would be clambering out of their hammocks ready for their day's work, and so she should too. She heaved a big sigh, as did Juno, and pushing back the tarred canvas, she emerged and jumped down onto the deck. First of all, remembering to walk like a lad—something easy for her as she had spent most of her life running around in her brother's clothing—she strode boldly towards the nearby beakhead, where the open privy was built—a seat with a hole directly over the sea and not for the faint-hearted. Juno trotted alongside her and squatted at the edge of the deck while Blythe, after a quick look around to ensure no one could see her, sat on the rather unsavoury seat. That over, and shoving her hair more firmly inside her cap, she and Juno made their way across the deck, loving the familiar roll beneath her feet, the wind in her hair and tang of the briny.

"Oi, yew! Wot you doin' wiv yer 'ands empty?" a rough looking tar with his rat-tailed hair in a queue shouted at her. "An' wot's that bloody great beast doing on board our ship?"

"I'm looking for the Captain, do you know where he is?" replied Blythe, lowering the tone of her voice as well as she could.

"Yeah, he's by bittacle if ya want 'im." Blythe was thankful that she had learned all the nautical terms as a child, knowing that this location is the stand where the ship's compass is mounted, so she wound her way across the deck where she could see a man studying the compass and making notes. As she walked towards him he must have sensed her and looked towards her. With a shock like a lightening fork coursing through her, Blythe realised it was Ambrose Bonnesby! She had wondered if he would be captaining this ship, though in all the frightening excitement of the night, she hadn't given it too much thought. Despite her feelings when she had first met him three years ago, she hadn't expected such an inner reaction to his presence.

"What the hell are you doing here Barnaby Brown?" Ambrose shouted. "God's Teeth! I knew your father wanted you to get some experience aboard soon, but you might have let me know, not just turn up out of the blue! What am I supposed to do with you? And what's that bloody dog doing here as well? We are not a zoo here you know!"

"I know, and I apologise—it was a very last-minute thing, and father gave me a note for you, as he wants me to work aboard, but look—it got wet and is now unreadable." Blythe pulled out the soggy paper. "Juno followed me and the gangplank was up before anything could be done. I'll make sure she is no trouble, and she is a good ratter—she will earn her keep!"

"And you bloody well will as well, young man. Don't expect any favours from me—you will be treated like any other ship's boy!"

"Yes, that is fine, I understand. I will do my best." Blythe was thinking fast now, her wits returning to her. It seemed it would definitely be best to stay in her disguise. Ambrose obviously thought she was Barnaby, and if he was fooled, so would anyone else. The only thing that bothered her was, being female in a male oriented ship, the thought of personal ablutions, relieving herself at the head, washing, and of course, her monthly courses—could be a difficulty if she were living in close quarters with the crew, especially if she had to sling her hammock cheek by jowl with the rest of them in the low ceilinged gun deck. Other than that, she looked forward to any work thrown her way.

"The only dispensation that Father asked for was a small cabin to myself," she told Ambrose, who snorted through his nose.

"Cabin! Cabin? You want yourself a cabin? To yourself? Well, this isn't a luxury ship you know and the stateroom is mine and you are certainly not having it! But if your Father insisted, you can have the small storage room by the bulkhead. You and that doormat will just squeeze in—but the crew won't like preferential treatment at all, so expect some harassment from them! And make sure you clean up after that wretched creature." The 'wretched creature' lazily wagged her long tail and leaned against Ambrose. He absentmindedly stroked her behind her ears, then realising he was somewhat losing face, he pushed her away. She just leaned back in again.

Blythe, feeling her pet was rather taking sides with the enemy said, remembering to lower her voice to sound more mannish, "Yes, that is alright—I didn't expect you to turn out of your own cabin. What kind of duties would you like me to attend to sir? I won't let you down."

"You'd better not!" said Ambrose, "I'll sort out some duties, but right now you can go up to the crow's nest and keep a look out."

"Yes sir!" said Blythe with a small salute and strode off towards the main mast pretending she wasn't worried, though she was feeling a bit anxious. She had scaled trees and climbed up the small mast of their own skiff, but shinning up the high mast on a tall ship was a totally different matter. She suspected Ambrose had done this on purpose (which he had) so she wasn't going to show that 'Barnaby' was a namby-pamby. Juno had decided to stay with Ambrose for the while, not worrying that her mistress was nervously approaching the biggest test in her life so far.

A small boy of around ten years nipped out from behind a barrel, with a couple of stolen apples in his hand. Handing one to her, he said, "Yer want to take yer boots orf. It's easier to climb in yer bare feet—yew can dig yer toes in loike. And never look darn!"

Pleased to have someone being pleasant to her, Blythe said, "Oh thank you—what is your name?"

"It's Billy. Th'ole Captin' he's awlroight—ee jest sarnds grumpy, just to keep us all in line, see."

Blythe smiled, saying, "Thanks Billy, maybe I can chat with you later? I shall need a friend while on board."

"Yeah, I'll be yer friend. Most of the crew are okay, but you 'ave to be wary of Old Nick—you can tell 'oo he is by his big black beard an' loads of little pigtails on 'is 'ed. likes young blokes and 'e'll be arter yew." Blythe couldn't think why, but out of the corner of her eye, she realised that the Captain was watching her with a scowl on his face, so she quickly took off her boots, grabbed hold of one of the ratlines, pulled herself up and started to climb.

Blythe had been restrained in the house ever since Arabella had arrived and had barely had the opportunity for escape to go sailing or any of her usual jaunts around the area, so she was already feeling her muscles protesting. However, she was not going to give in so early into the game so carried on, ever upwards. Taking Billy's advice not to look down, she kept her eye on the barrel at the top in the crow's nest, which had looked so small when she started to climb, but was getting larger as she grew nearer. The wind was whacking at the sails that cracked loudly and she had to be careful they didn't hit her head or sweep her off into the sea so far below. Luckily her cap was firmly pulled down, or it would have blown off in the wind exposing her hair. Maybe she should cut it off, she mused as she climbed ever upwards. She had to be careful, but guessed if she ever got used to this, after time, she would be able to scuttle up the rigging like a spider. Eventually she reached the platform and pulled herself up onto it. It was swaying back and forth with the swell of the waves and the wind was really keen up there. Still not looking down, once on the platform, she climbed into the barrel and once safe inside, clung to the sides. She didn't know how she was going to get down again, but she would face that when the time came. In the meantime, she was gasping for breath, her heart was pounding—especially now as she looked down to the deck below—but eventually her breathing became normal. She looked around at the sea that stretched in all directions to the horizon. What was the Captain expecting her to look out for? They were not yet into the English Channel. There would be no icebergs or pirates, but she supposed she should look out for other vessels and make sure they were not in line for a collision. Gracious, she thought, this is heady stuff! She felt so free and carefree in her barrel, nice and safe and secure, and felt she had the whole world in the palm of her hand. Juno, she noticed, looking the size of an ant, had settled down at the base of the mast, waiting patiently for her return down to the deck.

How good it was to be away from the stifling house with those awful women ruling the roost. She hoped her father would question the integrity of his new wife and be more cautious of her.

She thought of poor Goody Truman—she was probably dead by now, with the vicious crowd revelling in her torture. She wondered if Simon was alright— he would have been devastated to see his mother hang, but would he be arrested as a witch too? And, what about Barnaby? As her twin, Hopkins might say that he was in league with the Devil too, just by being her sibling. She hoped both young men would keep well clear of that evil man and it would have been a good idea if they had planned to go aboard the *Morning Star* together in any event, to put a good distance between themselves and the Witch Finder General.

Blythe eventually began to feel hungry. She didn't know how long she was supposed to be on watch up in the sky, then remembered the apple Billy had given her, which she had thrust deep into her pocket. She fished it out, with lots of fluff too, and after buffing it on her backside, she bit into it with a satisfying crunch. Some screeching gulls swept down and landed on one of the sail beams near to her, eyeing her apple greedily. She finished it off as quickly as possible and threw the core towards the birds. They all dived off the mast, battling each other for the morsel, and once caught, they circled around for a while, screaming at each other, then flew off and sat on the top sail, adjusting with ease to the dipping and rising of the vessel.

By the time the sun was getting quite high, Blythe calculated it was around 11 hours, she heard the bosun's whistle from the deck, and on looking down, noticed him gesticulating for her to come down. Oh, she thought, this is going to be the difficult part, but she was not going to fail on this—she knew nobody was going to help her. Deciding not to look down at all, but to keep her gaze fixed on the barrel, she felt her way down with her feet, clinging hard onto the ropes as she descended. It took a while, but she eventually reached the deck and jumped down. Billy grinned at her, busy at work coiling some ropes. "Yer managed that okay then. Bit scared wos yew?"

Blythe smiled back. "Just a tad!"

Billy jumped up and said, "Bosun said yer gotta swab the decks now. O'il 'elp ya. Usually oi 'ave to do it all."

Blythe's legs felt like rubber after her climb. She'd be glad when she toughened up a bit. She noticed she had a few blisters on her hands from gripping the ropes so tightly. She glanced around and saw no signs of Ambrose. Just as well, as the less he saw of her the better, in case he realised she was a girl. Billy showed her how to sling the bucket over the sides to get the water and bring it up without spilling it, and handed her a mop. "Just start there," he said pointing to a place at the edge of the deck, "an keep going until it's done! Yew 'ungry?"

"Yes, I feel starved—my stomach is rumbling like a thunderstorm!"

"Well, I grabbed yer a crust of bread to stop yer stomach cavin' in," said Billy with a cheeky grin, wiping his nose on his sleeve at the same time. He burrowed in his trouser pockets and handed her a chunk of rye bread. Blythe accepted it thankfully. She presumed she would be fed and watered at some stage, but in the meantime gratefully took Billy's offering. He looked very skinny so she realised he most probably would like to have eaten it himself.

"When do we get a meal?" Blythe asked Billy.

"Depends," he answered. "Depends on the weather. It's quite calm today, so 'ooever's cooking t'day will be able to prepare stuff—we get it around midday, so not long ter wait, and the food'll be decent, so soon out of port. When we'se been out for a long time, we jest gits weevils an' a bit'a brackish warta!" He spat nonchalantly over the side rails and watched it hit the water.

"Mind yew," the boy continued, "When we dock in the various ports of call, we always 'ave fresh food an' warta brung in. It all depen's on the winds, wevver they whoosh us along, or we get becalmed."

"Do you know our first port of call, Billy?" Blythe asked.

"Well, we usually go lickedy-split darn France and roun' Portugal an' through the Gibraltar Straits past Tangier. We usually stops there, an' right excitin' it is an' all—all them dark skinned geezers swarming all over the place. Cor, an' all the pongs wot they make. Sometimes we stop first at Portugal—it depen's on the winds and what the cargo is."

Blythe nodded, thinking that the further away from England, the better for her. She glanced over at Juno, who was curled up in the skiff they had sheltered in overnight. She was guarding Blythe's bag, and it was a good place for her to be out of the way. Blythe would inspect the storage room at the bulkhead later. If it was dreadful, they could always creep into the small boat again.

As Blythe and Billy were swabbing the deck, various tough looking members of the crew passed by intent on their errands. They looked a motley bunch, but

Blythe was used to sailors and as she had always intermingled with the 'low life' of the town, she didn't feel embarrassed. She greeted them, asked their names, telling them her name was Brown. She didn't tell them she was the owner's offspring, just briefly told them that she had run away from home, which was true enough. Sometimes, to fit in better with the men, she dotted her sentences with some of the swear words she had learned on the docks.

There was a fair breeze and the ship was rattling along smoothly over the waves. Men climbed up the rigging like monkeys every now and again, adjusting the sails to the bosun's orders. Blythe looked up at the clouds and there was no sign of rain nor storm. Despite all the odds, she felt deliriously happy.

Chapter Nine

Back at The Exorcist's House, Matthew was sitting wearily in his chair. Mary Phillips coughed as she entered the door, saying, "Oh my dear, you do look fatigued. Let me massage your shoulders—that is where the tension feels the most." Mary walked neatly past Matthew to stand behind him, and he could smell a waft of virginal lavender from her sombre clothing, which he found pleasing.

"Thank you, Mary, I *am* tense. That sly baggage Blythe Brown managed to evade me last night—she slipped into thin air with her familiar. I suspect she flew onto her father's vessel and is now far away, dammit." Mary began to manipulate the corded muscles at the back of Matthew's neck—she could feel the tension and was pleased to eventually feel them relax under her fingers. "Matthew, if it is alright, that is, to call you by your first name?"

"Of course," grunted Matthew.

"Thank you. Matthew, you could do no more. You are doing such excellent work at needling out all the evil women. Many have gone to the assizes at Norwich and returned for hanging in Lynn. Goody Truman hanged this morning, thanks to you, and that is one less harpy from Satan's list. Blythe Brown will have to return sooner or later, and you can strike when she does."

The woman's manipulations were soothing him into a nice reverie. He saw in his mind's eye Blythe Brown's body strapped to the table in the dark cell and imagined what he could do to her then. He realised his carnal thoughts were due to her evil influence but could not stop his fantasy. He wanted more; he wanted to possess her too. His fantasy was growing, as was the bulge in his black trousers, of which Mary, peeping over his shoulder, was well aware.

"I was thinking," she murmured, as she softly caressed his shoulders, "what God would want you to do in the circumstances when the witches have you in their evil thrall. I know that I am not an attractive woman and that you have no desire to bed with me, and the Lord be praised for that, for that would be sinful, but I would be quite willing, happy even, to offer myself to you, in order that you could more satisfactorily rid yourself of the evil humours these dreadful women send you."

Mary noticed a splendid twitch from Matthew's member, smiled to herself and licked her lips lasciviously behind his back, and continued stroking and caressing away at Matthew's tensions.

She continued in a soft voice, "I think, so long as we pray to God that we are doing his work in the way he wishes, he would certainly require that you cast away your seed, contaminated by the women's evil, in the *natural* way and I am willing to be that vessel, into which that wickedness is cast. I offer myself, even if I am cursed, in order to cure you."

There, she had said it—would the man see through her ruse and not think she was a tempting witch too? As Matthew did not demur, she continued, "Maybe we should attempt the dreadful deed in your bed—I am willing to sacrifice myself to the cause of casting out the evil. You are such a splendid, religious, hardworking and Godly man…"

Matthew rose from his chair, and gruffly said, "Follow me" and walked quickly to the stairs. Mary followed swiftly behind. Once in his bedchamber, Matthew wrenched the curtains across the small windows to darken the room and pointed to his bed. Once Mary was lying upon it in a virginal pose, he shed his jacket and shoes and lay beside her, drawing the heavy red velvet drapes all around the bed, leaving them in a dark rosy space. Mary was exultant, but did not wish to show her feelings to Matthew.

"What shall I do? Do you wish me to raise my skirts?"

"Of course," replied Matthew curtly, "ready yourself. We must get this over. I shall not look at you."

Matthew plunged straight inside her, his eyes tight closed, thinking only of the vision of Blythe underneath him.

Afterwards a fit of coughing beset Matthew as he climbed off Mary, so she quickly neatened herself until his coughing fit was over, when he then buttoned himself up. She neatly jumped from the bed and helped him replace his jacket. They both became efficient and business-like.

Mary whispered slyly, "That will have pleased God, to see you cleanse yourself so thoroughly. Let us pray before we return downstairs. Do you think this is something God would want us to do more often, to assist you in your spiritual work?"

"Yes, I do believe he would, Mistress Phillips—it's not as if we were enjoying ourselves. Thank you so much for your assistance. You are of great help to me." He took out a hefty coin from his purse and placed it in her hand. "This is just a small payment for undergoing such an unpleasant experience. Any other, er, intercourse, that we may have, I shall recompense in kind. It cannot be any more pleasant for you than it is for me."

"That is very kind of you, Master Hopkins," said Mary primly, going along with the lie, "I only wish for what is best for you, and of course, if we can assist God in such a manner, then it must be done, however unpleasant."

So, appeasing any guilt from their souls, Matthew clattered down the stairs, Mary following neatly behind. Matthew threw himself back to his chair to doze and, bidding her farewells, Mary stepped across the portal out into the streets of King's Lynn, to glide like a virgin, her sharp nose sniffing disapprovingly at all and sundry as she traversed her way back to her home. She entered her house, removed her bonnet and in her mind praised God to the highest, at the same time reliving every moment of her union with Matthew.

**

Meanwhile, the next day, the *Morning Star* had disgorged Barnaby and Simon onto French shores where they fetched themselves to the nearest inn to ply themselves with strong coffee before deciding what their next step would be.

On the *Evening Star*, after a somewhat uncomfortable night sleeping amongst all manner of clutter, Blythe awoke early, and started to improve her quarters. She piled stuff tidily on one side of the small space, leaving room to make a bed of sorts, and pulling out some spare canvas sails, folded them into a cosy and comfortable nest to sleep in. She intended to use her bag as a pillow, but something made her take it out to the rowboat she had previously slept in, hiding it away from any passing eyes. Back in her cramped little room, she shoved her hair more firmly back into her cap. Apart from her breasts, which she had flattened as much as she could with binding, and were well covered with Barnaby's baggy waistcoat, it was her hair that was going to be her big giveaway, and she wondered, once again, if she should get her knife and saw the lot off.

"You'se a gal, 'int yew'!" came Billy's voice from the doorway.

"No, of course not—I'm Barnaby Brown, son of Peter, the owner of this ship."

"Yeah, and I'm the King of England," grinned Billy, leaning on the side of the door. "You gotta be more careful that the others don't ketch yew out." Blythe looked at him worriedly. "Don't fret, I ain't gunner tell on yew, but you gotta look out, or them sailors will soon sniff yer out—they're like blimmin' dogs on heat at the best of times. 'Ere, 'ave 'n apple." Billy grinned as he handed over another nicely shining Bramley and nodded sagely as she poked her hair more firmly into her cap. "Yeah, that's gotta go—I noticed it 'anging down all around you when you wos asleep—it's a dead giveaway. I'll 'elp you get rid of it when it's lights out later. In the meantime, we've gotta splice some ropes, swab some decks and mend some nets. Come on, getta move on!"

Blythe, pleased she had an ally in Billy, got through the tasks of the day, greeting sailors she met cheekily, keeping her head down, keeping out of the way of Ambrose, and doing all the tasks given. As a new 'boy', there were many unsavoury and difficult tasks put her way, but she was up to it all, in her element, back to her boyish ways with eagerness and not even worried about losing her beautiful locks at the end of the day.

There was not actually an awful lot necessary to do, but work kept the sailors busy, kept them out of mischief and stopped them fighting. Apart from the man at the helm, the look-out, and sails to be furled and unfurled according to the wind, whatever else they did was just keeping things 'ship-shape'. Sometimes the men knitted. They were all capable of doing so, and they made their own socks, and the occasional scarf or hat. Others whittled on driftwood they found either floating by, or on beaches when they stopped for supplies.

Eventually, after a hard day's graft, she and Billy crept into her stuffy cabin, and with only the light from the moon coming through the slit in the door, Billy hacked away until handfuls of tresses lay on the floor. He had cut her hair off just around shoulder length, so she could tie a bit of twine around it, making it into a queue. Billy thought she still looked pretty, so suggested dirtying up her face, especially around her chin and over her lips to make it look as if there was a burgeoning beard on its way. "Mebbe you could make yerself a beard wiv yer 'air?" he quizzed.

Blythe laughed and said, "I don't think anyone would believe I grew one that quickly! Anyway, I am still young enough to be unshaven—but dirty I can do!"

Billy crept away to wherever he slept, and Blythe rolled up her tresses meaning to throw them overboard, but just couldn't—so crept out to hide them at the bottom of her bag, stowed away in the small boat. She was tired out after her adventures, and was soon back in her little stuffy room, fast asleep on the wedge of canvas, the sound of the waves slapping on the sides of the ship soothing her like a lullaby and she slept like a log until the bosun's whistle woke her with a start.

As she sat up and stretched, Blythe felt quite lightheaded with the weight of her locks gone. She had noticed some gun oil on one of the shelves, and quickly opened it up, smearing some of the grease onto her hands, which in turn she rubbed into her hair, then combing the lot back with her fingers, and using some twine, also found on the shelf, she tied her hair back into a queue and slapped her cap onto the back of her head. As she had slept in her clothes, there was no need for a wash—she didn't want to stand out from the rest of the men, and they were quite a smelly bunch! She decided to do a bit more clearing up in her small space. It appeared, amongst other things, to hold guns and cutlasses and other weaponry needed in case of attack. Most ships that held expensive goods needed to be armed, and on the deck below were a couple of small cannons, but it was by no means a fighting ship. Blythe felt it a good idea to sort out the clutter, for if there was a skirmish, better that weapons could be more readily found. She set to with zeal, organising and counting, using some chalk found on a shelf to itemise everything, using the wall for her tally. She dragged an empty barrel and put it at the side of the door, and arranged the muskets in it, ready for any emergency. She wondered where the shot was, and eventually found it in boxes under a pile of canvas—had pirates with grappling irons swept overboard in the night, even if the crew had managed to grab some firing irons, they wouldn't have found powder, flint or shot. Some of them were rusty too. She decided to begin oiling and cleaning. There were some swords and daggers amongst all the clutter too. She tutted to herself, feeling surprised that the Captain had allowed such a state of disarray on his ship and as she progressed, began to enjoy herself. She knew enough about firearms to know what she should be doing—her father's education had covered this too—thank goodness for an eccentric father. She felt a twinge of sadness as she thought of him, and wondered how he was faring with his dreadful new bride.

Her little space was just about completed and she was kneeling back on her heels admiring the neatly ordered space when she was aware that the doorway had been darkened by a figure standing there.

"What are you up to, Brown?" questioned Ambrose curtly as he leaned against the door limb. Blythe felt her neck redden, and rose to her feet, remembering to lower her voice said, "Oh, sorry Sir, I had forgotten the time—I just decided to clear up her and itemise things, then started to clean the guns as they were all a bit grubby."

"Oh, you just decided, did you? I hadn't realised you were in charge here—but then it IS your father's ship, isn't it? I suppose you feel you can do just what you wish then."

Blythe stammered a bit as she replied, "Oh, I really am sorry, but I thought it would be helpful if I tidied it up so that firearms and so on could be readily accessed in case of attack. I should have, of course, reported for duty and not just made my own plans. I do apologise." She felt terrible. A lifetime of doing just what she wanted, when she wanted, had not made it easy for her to begin a life of taking menial orders.

Ambrose looked around the small space, mentally appreciating what the lad (as he believed Blythe to be) had done. He had made a good job of it, and itemising everything was an excellent idea. It should never have been left in that state in any event. Someone's head would roll. However, he was angry. He was angry, not for what Barnaby had done—he was using initiative—but because of how the lad made him feel. Barnaby was stirring up a host of emotions that horrified him. At close quarters, he could not help but inhale the aroma of the boy's skin, and to him it was delightful. He even liked the look of the boy, but didn't like the way he was feeling—that's why he had kept out of his way. He had never thought he had unnatural desires, but that was how he was feeling at the moment. This had to stop!

"Get up the rigging at once and take your turn in the crow's nest. And next time you have any needs to be helpful, ask first, before presuming!"

"Yessir!" replied Blythe, standing to attention and feeling disgusted with Juno, who was pressing against the Captain's side, while he absentmindedly stroked the soft hair around her ears.

Blythe stumbled out into the fresh air and made her way to the main mast. She hoped she could get up it all right, as there was quite a swell on the sea. Billy grinned at her from behind the apple barrel.

"He fancies yer, even though he thinks yer a fella! Cor, wot a turn up for the books!" He handed Blythe an apple and a chunk of bread from his copious pocket, which she thrust, grinning, into her own, before setting her bare feet into the base of the rigging.

"Don't be silly, but thanks for the sustenance," she said out of the corner of her mouth and proceeded to climb up the ratting. As before, she didn't look down, and this time her legs didn't feel quite like the jelly they had previously. Although she had not been onboard long, she was already toughening up again. It felt good, as did the wind on her face as she climbed higher and higher. A sudden gust of wind blew her cap off, which sailed off into the ocean. Part of her disguise had blown away, but thank goodness her hair was now like a man's. God bless little Billy for his friendship.

Once up in the safety of the crow's nest's barrel, Blythe looked down at the tiny deck below. She noticed Juno was keeping close to Ambrose's side and felt a twinge of annoyance. However, Ambrose did seem to take kindly to the dog, which was a good thing. Thank goodness Juno hadn't taken a fancy to chasing any of the chickens cooped up on the top deck! She set her eyes to the horizon, the sun and wind already turning her face a nice even tan. She watched some seagulls squawking and fighting for space on one of the spars. After an hour or so, she began to feel restless—just standing still and doing nothing, other than scan the horizon, was getting boring, but she couldn't complain. She then noticed a dot on the horizon, which after a while she could see was another ship. She yelled down the mast "Ship to starboard!" Some of the crew stopped what they were doing to lean on the rails, while Ambrose focused on the clipper through his telescope. He could see it was a Dutch trade ship, but best to keep an eye on it—one could never be too careful. However, the two ships sailed past each other with quite a distance between. After her four-hour shift, the bosun waved Blythe down and once she had reached the deck, he told her to mend some nets with Billy. One of the other crew climbed up to take her place. Ambrose kept to his cabin, where Juno had taken to sleeping at his feet, while he wrote his ship's log. He was determined to keep that lad working hard at the most menial tasks, but having noticed the good writing and tallies he had executed in chalk, he wondered if it would be worth getting him to help out with the checking and tallying of the ships cargos. Nobody else on the ship could count or write. It was something worth thinking about. If only he could rid himself of the attraction he found when confronted with the wretched lad. That, he mused, must be the problem, brushing shoulders with men day after day—it made one's thoughts run amok in strange directions!

While Blythe kept on good terms with the men, she tried to avoid making any real connections with them. They thought she was a lad, but if she got friendlier with them, they might realise she was a girl, like Billy had so easily. She had to keep on her toes, so only chatted with Billy, with whom she became very fond. He told her he was 'an orfin' that Capt'ing had rescued after a dice with death in Town, when he had nicked a pie off a stall and was being pursued by the wrathful pie man. Ambrose had apparently picked him up by the scruff of his neck, paid off the pie man, and after a stern telling off, ascertained that Billy had no parents or home, had asked him he if wanted to be ship's lad on his vessel. Billy said, "Cor, YES!" and followed Ambrose like an excited puppy onto the boat, where Ambrose had instructed some of the men to strip the boy off, throw some water over him, shave his head, rid him of lice and fleas and find some cast off clothing for him to wear. Since then, Billy had idolised the Captain and made sure he was useful around the ship. That he was a bright lad, there was no doubt, and after he had seen Blythe's writing and sums chalked on the walls, he said to her,

"Cor, I wish I could read and write. Would you learn me?" So in the evenings, she and Billy would settle down on the nets that they had been mending during the day, and using some of the precious chalk from her quarters, she taught Billy by writing the alphabet on the deck, and getting him to copy and memorise. They always cleaned away any marks they made, so while Ambrose was aware what the pair were up to, he saw no reason to stop it.

It didn't take Billy long to be able to write his own name, much to his excitement, and Blythe enjoyed watching the little boy's agile brain springing into life with its new challenge.

Blythe by now had completely adapted to life on board the ship—she could shin up the ratlines like the best of the crew, had no fear at all of heights now, could help raise or lower the sails with no problems, enjoyed all the tasks, however menial—her face, arms and lower legs were deeply tanned, her muscles getting toned—indeed she was a picture of health. Food on board, thus far, was not too bad. They supplemented supplies by catching fish, throwing their nets over the side, especially when shoals of fish were sighted. She helped gut and scale them, some were strung on lines to dry in the sun, some were salted and stored in barrels, some were cooked straight away. Food was cooked in a small galley either in a brick oven with sand nearby in case of fire or upon a spit. There was no resident cook—if any crew member were injured or poorly, they usually had to act as cook, so food was very basic. Sometimes Blythe took over, making bread or cooking the fish, but she didn't want to show her skills to much advantage in case it was realised she was a woman—not that she had done much cooking at home but during her times in the kitchen chatting to cook, she had seen how food had been prepared and cooked.

Ambrose noticed how much Barnaby was doing around the ship and was pleased to see that he was no shirker. He seemed to get on well with most of the crew—friendly, without making any particular friends, other than Billy. Billy was getting on well with his writing and reading—Ambrose had let them practice with the Bible from his cabin—and surprisingly, a few more crew asked Barnaby if 'he' would teach them too.

Blythe approached Ambrose one day, remembering to accentuate the slight boyish swagger and stride, and once his attention was on her, she said, "Some of the crew have asked me to teach them the rudiments of writing. Would that be in order, Captain?" Ambrose stared down his nose at what he thought was Barnaby, then looked out to sea.

"I don't see why not," he replied haughtily, "if all their tasks have been seen to, it's better they have something to absorb them, instead of picking fights with each other."

Blythe hoped she wasn't blushing too much—she could feel it starting at the back of her neck. She didn't know why Ambrose had to be so cold with her—or rather, with Barnaby—if only she didn't have such strange feelings whenever she saw, talked to, or even thought of him. She wished she could dislike him, for he really hadn't been pleasant to her, though she had to admit, he certainly hadn't been exactly *unpleasant*.

"Thank you, Captain," said Blythe, swivelling round to return on deck, when Ambrose said,

"I've been thinking, Brown, as you seem to be a penman, you might as well help me with my paperwork. There is plenty of work to be done with checking the dockets with the cargo, bills of lading, the men's pay and so on. Is that something you feel you could assist me with?"

"Certainly, Sir, I would be happy to help." She felt her heart leap within her, at the thought of closer contact with this man whom she seemed to have lost her heart to. She must make sure he didn't suspect her secret.

So began a new regime for Blythe. Ambrose took her down into the hold to show her where all the cargo was stored. He explained that while their intention was to bring back lots of silks for her father, on their outward journey, rather than just fill the holds with necessary ballast, it was more sensible, and of course profitable, to take goods to sell en route. Everything was accounted for on paper, but it was necessary to check every now and again that no water had seeped in to ruin their goods. Currently they were carrying sheep fleeces and tanned cowhides, some iron ware and other household goods that they hoped to sell on the way to Constantinople. Everything had to be crated and held down so nothing moved during bad weather and upset the balance of the boat. The ship's cat, whom Blythe had already befriended, was let loose in the hold to catch the ever-present rodents. Blythe was not a skittish female and didn't leap on chairs at the sight of a mouse, but she didn't like rats and mice. She and Goody Truman held the belief that they were carriers of disease, so she was ever vigilant and annoyed the men by covering up food that was left out, to stop the mice and rats scuttling over and contaminating everything.

"By the saints Brown, stop acting like a girl!" yelled one of the men at her, as she carefully covered the remains of the fish stew. Blythe recoiled, thinking her disguise had been uncovered, but thinking quickly, she retorted,

"Girlish? You dare to call me girlish?" she yelled, eyes flashing—"those creatures carry disease on their feet and their droppings too can kill you!"

"Don't be daft, sissyboy," replied the scruffy seaman, who deliberately picked up a rat dropping and placed it in his mouth. "Yum yum, delicious." He made a great show of chewing it while his shipmates all roared with laughter and slapped each other's backs.

Blythe glowered at them. "That's so foolish Sam. I hope you don't get ill on it. You can call me a sissy if you want, but my sister was taught by the local wise woman and she learned a lot from her."

Sam glowered, his black eyebrows meeting, and spat onto the deck. "Hung as a witch, was she? The wise woman?—Heard as one was hung the day we sailed. Not so wise, was she!" His words were greeted by laughter from the crew.

Blythe's shoulders dropped and she blinked away a tear, turning slightly so the men didn't notice it.

Sam continued. "Is your sister a witch then, Brown? Has she taught you any tricks?"

Blythe thought the conversation was getting too close for comfort, so threw a roguish grin at Sam, and just said, "Don't be a coze, Sam—it's just a question of being careful, that's all."

Billy had been quiet through this discourse and broke the tension by digging Blythe in the ribs and saying,

"Wot abart me reading lessons then? Anyone else wanna join in?"

Most of the men moved away, not wanting to go to the trouble of learning, but the two who did waited near Blythe, who agreed to doing so in their spare time. They were only keen to be able to write their names, but Blythe felt they might want to learn more after that.

Ambrose had noticed this discourse and while he didn't think Brown was a sissy, it did make him realise that the lad was in fact a bit girlish. He was far too slender; despite the hard work he did. He had muscles, but they didn't show as manly, and he was altogether too handsome. Because Ambrose was aware of the boy all the time, he had seen that sometimes the swagger dropped, making him look more vulnerable. Maybe the lad wasn't as manly as he made out…

Carnal thoughts drifted into Ambrose's head, which he tried to banish immediately. He became angry with himself, and consequently with everything around him. He swooped down on the men and shouted at them, "Get off your lazy backsides and get on with your work. You are here to man a ship, not learn to read for God's sake! I've given permission, yes, for odd occasions, but the ship comes first and foremost, and don't you forget it. Brown—haven't you got work to do?" His gaze at Blythe was thunderous and as he had emphasised his words by thumping on the rails, she jumped up, saluted, and began to scurry off, feeling mortified, and angry too. How dare the wretched man have a go at her? She hadn't done anything wrong. "Permission to get my writing materials from your quarters, sir?" she asked. At his nod, she strode off to her duties, hating the man with one part of her soul, while the other asked, "Why does he dislike me so?"

Blythe took herself down into the hold to check out the cargo. It was as black as pitch down there, so she had taken a lantern that only threw out a dim glow. It wasn't a particularly pleasant task, trying to see what was there, and to check the chalk marks on the outside of the various crates. She inspected, to see they were all firmly tied down, but noticed that some of the ropes were distinctly gnawed and saw some of the culprits slinking off around the bilge pumps. The water at the bottom of the boat was fetid and stank to high heaven. As the ship ploughed through the water, the stinking bilge water sloshed back and forth and Blythe had to tread carefully. She wondered if the level of the water was a bit high and thought she ought to report back to the captain, though she didn't really want to come face to face with him again, hateful man. He was pompous, standoffish, and altogether too handsome. She wished she could put him out of her mind and forget all about him. She skirted around most of the cargo in the hold, jotting down as she went, and once she was done, was pleased to get out in the fresh air again. The first thing she wanted to do was to wash her hands—her belief in ill humours from filth was uppermost in her mind, as she strode back to her tiny quarters, where Billy always left a bucket of water for her ablutions.

Blythe wanted to be clean, but only kept washed what was not apparent. She needed to keep up her disguise, and even as the son of a wealthy mercer, she was here as crew, and didn't want to stand out in any way, especially as she wanted to maintain her disguise. If Ambrose realised she was a woman, it was not too late for him to send her from the next port back home into Matthew Hopkins's clutches. She was pondering on what would happen to her, as she washed her hands, when she came over all dizzy and slumped down onto her makeshift bed. Before she knew it, she seemed to be in the midst of a terrible storm. Thunder and lightning rent the heavens, and she could see, as if from above, the ship listing terribly into the waves. Lightning struck, all she could see were huge waves thundering over the ship, and a vision of Ambrose, blood all over his face, being washed into the malevolent mouth of the ocean.

Blythe came to, her arms outstretched, her body shaking all over. At that moment, Billy came in and rushed to her side. "Wot's going on, Miss? Yer face is as white as a sheet!" He flopped onto the ground next to Blythe and held her hand, patting it at the same time.

"There was a terrible storm, Billy, and the Captain was swept overboard."

"No there wasn't and no, Capting wasn't washed over neither—the sun's shining and everything's fine." Billy looked closer at Blythe, who was coming out of her peculiar state.

"Oh dear, Billy, I know everything is fine at the moment, but I think there WILL be a storm, and we must keep our eyes open for the Captain, for he is in mortal danger!"

"Ow dew yew know that then?" asked Billy with his eyes opened incredulously.

"I don't know how I know, Billy, but I just do. Every now and again, I have these visions, or knowings, and they always come true. Please don't tell anyone, or they will say I am a witch. I am not a witch, but I do seem to know some things in advance."

"Well," said Billy anxiously, "when do yew think this 'ere storm is gunna 'appen? Is it a long time in the future, or soon?"

Blythe looked out of the door at the blue sunny sky above and narrowed her eyes. "I think it is going to happen very soon—and first, I must tell the captain that some of the ropes are frayed in the hold. It won't help in a storm if the cargo is smashing holes down below." She nimbly leapt to her feet and picked up the papers she had brought back from the hold and strode off to the Captain's cabin.

She rapped on the door, and on hearing Ambrose's curt, "Enter," she stepped into his chamber. As he looked up at Blythe, she noticed a quickening to his eyes, that soon changed to a hard stare.

"What do you want?" he curtly demanded.

"I've checked the hold, and written down all that you asked, but I did note that some rats have gnawed through some of the ropes tying down the cargo. That could be a problem with the oncoming storm."

"What oncoming storm?" Ambrose snapped at her, and continued writing.

"Well, I know it sounds ridiculous, because everything is very calm out there," answered Blythe, "but I have a sixth sense when it comes to storms, and I predict one is imminent. We ought to reef the sails."

"Oh, you predict, do you? What can you possibly know about storms? And have you been promoted to Captain now? You are telling me that the sails need reefing? My God, I should give you a lashing for impertinence. Just because you are the owner's son, doesn't give you the authority to issue commands to me!"

Blythe felt terrible, and realised she had overstepped the boundaries, but she was actually terrified that Ambrose was going to die, let alone the ship be wrecked—and how could she tell him that her visions came true?

"I'm sorry sir, but sometimes I see visions of events that happen afterwards, and I saw this terrible storm come up out of nowhere, and I also saw you swept overboard. I'm not trying to undermine your authority, just warn you that a storm is going to hit us so that you can be prepared and not die!"

Ambrose could see that the lad was overwrought and seemed genuine in his distress, but of course he didn't believe that the lad had visions that came true. That wasn't possible. He was at a bit of a loss as to what to say next, especially as Brown looked so endearing standing there, twisting the end of his sleeve.

"You say the ropes are frayed?"

"Well, that definitely needs fixing—I'll get some of the men onto that straight away. Get back to your duties." He frowned at Blythe, who nodded politely and backed out of the room as quickly as she could. She went back to Billy and drew him to one side.

"Look, Billy, we must act quickly. The Captain won't listen to me, he doesn't believe me, but I think we must make sure the skiff is ready to be launched, and that all supplies in it are tied down and waterproofed securely, and go get some food and store it away—no, I'll do that, just get anything else you think we might need. My bag is already in there, but check the oars, mast and sails are tied down and then fasten Jupiter in the skiff as well. Make sure there is a baler in there too. Think fast, Billy, for I know that a terrible storm is going to hit at any moment."

The ship was sailing along quite peacefully in the light breeze and the sun was bright and hot, and while Billy raced around doing what Blythe had asked him, he was thinking that maybe she was out of her head, but then, what did he know?

In ten minutes' time, darkness suddenly hid the sun and the temperature plummeted, while at the same time a terrifying wind blew up from out of the blue skies that swelled the sails fit to bursting and rattled the rigging furiously, while huge waves suddenly appeared from nowhere. The ship surged forward, at the same time being knocked by the waves from side to side, so that men were slipping and sliding, cursing and panicking as mayhem suddenly took over. Rain and hail poured from the heavens, lashing every which way while men tried to climb the rigging to reef the sails which were already getting ripped by the wind. Some men fell into the furious sea while others had to ignore their screams as they battled uselessly to get the ship under control. Blythe watched with horror and managed to pick up a coil of rope that she threw over her shoulders, one end tied to a hook on the rowboat. She saw Ambrose come onto the deck, shouting orders to the men while Billy was tying Juno in the boat as she had asked. Billy staggered back to her side, barely able to walk against the buffeting of the wind and they both clutched onto a rail as a huge wave broke over their heads, sweeping their feet away from them.

"Bloody Hell, you *must* be a witch to know this was gunner 'appen!" yelped Billy as they clung for dear life. The wind was ferocious by now yet strangely Blythe didn't feel frightened. The elements exhilarated her, and while there was a chance to move towards Ambrose, struggling with the men to lower the sails and save the masts, she did so. "Get to the rowboat, Billy, hold on for dear life and be ready to cast off if necessary." A sudden crack of loud thunder almost deafened them and immediately a bright fork of lightening zig-zagged its way down from the dark, seething heavens and struck the main mast. One of the spars thudded downwards and Blythe could see, in slow motion, it was going to hit

Ambrose. She tried to get nearer, but the ship suddenly listed and she was thrown to the wet deck, clinging onto the rope to save herself from sliding into the sea. Then the ship crashed down once more. Blythe wondered if those great crates in the hold were making things worse if their ropes had frayed right through. That would make further chaos and upset the balance too.

Blythe had seen Ambrose fall as the heavy wood struck him, and as the deck tilted, he began a crazy slide to the edge of the deck. Blythe threw herself towards the man and caught hold of his leather belt trying to stop his momentum, but even as she tugged for all her worth, felt herself being swept over the deck with him into the mountainous fury of the sea. She clung onto Ambrose and felt them both being sucked down into the frothing depths. She could feel the rope unfurling—hoping that it was still secured and that she might be able to haul them both to safety once they reached the surface again. Her lungs were bursting and she pushed with her feet to rise upwards, but clothing and Ambrose's weight dragged her back. After what seemed like hours, they did break through and she was able to gasp some air into her lungs, only to be crashed on by another huge impossible wave. She couldn't see the ship, but concentrated on keeping them both afloat. She looked at Ambrose's white face with a gaping wound on his head and didn't know if he were alive or dead. The sky was a bilious yellow-black and she despaired. Trying to keep Ambrose's head out of the water, she kicked with her legs, but her boots were hindering her and were too tight to push off. The waves were so huge and kept crashing down on them as she tried to keep them both afloat. She felt the rope and gave it a tug, but it did not feel taut. Had it come away from the rail? There was no hope for them at all then. Maybe she should cut the rope away, for might the weight of it pull them down into the briny?

Just then, she thought she heard a bark. Was that Juno? Had she fallen into the sea as well? The barking got louder, then she heard a faint cry of, "Where the bluddy' 'ell is yer then?"

"Over here!" shouted out Blythe. "Over here!" Then as the waves rose and fell, she saw the prow of the skiff ahead. Then she felt the rope tightening as it drew them towards the boat. There it was, rising and slamming down as waves hit it, and there was Billy, pulling on the rope and bringing them close to the side of the vessel. Her strength was almost gone, but she managed to push Ambrose towards the rim of the craft on a down wave and Billy managed to haul him in, and then she had to try and get herself onboard. Billy pulled on the rope and she scraped against the side of the boat and felt herself being slammed time and time again against the edge, but after much heaving and pulling by Billy, she fell in a heap on top of the inert form of Ambrose.

"Is 'e dead?" shouted Billy against the tempest. "I don't know," gasped Blythe, "but he'll need to be pumped out as he must have swallowed half the ocean."

Juno was barking wildly, still tethered to a seat of the craft, pleased to see her mistress. Nodding towards Ambrose, Blythe gasped out to Billy, "Push him onto his stomach and I'll try and thump the water out of him."

The skiff pitched and plummeted in the lashing waves. The elements resounded—the dark sky spasmodically lit by lightening while the thunder, so close, nearly burst their eardrums. Rain was lashing down so heavily that it actually hurt their skin. The boat was filling with seawater, but Blythe was concerned only about Ambrose. She made sure his face was out of the water and pushed on his back until eventually a rush of sea spewed from his mouth and after that he took a deep breath and resumed breathing.

"Thank God for that!" exclaimed Blythe, and began to rub at his icy hands. "Bale like mad, Billy, that's all that can be done at the moment—there's no point trying to row the boat until the sea calms!" She pulled and pushed Ambrose into a more covered section of the boat and tried to warm him. It was no good—she was wet through and frozen, the boat was filling with water as waves crashed over them, and she thought that there was little hope of survival. "Rope yourself to the side, Billy" she shouted over the noise of the storm. She did the same to herself and to Ambrose, and just prayed that the tempest would soon die down and that they wouldn't perish. Ambrose remained unconscious, while Blythe fell into an exhausted slumber, despite being thrown from side to side as the boat was buffeted this way and that. Little Billy, keeping one hand clasped to the side of the boat, kept bailing with the other, while Juno, wet through like them all, shivered and whimpered, her teeth chattering with cold. Eventually even Billy fell into a sleep of exhaustion, sitting at his point of duty, bailer still in his hands.

***

Blythe blearily woke to the sound of Juno's barks. She could hear surf pounding and felt the rocking of the boat and wondered why she felt so sodden. Opening her eyes, she realised she was in the rowboat and remembered the fury of the storm. She could see the blue sky and feel the sun on her face that was beginning to warm her cold body. She quickly turned to see how Ambrose was, and noticed he was still deathly white, with blood congealed all over his face. She shook him, but he made no response, though she noted that he still breathed, thank God. Next, she appraised Billy, who was still stuck in his bailing position, the bailer now floating in the water sloshing in the bottom of the craft, while he was still fast asleep with his little mouth wide open. He, too, was wet through, as were Juno and Ambrose. Blythe eased her bruised body up to enable her to look over the side and see where they were. The sea, with the aftermath of the storm, was still quite choppy, and their boat a-bobbing, but the horrendous lashing waves were thankfully gone. At first, she saw nothing but ocean in front of her, but as she turned around, she saw to her astonishment that they were at the edge of a sandy beach, their bow stuck and keeping them fast. They had survived!

"Billy!" she shouted out, making the boy jump, which splashed water everywhere.

"Bluddy Hell miss, we're ashore!" he excitedly replied as soon as his addled wits were working. "Quick, Miss, we must jump out and pull the boat ashore. We don't wanna go drifting out agin!"

Untying Juno first so the dog could jump out with them, they splashed into the shallow sea and between them dragged the boat up beyond the tide line, Blythe noting at the same time, lots of flotsam and jetsam, as well as trees and branches that lay scattered on the sand and left there by the furious tempest. What looked like a body lay at some distance further along the beach, but Blythe pushed that to the back of her mind as they had to tend to their own safety first.

Once the boat was safely secured Blythe said, "Billy, we have to get the Captain out now—he's still unconscious and we must get him out of those wet clothes and get him warm and safe." She looked quickly around noting a space in some trees at the edge of the beach. "If we can get him up there, we can make a shelter, just in case the weather turns again. The sun will warm him up in the meantime, but he mustn't lie out in it too long. How are we going to get him out of the boat and up there? He'll be a dead weight."

"I dunno Miss, but we could drag him up the beach on some canvas I reckon, once we figure how to get 'im outta the boat, there's as much bluddy seawater in the boat as there is in the bluddy ocean."

Nodding, Blythe said, between her chattering teeth despite the sun, "Let's try and sit him up first, Billy, and we will have to pull him over to the side and manipulate him somehow." She began immediately putting her plan into action with great difficulty. Ambrose was indeed a dead weight, and his head was falling down on his chest, his limbs limp and useless. Billy pulled on his legs and between them they managed to pull and push their captain over to the edge of the boat and dangle his legs over the side. Blythe jumped out and yelled at Billy to push Ambrose as far as he could and she would try and catch his weight as he fell down. In the end, Ambrose fell onto Blythe, but at least she broke his fall, and Billy, after throwing out some canvas, nimbly jumped out and helped Blythe to her feet, and together they rolled Ambrose onto the canvas and once he was in position, pulled the senseless man up the beach until they were panting with exertion. Blythe noticed that the wound on Ambrose's head had begun bleeding again, so she yelled at Billy to go to the boat to bring first of all her duff bag, and then to bring out as many useful supplies he could manage as fast as he could, adding, "We'll have to get all that water out too, later on."

Once Blythe had her bag to hand, she delved in the bottom to find that thankfully, her herbs and supplies were still dry—everything had been wrapped in waxed calico—and after stopping the bleeding with a clean rag, she was able to spread some herbal ointment onto the wound that would help the healing. She then tenderly wound a bandage around his head. Billy, by this time had brought up as many supplies he could manage from the boat and Blythe took quick note of the stock. "Bring those blankets over Billy—we have to get the Captain warm, but first we must take off his wet clothing."

She began to unbutton Ambrose's jacket and together Billy and she pulled it off, and then his shirt. Next they pulled off Ambrose's pantaloons and underpants—Blythe had seen her brother naked many times, but she wasn't prepared for the shock of seeing the beautiful body of a large man. Quickly putting her emotions aside, she covered him with a blanket. Blythe next made a cushion out of another of the blankets, and placed it gently under Ambrose's head. He let out a gentle groan, but his eyes didn't open.

After Blythe had done all she could to make Ambrose comfortable, she said,

"Right Billy, we must now make ourselves a shelter. I don't know where we are, and what the weather is going to do. We must prepare for more storms, get our supplies covered and make ourselves a camp. First of all, we can make a roof by tying one of the sails from tree to tree, and then use the others for the sides. We will find some rocks to hold them down in case a wind blows up."

The two bedraggled sailors didn't take long to construct a make-shift shelter, into which they dragged Ambrose, and then while Blythe kept an eye on him, she asked Billy to go and drag some wood off the shoreline in order to make a fire. The sun was warm, but she wanted to get their clothing dried quickly, and also be able to heat some water and cook something—she didn't know what yet, or where they would find water—but first things first! They both needed to be organised, to do things that made sense.

Billy raced around pulling branches and driftwood up from the plentiful supply on the beach and stacked them near their shelter. Blythe searched for some flint stones, and luckily found some stored in the boat's locker. Thank God someone had the sense to put them there—she hadn't thought of it!

Once everything was to Blythe's liking, she rummaged in her bag for a change of clothing, told Billy to run over to what she had thought was a body along the tide line. Whilst he ran off to fulfil that errand, she took off her wet clothing and laid it on the sand to dry, in the meantime climbed into one of her gowns that were bundled in the bottom of her bag. It wouldn't take long for her trousers, shirt and waistcoat to dry and she could change again. Once she was in dry clothing, she felt a lot better by which time Billy returned to report,

"Miss, it *is* a body, and it's one of the crew, an' 'e's as dead as could be, an' you should see all the flies buzzin' around the poor bugga."

"Well," said Blythe pulling a face of remorse, "he will have to stay there for the moment—we will try and bury him once we are organised. In the meantime, will you stay with Ambrose, for I'm going with Juno to see if we can find some food of some sort, and hopefully some fresh water. I can also see if there is any habitation nearby. Shout if the Captain awakens, or gets worse."

As Billy nodded, Blythe stuck a knife in her belt, picked up a leather bucket, gave Billy a hug, for she noticed that now the danger was over, he was shaking a bit.

"Billy, you are doing so well! I couldn't have done this without you and I still don't know how you came to save me—as soon as I come back, hopefully with some food to fill our bellies, you must tell me what happened."

Billy grinned at the praise and puffed his bony little chest out. "Don't you worry, Miss—I'll look arter you, an' the Capting of course!"

Blythe smiled, hitched her skirts and strode off up the dunes and into the woods behind the beach. Billy shouted after her, "You look right pretty Miss, dressed as a lady!" Even though their situation was dire, Blythe was relishing the adventure and felt alive for the first time in ages, after her dreadful stepmother had clamped down on her activities.

A lifetime of running wild with Barnaby in and out of their skiff had prepared her for survival and she had no fears that she couldn't cope with the situation she and her shipmates were now in. Turning around before she disappeared into the wooded area, Blythe smiled widely and blew Billy a kiss, then pressed on, keeping her sharp eyes focused in all directions. Her skirts annoyed her, hampering her legs after having felt so free for such a long time, but she made sure she didn't tear the material, after all, there was no way of knowing how long they might be shipwrecked and how they would cope, or indeed what lay ahead of them all.

Juno trotted ahead, looking back every so often to make sure her mistress was still there. Blythe could hear birds in the trees calling out their alarm as she walked underneath the boughs. The gradient was quite steep, and she could see that it was quite rocky with some climbing involved. She wondered if there would be a cave, perhaps, that would be a better place for them, until she found habitation and people. Was this a small island, or were they on a mainland somewhere? She climbed up over loose scree, hanging onto bushes to aid her passage, hoping to reach the top where she might be able to see the lie of the land. Suddenly, Juno shot off into some bushes and Blythe could soon hear the dog slurping at water. Pushing aside the greenery, she could see that the hound had found in the rocks a natural indent filled with water that splashed from the rocks above, to continue downwards, forming a little stream. Water! Blythe realised how lucky they were to have fresh water. Blythe filled the bucket and left it by the stream to pick up on their return. All they needed now was some fresh food, but that shouldn't be a problem. Juno was used to catching rabbits when she and Barnaby had been out adventuring and which they had cooked over a camp fire. After cupping her hands and filling them with the sweet water to drink, Blythe pushed on, telling Juno to 'go seek'. The hound pricked up her ears, keen to hunt for her mistress and ran off, her nose to the ground, while Blythe continued upwards, checking the ground to see if she recognised any of the vegetation that might be edible. She noticed there were plenty of herbs that smelled delicious as her feet trod over them, and she plucked some and pushed them into her pocket. It wasn't long before Juno returned a short while later, dragging a small red deer.

Blythe praised the dog and told her to 'bring', and the pair triumphantly returned back to the camp with their spoils, retrieving the bucket left at the waterfall, Blythe could not believe the ease in which they had found sustenance.

Billy greeted Blythe excitedly. "Cor, we got dinna!" he exclaimed, when he saw Juno dragging in her prey.

"And water," replied Blythe, brandishing the bucket with a huge grin on her face. "How's the Captain?" As she rounded the corner, she noticed that Ambrose now had some bright pink colouring on his cheeks, which worried her, but he did seem to be breathing more easily now. She also noted that bruising was now coming out on his face around his eyes. She knew that was a good thing—better to have a puffed up face than bleeding on the brain.

"Right, Billy," she said as she carefully placed the bucket of water in a shady position, and then relieved Juno of her prize. "Will you put some more wood on the fire please, and get it really hot in order to roast the deer. Then, find some sticks to use as a spit over the flames?"

"Yeah, I can do that, Miss—and shall I cut orf the deer's skin so it's useful?"

"Good idea Billy—I must check on the Captain's wound first, but you get it all going. You have to gut it first. Can you manage that?"

Billy had never done anything like that in his life, but called out "Just you try an' stop me Miss!"

"Just cut off some hunks of meat first so they cook more quickly, and once I have seen to the Captain, I'll boil some of the flesh too, which will be easier for him to swallow. We are very lucky, you know, to have reached this place and found food and water immediately. We are not going to starve to death, thank goodness, after nearly losing our lives in that storm."

As Billy busied himself arranging wood and setting up the spit at Blythe's direction, he threaded the meat onto the sticks and it wasn't long before the meat started to sizzle and smell wonderful.

Meanwhile, Blythe carefully unwound the bandages from around Ambrose's head. The bleeding had stopped and congealed, but it was a nasty wound, and really needed some stitching. She knew she was capable of that, and thought she would do it as soon as possible before Ambrose woke—so she rummaged through her bag and found her needle and thread. Always liking to keep things clean, she first washed her hands then held the needle in tweezers and let Billy's flames heat and cleanse it, and then swiftly threaded it with strong thread.

"Billy, you had better come and hold the Captain down, in case he wakes up in the middle of my sewing."

Blythe had pulled Ambrose's back into her lap, with his head resting on her breast, so she was able to more easily reach his wound to sew it. Billy watched in fascination as Blythe carefully held the torn flesh together, pushed the needle in and began to place neat stitches that pulled the loose skin into place. As she did this, Ambrose began to groan, so she quickly finished the job by covering with another clean bandage. Ambrose began to cough and groan again, so Blythe began to sooth him by stroking his hair like a mother would her babe.

Ambrose was slowly reaching consciousness. He could feel that his head was encased in what felt like a soft bosom and that his hair was being gently stroked, but the pleasant sensation was overridden by the pain in his head. He tried to open his eyes, but failed, though he could hear a soft voice soothing him and telling him everything was alright, and just to relax. He was aware of wood-smoke, and the wonderful smell of food cooking. Not able to think clearly, he imagined himself a child again, soothed at the bosom of his mother. He groaned and nuzzled his nose into Blythe's soft flesh and let oblivion begin take him over again. His Mother had just told him he was fine, so he snuggled back into her comfortable body and allowed himself to drift off. At the back of his mind, he could hear the gentle sound of surf hissing back and forth on the beach and could feel the warm sun on his body, and groaning again, drifted off into a healing sleep.

Blythe kissed the top of Ambrose's hair, avoiding his cut, and gently eased his body down onto the makeshift bed. Her heart really went out to this man, now so vulnerable and in her charge. She hoped he would soon recover and gain all his faculties—Goody Truman had taught her that injuries to the head could often leave people befuddled—if they survived.

The fire was roaring merrily and Billy was having a wonderful time feeding it with more and more wood. It was wet after the storm, but had ignited and once lit, had eventually got going well, if rather smokily. That made Blythe think of smoking some of the deer so that nothing was wasted. She would set to after they had eaten, and by the look of it the chunks of meat skewered on the stick were dripping juices and looked about done. Once she and Billy had broken their fast, she would make a broth for Ambrose. She had already the fresh herbs gathered on her walk that would make him a tasty drink.

Billy had found a couple of battered bowls in the longboat's lockers as well as some knives, so he hooked the hot meat off the spit and let it fall into the bowls. He put a ship's biscuit at the side and looking very proud of his efforts, handed Blythe her meal. They settled down in the sunshine and hungrily chewed at their meat which tasted absolutely delicious. Juno had already had hers raw, and was spread out in the warmth of the day, enjoying firm land and a full belly at long last.

"First of all, Billy, now that we are settled, safe and eating, tell me how you managed to get the rowboat to us so soon? I think there must have been a bit of a miracle going on there!"

Billy grinned, and flicking his greasy hair from his brow, said, "Well, I sees you and the Cap'ing bluddy well skidaddering orf the deck and inter the briny, so I jumped in the skiff as quick as Jack Flash and got art me knife and cut through the ropes holding it darn, and Juno and me 'ad our stomachs and kiddilies bumping around as the boat hit them huge waves. I thoughts we wus both gonners then. I'd kept me eyes where you'd went, but there was no ways I could steer or use the oars or anything, but I'd clung onto yer rope all the ways, knowing that if all went well, I could pull yer both in!"

Blythe smiled at Billy and said, "I think some angels must have been looking after us, don't you? It was an impossible task, and yet you managed it!"

"I was bluddy scared, I can tells yer Miss, but I was 'termined I'd save yer!"

"Well, I can't thank you enough, and nor will Captain Ambrose when he comes round. I don't think we can call you Ship's Boy any more Billy, you have proved yourself to be a man!"

Glancing over at Ambrose for the umpteenth time, Blythe noticed Ambrose's cheeks were pinker than ever. It wasn't a healthy colour, yet she could see he was shivering at the same time. She went to check him, and his skin was both clammy yet hot. She knew these were the signs of fever, but hopefully he would wake soon, and she could reassess the situation. In the meantime, dragging over an old iron pot from the heap of possessions, threw in some of the meat, and the herbs she had gathered, covered it with water, and said to Billy,

"Billy, will you place the pot amongst the embers, away from the main flames. We don't want it boiling too fast—a gentle simmering will make the meat tender. I think I saw some garlic flowers back along the path—I'll go back in a minute and dig them up for the bulbs—they will make the flavour even tastier."

Billy saluted, with a grin from ear to ear. He was feeling really important with all these new duties, knowing that he had saved the lives of the two people he most respected in the whole wide world.

Just as Blythe set off to collect the wild garlic, she asked Billy, "Where do you think we are, Billy? I know that we were in the Mediterranean Sea, but don't know where the wind has blown us."

"Dunno, Miss, could be anywheres—look at the sun, is wot the Captin' always told me, an' feel it too—it's getting 'andsome 'ott—but it depends where we've landed as to wevver the natives are gunna kill us or not! Maybe we are near the Adriatic Sea." He grinned at Blythe, who pursed her lips and said,

"Well, let's not worry about that while we don't have to. Just keep an eye on that meat simmering, and while I am gone, cut some of the raw meat into thin strips, so we can dry them in the sun and smoke them over the fire. Try not to get sand all over them."

Billy nodded and waved as Blythe and Juno wandered off, and he looked around to find some large leaves that he could use on which to place the slivers of meat as he cut them. Ambrose continued sleeping, but Billy could hear him groaning and muttering, and hoped his Captain was going to regain his senses soon. By now, his eyes were really purple and very swollen, and Billy could see that blood was seeping through the bandages. Flies buzzed round, and Billy tried to wave them away into the direction of the meat, rather than his Captain's head.

Returning to find the garlic, Blythe didn't want to stay away from their camp for too long, so plucked at any herbs that she saw. Their sweet aromas wafted into the hot air as she walked over them, so it didn't take long before she had a good supply. She saw the garlic leaves, and using a stick, managed to dig up some bulbs. "This will make the stew taste delicious" she said to herself, and Juno waved her long tail in agreement. As she had enough for the immediate job in hand, Blythe returned to what was now becoming 'home' and strewed some of the herbs and garlic into the pot.

"Cor," said Billy, "That smells bluddy good. Will there be enough of that for us an' all?"

Blythe laughed, and said, "Yes, Billy, we have enough here for a few days, so long as it doesn't go off in the heat—we have been so lucky this far." She bent over the pot and stirred with one of the spoons Billy had found, then checked on

Ambrose, deciding to loosen the blanket around his neck and pulled it down to his waist. The day was becoming very hot now, and she didn't want him to get overheated. She noted that her clothing was now dried and decided to change out of her dress and back into her comfortable breeks and shirt. She decided not to bind her breasts as Ambrose was in no state to notice her, and anyway, what did it really matter now if he found out her gender?

Telling Billy to turn his back, she disrobed and stood naked, stretching in the sunshine, enjoying the warmth of it on her skin, revelling in the heat after the cold of the terrible storm yesterday. At that moment, Ambrose had managed to open his eyes and was puzzled to see a beautiful nude woman outlined against the sky. He wondered if he were in heaven, and closing his eyes against the sun, tried to shift his position to see more clearly. By the time he had managed to re-arrange himself so that he was propped up on his elbows, Blythe had wriggled into her breeks and had just finished tucking in her shirt when she heard Ambrose coughing behind her.

"Oh, you are awake!" she cried happily, and ran over to his side. "How are you feeling? You had a terrible blow to your head."

Ambrose blinked at her with a puzzled expression on his face. "Oh, it's you, Brown—I was sure I saw a naked woman in front of me—I must be hallucinating."

"Probably," she answered, kneeling down at this side. "Do you remember the terrible storm? We were washed overboard by huge waves, but Billy saved us."

From the corner of her eyes, she noticed Billy's chest swelling with pride.

"You had a spar fall on your head and knock you over. I've had to sew up your head wound, and the bruise is now coming out beautifully. You look as if you have been in a fight! Do you want to try and sit up? Do it carefully, for I don't know if you have any other injuries."

Ambrose blinked, barely able to take in what Blythe was saying. He tried to push himself up, but groaned with an intake of breath. "Ouch!" he grimaced, "My ribs hurt!"

"Maybe they are cracked—do take care as you sit up, we don't want you puncturing a lung!"

Blythe motioned to Billy to bring a stack of canvas to put at Ambrose's back, and she helped him settle into a comfortable position.

"God, my head feels like it's splitting, and I am seeing double at the moment," Ambrose groaned, "and I need to relieve myself and I also want my trousers—I'm completely naked!"

Blythe wasn't going to help him relieve himself, but swallowing her embarrassment, she did assist him stand even though she averted her eyes. She couldn't but realise what a fine figure of a man the Captain was, and felt a delicious tingle run through her body. She busied herself with the fire while Billy led his Captain, who limped badly, over to the wood area. When they returned, Ambrose managed to get his dried trousers and shirt back on, after which he was ashen faced, so Blythe made him sit again, and fussed while he did so.

"For God's sake Brown, you are fussing like a woman! Just leave me be, and I will soon recover."

"I'm sure you are ready to eat something?" she grinned, knowing that men hated fuss, but she couldn't help it. At his careful nod, she strolled over to the glowing fire and pulled out the pot. Once the lid was off, a delicious aroma filled the air, which made them all feel ravenous.

"First things first," said Blythe, spooning out the broth into bowls. "We all need sustenance, and once we have eaten, we can plan our next step. Well, in fact, the first thing is to bury that poor man."

"Bury whom?" asked Ambrose, still befuddled.

"One of the crew—he must have been washed overboard, as I am afraid many were. Billy and I will go and dig a grave after we have eaten and get him covered as soon as possible."

Despite the pain in his head, Ambrose wits were arranging themselves, and as soon as he had emptied his bowl, he said, "That was delicious. I already feel better. And now, Brown, you must tell me what happened, as I don't remember anything except the storm blowing up and the need to reef the sails."

Blythe told him a brief version of what had happened, finishing with, "And I don't know what has happened to our ship—whether it foundered, or if it is still intact. If it is, the men might send out a search party, but we can't rely on that. Nor do we know where we are, whether we are in hostile territories or friendly, but at this stage, you have to recover fully before you do anything, especially if you have a broken or cracked rib."

"At the moment, I don't think I can do anything," said Ambrose smiling wryly, "so while it seems you have already been in charge, I appoint you my deputy until I can think straight. That blow has certainly addled my brain, and

I'm seeing double at the moment, though I am sure it won't take long before I am compos mentis again."

"Compost wot?" asked Billy.

"Thinking straight," said Ambrose. His chin then dropped onto his chest, and he fell asleep, his hair flopping over his poor bruised face.

"Sleep will be his best medicine," said Blythe to Billy. "You'd better stop calling me 'Miss' or he'll soon twig I'm not a fellow. It's easier to leave it that way. Just call me Brown, like he does."

"Okay," grinned Billy, "Brown it is then. We gunna go and bury that dead geezer then?"

"Yes, I think we had better—the sun won't be doing him any favours." Blythe picked up a couple of shovels that Billy had retrieved from the boat and they went to find a suitable spot to dig a grave, which they found just beyond the dunes. The soil was soft enough to dig easily and they toiled in the hot sun until Blythe deemed the space large enough.

"Now, let's get that canvas to drag him along." Leaving the spades by the grave, they collected the canvas and walked across the hot sands to the distant corpse. As they neared they could hear the buzzing of a multitude of flies and could already smell a horrible stench.

"Oh Gawd!" exclaimed Billy. Blythe retched—it was indeed a horrible sight, but it was something they had to do. They rolled the fly-ridden body, fly eggs already laid in the poor man's eyes, nose and mouth, onto the canvas sail and covered it as well as they could and then set to, dragging the body up the beach towards the grave. Flies buzzed all around them making the task even more difficult. Eventually they stood by the open grave, trying to get their breath back.

"Shall we leave 'im in the sail then Miss—er, I mean Brown?" asked Billy.

Blythe had been wondering about this. It seemed more appropriate if they could, but she thought the sail would be important when they left in the skiff, so she said "No, we'll have to roll him out. He's not going to know, is he?"

So, the small boy and the lean young girl tipped the drowned corpse into his last resting place, a buzzing cloud of flies following him down.

"Quick," instructed Blythe, "get shovelling!" Once the body was covered with soil, Blythe said, "I think I should say a few words—I don't know the correct way, but lower your head Billy, we will say a prayer for that man. Do you know what his name was?"

Billy replied, "I jest knew him as Dirty Dick from Diss."

Blythe smothered a smile, and said, "Well, it must have been Richard, then, mustn't it. Alright, here we go."

They both lowered their heads respectfully, and Blythe said, "Richard from Diss, we pray that you have a safe journey to heaven and that the Lord is there waiting for you. We are sorry that your life was cut short so swiftly. Rest in Peace. Amen"

Billy added his Amen too. Blythe picked a few flowers growing nearby and placed them on the grave. In silence, they picked up their shovels and dragging the canvas behind them, they made a return journey to the camp. Once there, and noting that Ambrose was still sleeping, Blythe motioned to the seated Billy,

"I'm just going to go and douse this canvas in the sea and have a swim. I feel so hot and stinky and need refreshing and that was all a bit too much for me. You keep your eyes on the Captain, and not me. Alright?" Billy grinned, and said, "Yes mate, 'ave a good douse. See yer in a minnit."

Blythe walked slowly down to the edge of the sea and disrobed. She felt exhausted, the events of the last days had drained her. She pulled the soiled canvas into the water and found some rocks to hold it down—the sea would clean it. She waded until the water covered her breasts, and then flopped down so that she was floating on her back. She let the sun caress her body, she allowed the gentle waves to soothe her and let her mind drift. How her life had changed!

From a carefree child, running wild with her twin through the town of King's Lynn, watching that poor woman, accused as a witch, being hung by the neck in the marketplace, being almost in the same position when Matthew Hopkins' eye lit on her, and only just escaping his clutches, then racing along the foggy docks in the dark of the night to leap onto the wrong ship, and then live a sailor's life disguised as a lad. She had survived a terrible storm, she had been shipwrecked, and worst of all, she had just buried a man covered in flies with wriggling maggots in his eyes, and to end the litany of woes, she was in love with a man who believed her to be a boy. Yes, she admitted to herself, "I must be in love." Not only did she feel desire for Ambrose, she cared for him too.

She splashed her arms in the warm water and rolled onto her tummy and did a few lazy strokes to propel her along. What would happen next, she wondered? Well, as soon as Ambrose was recovered, they would be able to sail off in the skiff to the next port, and soon find out if their ship was there or not. If not, they would eventually be able to wend their way back to Norfolk—though she was in no hurry to return to be captured by Matthew Hopkins.

She hoped the ship was not perished, for if so, that meant her father faced considerable financial ruin. She also wondered how her twin, Barnaby, was faring. She felt he was alright, and safe—had 'that feeling' that all was well with him. She thought she would know if not.

After a delicious time of carefree floating and splashing, Blythe returned to the shore and pulled the cleansed canvas out of the shallows. Once it was rolled up, and the sun had dried her, she climbed back into her clothing, and strolled back up the beach to their little camp.

Ambrose, his head propped up against some rolls of canvas, peered through his swollen eyes with difficulty. His head hurt like the blazes and it was difficult for him to think, but he could swear on his mother's life that young Barnaby, who made his heart quicken, was displaying breasts and female parts. He groaned, shut his eyes, endeavoured to make himself comfortable whilst trying not to move his body because of the pain. A thousand curses on the lad.

***

In King's Lynn, Arabella was viewing herself in the mirror, very pleased with how she looked. She ran her hands over her breasts and couldn't help but touch her nipples, making them hard. She plunged her hands down her corset and drew her breasts further up so that they were displayed fully. She liked to see her body and bring it to fulfilment. It's a shame Peter hadn't been an ardent and rough lover—fie on the stupid man—but then, she will soon have got rid of him. The belladonna drops she had been placing in his food would do their work. Already his face was pale, there were dark rings around his eyes and he was doubled up with pains in his stomach.

Tonight, she was going to a dinner with a ball afterwards, and she would go without her spouse—with luck, he would be dead on her return. She rearranged her bosoms so that they were displayed becomingly, with the nipples only just within the bounds of decorum. She would make sure the richest men were aware of her charms—she intended rising up the rungs of the social ladder and eventually away from this pit in Norfolk and into a landed estate, the wife of an Earl and a Countess to boot. She called to her maid who tweaked her hair and added some adornments, and then she was ready.

Arabella made her way down the stairs, clutching her fan and vanity bag, and summonsed the butler to arrange her cape around her shoulders.

"Is the carriage at the door?" she snapped at him.

"Yes, Mistress, all is ready for you." He opened the door for her, where she could see the postilion holding open the carriage door, and she stepped daintily towards it, making sure no dirt was in the way of her feet to sully them. She arranged her beautiful gown around her once inside, and tapping the roof of the carriage to declare she was ready, she held on to a tasselled cord as the horses lurched off towards the ball. It was unusual for a woman not be accompanied to a social occasion, but Arabella didn't care one whit.

Arabella had her eyes on a local Earl whose wife had unexpectedly died recently. Thinking about it, Arabella tittered to herself. It had been so easy to slip the potion into the woman's drink, and it had done its work rapidly. She had visited the Earl to pay her respects, and played her part beautifully as the concerned friend and the fool of a man was already eating out of her hand. She had to wait before her own husband died, when she would then act the part of the grieving widow, before she could pursue the course she had set herself to ensnare the Earl, but she knew she was now *almost* part of the aristocracy. She wiggled with excitement. She also wondered who else would be at the ball. She hoped that she would get many dances and have the chance to press against all those ridiculous men and feel them harden at her innocent pressure. They were all so very predictable.

"Where is your husband, Mistress Brown? I trust he is not unwell?" enquired the genial host as she entered the wealthy establishment.

"Alas, he is abed, I am afraid," replied Arabella, with enough worry in her eyes to convince the devil himself that she was in earnest. "He insisted, however, that I came tonight, despite my pleas that I stay by his bedside. He told me that he is only inconvenienced and should be fine in a day or so. He said it would be rude if I didn't attend your function."

She smiled sweetly at the host knowing perfectly well that she was acting out of the bounds of convention by arriving on her own without an escort. After allowing her cape to be taken from her shoulders, she swept through to greet all the other guests and made sweet small talk with the women folk to allay their fears that she might grab their husbands. She intended to play the floor with them later! Her Earl had not yet arrived, so she circulated freely, throwing her head back on occasion with what she considered a tinkling laugh.

A sudden hush took over the room as a last guest entered bringing in with him a rush of cold air and the harsh cry of a raven. Quickly, the conversation began again, with furtive glances towards the newcomer, who by now was a person of dubious renown—a man who made people scurry by quickly, a man who was feared greatly, a man named Matthew Hopkins.

Matthew was still being paid a great deal of money from the town coffers to rid the county of witches, and he had already had hanged many innocent women on the gallows in Tuesday Market place. Matthew by now had many cohorts, including his old friend John Sterne from Manningtree, to help him find and take witches to trial. As well as the moles that didn't bleed when pricked, those on trial were taken to deep water and had their thumbs bound to the back of their heels before they were thrown in. Anyone who survived and floated were deemed guilty and taken in a tumbrel to the gallows in the market square.

In order to escape the steely gaze of Hopkins, people would stammer when speaking to him, and would invariably tell him the name of any person, with a concocted story of how, perhaps, after a woman had looked at their hog, it had died within hours…anything to deflect Matthew's probing eyes from themselves.

Arabella felt a shudder of unease when she noticed Matthew making his way towards her through the throng. She was not frightened of him, for she knew men and recognised him for a bully, and bullies were usually men with problems and often strange sexual desires. She could soon sort him out if he became difficult with her.

"Ah, Mistress Brown, we meet again," said Matthew as he made a neat bow to Arabella, who curtsied back prettily.

"Yes," she replied. "That was an unfortunate occasion when that wretched girl fled the nest."

"Indeed," replied Hopkins, his eyes lingering on the swelling orbs of Arabella's breasts.

Arabella gurgled and tapped her fan on Matthew's shoulders. "We are not sure, but we think that she escaped on one of my husband's ships. She will have to return eventually." She said no more, but fluttered her lashes at him with a pretended shy downward glance and hooked her hands through Matthew's arm.

"I am unescorted tonight as my husband has been taken ill. Perhaps you would walk me in to dinner please?"

Matthew did not particularly want to, but manners prevailed, and the two sauntered through to the dining room and were ushered into their seats.

Arabella questioned Matthew on his work, being sure to flatter him at every slight pause.

"Do you accompany these wretched women down into the dungeon and interrogate them yourself?" she asked tremulously. She was sure that he would do, and felt he was one of those who liked to inflict pain.

"Yes, I do, for although I have a team who work for me, it is my duty to ensure that we are not committing innocent women to the gallows," said Matthew in sanctimonious tones.

"Oh, quite, quite—you must know the truth of things, mustn't you?" she breathed.

"What do you do? Do you strip them naked and whip them until they scream?" She licked her lips as she said this, imagining the scene, "And do you," she whispered in his ear, "tweak their nipples until they bleed? And then, do you… " she didn't have to finish her sentence, for the man was already breathing heavily with a glazed look in his eyes. She placed her hand under the tablecloth and let in rest at the top of his thigh where she could feel an interesting stiffness by her fingers. She withdrew her hand and raised her glass and said to Matthew, "To your witches, Matthew," and smiled beguilingly into those lust-filled black eyes.

Arabella felt a tinge of unease. She knew men very well, and realised that Matthew was not one whom it would be sensible to anger. He was a religious fanatic with dark sexual urges. She was not interested in him as he was not what she had set her aims upon, and she should tread carefully around him.

"You are a good man, Matthew, and I for one am very grateful that you have almost rid the town and surrounding countryside of evil women. May God go with you."

Matthew's eyes focused again and lingered again on her breasts. "Indeed Madam, and I thank you." The woman was a temptation. She was showing her breasts and luring him with her words and her eyes. She had made him think lewd thoughts and all he could think of right now was an image of her on the block in his dungeon, naked and completely at his mercy. She was no woman of God.

He looked Arabella in the eye and let his gaze drop to her bodice.

"Now, Madam," he said, "I declare you have a mole nestling there between those two temptations." His black eyes bored into hers and she felt a terrible shudder of fear, especially as his sardonic smile held malice.

"Oh lud, Sire, 'tis just a patch put there for fun! Drink your wine, do." Turning to her own glass, she pulled her bodice to cover the mole. Surely he would not arrest her? Not when she was so nearly in command of her life and coming riches? She looked around to see if her Earl had yet arrived, and could see him at the further end of the long table. She wiggled her fingers towards him, once she had caught his eye, and he raised his glass to her.

"Yes," Arabella thought, *"as soon as the meal was finished she would ensure that she managed a waltz with him and press herself against his fat stomach."* She wondered if Peter had succumbed to the belladonna yet. She smiled to herself, just as Matthew Hopkins rose from the table.

"Excuse me, Mistress Brown. I shall see you later." Arabella watched him as he left the room.

"Yes," she thought, "he is lusting for me too. They all are." She sat and finished off a lobster moose and pushed her plate aside, which was immediately removed by a flunkey. She looked forward to some marchpane that she could see set by on a side table. Then, she would dance with her Earl and praise his prowess on the floor, and hint that she was sure he was just as clever between silken sheets—but she mustn't be too obvious, she didn't want to put the fool off.

Matthew Hopkins hadn't gone far. His henchmen were waiting in a side room, and he gathered them together. "That Brown woman is a witch, I am sure. She has a mole between her breasts." The other men snickered and Hopkins glared at them. "Come with me now, I want her arrested."

First, he went to their host and took him to one side. "Sir, I am afraid we have to arrest one of your guests. To avoid an upheaval, I would request that you bring the lady to us, rather than cause an uproar within your dining hall."

The man paled, but left Matthew and his men and walked over to Arabella, where he whispered into her ear, "Madam, I am afraid there is some bad business afoot. Please come with me."

Arabella wiped her mouth delicately with her napkin, hiding a smile. Ah, it would be Peter's death, of course. She must look devastated when she was told, and weep copious tears. She followed her host from the dining hall, where guests were enjoying the feast and was then confronted by Matthew Hopkins's bulk and several grim-faced men.

"Madam," said Hopkins crisply, his pale face making his black eyes even blacker, "you are under arrest on suspicion of witchcraft!"

Arabella gasped, the colour draining from her face. "I'm no witch!" she screamed, causing nearby guests to turn and stare. "How dare you!" She shrieked again and spat and scratched as her arms were grasped and she was propelled towards the elegant door.

Unfortunately for her, a black cat just happened to race across the feet of them all, hissing and yowling, which gave rise in the following days of how her familiar had fled from her body and raced towards safety in the dark alleyways of the town.

Arabella was marched through the town in an ignominious manner, her screaming complaints knocked out of her by the blows of the men pushing her forward. Matthew felt the thrill of torture coming his way as they marched towards the gaol and its dungeon. Before he descended the dank steps, he turned to his cohort and said, "Go back to the Brown's house and fetch that French maid and the housekeeper as well as the daughter. I sense they are a coven and need to be interrogated as well. They are a nest of vipers and I would like to eradicate them all to please The Lord our God."

The men were quick to stride importantly through the town to hammer on Peter's door. The butler opened it, only to be thrust aside and told to fetch the housekeeper, the maid and the daughter. All three women were soon found and brought to the door, all asking what on earth was going on. Told that they were to be taken for interrogation at the Court where their mistress and mother was already undergoing questioning, all three paled and began to tremble. Dimity clutched on to the back of a chair wailing, but the men had no sympathy. "Master believes you to be a coven of witches!" he declared in a rough voice, pushing the women in front of him, where other gaolers soon took hold of them and thrust them through the streets of Lynn while unsympathetic market holders and local folk watched. Dimity heard one say, "Serve them right, stuck up women—never trusted 'em anyway."

One of the original staff, a young girl named Mary, took the stairs two at a time and raced into Peter's bedroom, where he was lying in his bed, eyes dark, skin clammy and looking near to death. "Sir!" exclaimed the girl, "they have taken away Mistress Brown and her daughter and maid and the housekeeper— they believe them all witches!"

Peter managed to gasp to the girl, "Well, they have behaved like witches, haven't they—I'm sure I am being poisoned—will you go to the apothecary and ask him to visit me quickly before I am dead? He may be able to help me. I have to get better, to ensure that Barnaby and Blythe come to no harm when they return."

The girl curtseyed and raced off on her errand and on the way bumped into the old cook, Mistress Gotobed, who had recently been dismissed by Arabella. "Oh, please go to the house—Mistress Brown and her nasty flock have been accused of witchcraft. The master is ill—he thinks they have poisoned him. I am on the way to get help, but we need people who love him to bring him back to life. I do hope it's not too late."

Mistress Gotobed took no time in scurrying along to the old house and entered through the kitchen door. "Wot are yew doing in here?" spat the current cook.

"I've come to help my old master and if I were you, I'd be gone as quickly as you can before you are arrested by Matthew Hopkins too. Your mistress and the others are in gaol at the moment, where you will be too if you hang around."

The cook quickly took off her apron, raced up to her attic room and collected her things, which included several silver items that she had secreted from the house, and made her way to get the London coach—she would be glad to get back to the city she knew and get away from this stick-in-the-mud Norfolk place.

Wheezing her way up the stairs to Peter's room the old cook was disgusted at the mess and smell in there. Clearly the poor man had been abandoned for some time. Pulling back the heavy drapes around the bed, she fussed with the pillows and made him more comfortable.

Smoothing back his hair gently, she whispered, "Don't you fret, my man, we will soon get you better. I'll get the girl to sort out this filth and go and make you some broth to strengthen you. I'll get you something to drink too—looks like you haven't had any help, have you."

Peter smiled wanly, pleased to see the familiar face of his old and beloved Cook.

Hope rose in his heart. "Thank you, Cook. I'm so happy to see you. I will be alright now." He held out his hand, which Cook took into hers, giving it a gentle rub.

"Shush yourself Sir—you need all your strength to get better. We will soon have you sorted out. Did you know that your new wife, her daughter and her retinue have been taken for interrogation by Matthew Hopkins?"

Peter nodded weakly, but having lost the love he had for his new wife, he had begun to suspect that she wasn't what she had portrayed, and while he didn't think her a witch, he was sure that his food had been interfered with and that she was trying to kill him. He was too weak to be able to do anything about any trial at the moment, his wife had certainly seen to that. His head dropped back on the pillow and he drifted into sleep.

Had the scheming Arabella realised she would be taken as a witch and probably hanged, she would not have poisoned her husband, but then, she was so far down the slippery slope with her plots and plans to elevate herself in society and riches, she had almost succeeded in killing the only person who might have helped her in her current situation.

With the alien folks gone from the house, the place was already taking on a lighter air. Cook got cracking, giving orders to clean out Master's room and make him comfortable, while she started assembling some food that would help his poor stomach and get him on the road to recovery. She was pleased to be working again, having been staying with her sister in cramped quarters and knew she was a burden on the family. She hoped the Master would let her stay, and for that to happen, she had to make him well again.

**

Blythe squatted by the sleeping Ambrose's side. He looked terrible. His face was so swollen and discoloured by bruising that he barely resembled the handsome man he had been before the storm. She noticed that his ankle was swollen—something she hadn't noticed before, as she had been concentrating on sewing up his head wound and worrying about the possibility of a cracked or broken rib.

She wasn't worried about herself in the predicament they were in, as she knew she was self-reliant and with Juno and Billy could easily cope in their make-shift camp. However, she did need to find out where they were and go out on explorations a little further afield. They seemed safe enough at the moment, but it depended on whether or not there were dangerous natives or wild animals nearby. She had listened to the sailors' tales on board the ship, intrigued to hear of dark faced and turbaned men with honed and curved scimitars stuck in silken waist bands who cut off the heads of innocent people just on a whim. They spoke too, of pirates and bandits, bears and wolves and even hordes of Mongolians who screamed as they rode to battle on the backs of white horses.

The sailors had talked of slaves being sold in marketplaces, of women who were chained at the neck and bound to posts while rich men came to inspect their bodies, look at their teeth and caress their breasts. Those whom they favoured were purchased then taken off to harems in jewel-studded palaces that were guarded by castrated men. The women would be perfumed and clad in diaphanous robes to await the summons of their owner.

Blythe didn't want to escape from hanging as a witch to then find herself being bought as a harem slave to a rich man with eyes as black as ebony and an eagle's beak for a nose. Nor did she like the idea by being stalked by a bear and being clawed to death, or herded into a forest corner by a pack of hungry wolves and being torn to death.

Blythe forced herself to think positively and not fear the worst. She might find some kind people in a nearby village, who would help them until Ambrose was better, then they could go and search for their ship. Or, pondered Blythe, they might have to stay living under canvas on the edge of the beach until they grew ancient and died of starvation.

Juno's nose nudged her in the side and she came out of her morbid reveries and looked around her. The woods they were in held different trees to those in Norfolk and were more gnarled and smaller leaved. The ground was dry from the constant heat but was aromatic from the multitude of herbs that grew in profusion. The aroma was quite heady and almost unconsciously Blythe was thinking how useful some of them would be to make unguents and balms—but first, she must press on and look around to assess their situation. As she pushed on up the steep hill, she found herself on a ledge and realised that Juno was no longer with her. The dog had been ahead of her, so where could she have gone? Blythe pushed forward until the ledge petered out, so she began to call to her dog. She heard muffled barks coming from behind some creepers that hung down the face of the steep hill, so pulling it back, Blythe was surprised to find a cave that from the outside was completely hidden from view. When sunlight entered the cave, Juno began to bark again, she seemed to realise she had made a good find. She was sniffing all the nooks and crannies, and Blythe realised the dog would sniff out any animal or snake that might live in there. She could see the hound's long tail wagging slowly which indicated all was well, so she entered inside and was pleased at what she found. The cave was dry, with an overhang above the entrance, bushes around it to shield it from enemies (if there were any) and deep enough for them to retreat to for safety.

Blythe could not see right into the back of the cave as it was too dark, but she had heard Juno blundering around in there, and it didn't sound as if it were overly large.

"Well," said Blythe happily to Juno, "This will be a better place for us to use as a home. We need to be safe, and are too exposed on the beach in case of danger. What is good also, is that we can have a lookout place near to the cave, so that we can see if a ship comes into view—how wonderful if it were the *Evening Star*. You are such a clever girl, Juno. Well done." Juno wagged her tail.

The more she looked around, the more Blythe realised what a safe haven the cave would be for them—it couldn't be noticed from afar and with the creeper left hanging down, wouldn't be seen by anyone passing by. She climbed back down the hill and returned to Billy and Ambrose on the beach. She noted with relish that Billy had managed to catch some fish that were sizzling on the spit and that Ambrose was sitting up, fully awake now.

"Oh, Ambrose, you are awake, thank goodness! How are you feeling?"

"Hungry," growled Ambrose with a wry smile. His face still looked awful, the purple bruising had now the added colours of yellow, all leeching down his face.

Blythe squatted beside him and adjusted his bandage. "I'll have another look at that after we have eaten—that fish looks too good to leave. Well done Billy!" She then sat next to Ambrose while Billy was proudly levering off the fish onto some leaf plates, and they all set to with gusto. Once they had completed their meal, Blythe said, "I've got some really good news. Juno found a cave further up the hill and it would be ideal for us. I think we should move camp to be on the safe side, and cover all traces of where we have been. We need to move the boat too and hide it in the undergrowth." Turning to Ambrose, she said, "Have you any idea where we might be beached, sir? I have no idea, and am worried that perhaps there might be hostile natives. I've searched the immediate vicinity and there is no sign of habitation, but I didn't want to go far while you were still unconscious."

Ambrose blinked. His head was still pounding, but he didn't feel so bad as he had when he had woken for a short while previously. He tried to think coherently. Clearly they had somehow become shipwrecked, and he tried to trace his thoughts back. He couldn't remember the spar knocking him out, but he did recall that they were probably near to the Barbary Coast, in which case it would be prudent to hide themselves away. Pirate ships sailed this way, and they often used such coves as this to careen their vessels, look for fresh water and hide their spoils. Barnaby and Billy had done well whilst he had been out of action.

"Brown, Billy, I can only thank you from my heart. Between you, you have done so well, and yes, I think we should get to your cave Brown, as quickly as possible. We just don't know what might happen, and while I am in this dozy state, I can't do much to help. I think you are right, Brown, my rib is either cracked or broken, and my ankle can't bear any weight without buckling. I am sure I will be better in a few days, but in the meantime, let us move all our goods and do as you suggest." This speech seemed to tire him, and his head drooped onto his chest again as he fell into another sleep.

"Billy, let's get cracking. We will leave the canvas shelter until last, so that the Captain is in the shade. Just grab what you can, and follow me to the cave. We might as well use Juno as a donkey too—she is so strong and can carry loads."

Blythe showed Billy how to make a structure out of branches that trailed behind the dog. They loaded quite a lot of their belonging onto it and off the hound trotted, easily pulling the load.

"Cor, I wisht you'd thought of that before Miss, instead of me lugging all this stuff up the beach!"

"Yes, Billy, but my brains were just as addled as the Captain's."

They both laughed as they toiled up the slopes to the cave. Billy was really excited when Blythe showed him how to pull back the creeper. He ran around inside whooping and hollering and that set Juno barking in excitement and even Blythe giggled. They tied back the creeper so that the cave was lit up by sunlight, and brought in all their belongings. Blythe designated areas for their bedding, placing Billy and the Captain away from her own. Then she had a lovely idea.

"Billy, I've been thinking. There are so many delicious herbs growing everywhere, lets pick lots of them and we can stuff out our bedding with them. We can use some grasses as well, and we will have really soft beds that smell fantastic as well."

"Bluddy 'ell, Miss, you'se acting like a bluddy housekeeper, 'int yew—fuss, fuss, fuss'!"

Blythe giggled, saying, "Well, I would never have believed it of myself, but it does seem rather fun, setting up home here! Let's go and gather those herbs then all we have to do now is to hide the boat and get the Captain up here, and then we are safe and dry from the elements and any passing pirates!"

After the cave was ready to Blythe's liking, they all set off down the hill again, where Ambrose was still asleep in the shade, so Blythe whispered to Billy, "Let's go down to the beach now, and get the boat hidden."

Billy nodded and before long, he and Blythe had heaved and pushed at the boat, pulling it up to the edge of the beach where the forest began, and covered it from sight with branches and undergrowth. By the time they had finished, Ambrose was awake again, and watching the proceedings with admiration. He acknowledged to himself that Barnaby seemed to be a born leader and Billy a willing member of the crew. He groaned, tried to shift his position and gasped at the chest pains.

Blythe heard Ambrose gasp, and ran over to his side.

"Let me feel those ribs, sir. I don't think there is much I can do, but maybe some rags tied around might make things a bit better." As she spoke, she gently felt around Ambrose's chest, her fingers gently testing the skin to see if she could feel any break in his ribs. He groaned at her touch. "Oh, does it hurt there, Sir?"

"No" said Ambrose, for in truth, the lad's touch had made him feel desire, which he loathed. "No, it just hurts in general." He pushed Blythe away. "Enough lad—I've just got to take care—I will be alright. Billy, help me up, for I'd like to get to the shelter of the cave you speak about."

Blythe felt upset that Ambrose had pushed her away so roughly, but guessed that he probably didn't want to be babied, and tried not to take offence.

It didn't take long to pull down the canvas shelter and roll it up ready to move. Both Billy and Blythe pulled Ambrose into a standing position and Blythe handed him a hefty stick to use as a staff to aid his progress, then walked ahead with Juno, who now carried the sails over her back, up to their new cave home. The sun was blazing down fiercely now and they were all sweating. Blythe thought how lucky they were to have a small stream flowing near to their cave to drink from.

Blythe had prepared a comfortable seat for Ambrose at the entrance of the cave under the overhang, which kept the sun off him. She had delegated a space for the fire underneath some nearby trees, which would filter the smoke away from any eyes that might otherwise spy it and come and investigate. When Ambrose reached the cave, she indicated where she wanted him to rest, and he sank blissfully down onto his comfortable couch. As he did so, wonderful wafts of herbs and soft foliage hit his olfactory senses—"Gads, man, what have you been doing? Padding my seat with attar of roses?"

Blythe laughed. "No, Captain, just herbs that grow in abundance around here. I thought it would make your seat soft and comfortable and the aroma is good for your wellbeing."

"Hmpth!" replied Ambrose with a groan as he settled himself down gingerly and got himself comfortable. "You look like a bloody girl, and you act like a bloody girl, but then, no girl could take command of a situation like this, so I shall forgive you!"

Blythe flushed with annoyance, thinking how little he knew, and swept her greasy hair out of her eyes. She looked around and was pleased with what they had achieved.

"With your permission, Sir, I think Billy and I should now go back to the beach to sweep away all evidence of our camp and make sure everything looks normal should any undesirables find their way ashore. I think we should take it in turns, though, to look out to see if our ship does come this way, just in case all is well with it, and they are looking for us. There is an ideal spot just over yonder."

"Yes, Brown, that is a good idea. I can take my turn at that, it will make me feel useful. Is it far?"

"No," replied Blythe, "it's just through those trees, but for the moment you must rest after the exertion of the climb up here. Billy and I will go now to finish off eliminating any trace of our stay on the beach. We won't be long, and once we are back, we can get into a routine while you recover, and then we can find a way out of this situation. We have the skiff with both oars and sail, so our situation is by no ways grim." Turning to Billy, she said, "Let's get started then. Juno, you stay with the Captain."

Ambrose nodded, and leaned back against the smooth rock, every movement that he made causing pain, that was somewhat allayed by the sweet smell of the herbs. He watched as Billy and 'Barnaby' left the cave to walk down through the rocks and tree growth, while Juno settled herself against his side. Ambrose placed his good arm over Juno's back and as he got his head comfortable, he gazed up into the branches of one of the trees a little distance away from their cave. He had watched some bees that seemed to end their destination at the trunk of the tree and noticed that a lot were disappearing into a hole and that others were coming out and flying to some distant destination. "Ah ha, there must be honey in there. I wonder if that lad will have the guts to go and ferret it out? If so, at least I have contributed something to this situation we have found ourselves in."

Blythe and Billy on their return to the beach cleared up any tell-tale signs of their stay at the camp.

"What we will do, once we have everything tidy again, is to use some branches to sweep away all our footprints. It's a shame this is a relatively tide-less beach, otherwise the sea would do it for us, but we don't want to be found by scimitar wielding Turks, do we!"

"Cor, bluddy well no, Miss—er, Brown—I 'erd enuff abart them when the crew wos telling their tales on board—load of infidels they called 'em, cutting orf 'eds at the drop of a 'at. Well, I suppose 'ats would drop if they wos on the cut orf 'eds, wouldn't they!" Billy chortled and Blythe laughed.

"Yes, we don't want to be discovered by any of them, do we Billy. Look, I'll finish off here—it's mostly done now. You take your makeshift spear and see if you can get us some more fish, and if you leave your branches at the edge of the sea, you can brush away your footsteps on the way back."

Looking around at their work, all look untouched, unless people were searching carefully, so Blythe returned to the cave, her eyes ever watchful for herbs and edible growth. This landscape was very different to Norfolk and she didn't recognise any trees, but she wasn't worried about anything. They had food, they had water, Ambrose was on the mend, and it wouldn't be too long before they could set off in the boat and find out where they were.

Over the next week or so, Billy and Blythe had combed the area and discovered that they were on an island that, luckily for them, had deer, rabbits and birds that Juno caught easily. Billy did well spearing fish, and they had even found some turtle eggs on the beach, so they certainly were not going to starve. Blythe had found and dug up various roots that were delicious when cooked.

In time, Ambrose's bruising had gone and his ribs were healing. So long as he was careful, his breathing was easy. His ankle had improved as well, and he could hop around with the aid of his staff easily enough to go to the lookout point for his duty hours.

The three of them had formed an easy relationship, though both Ambrose and Blythe were trying their best to keep their desire for the other at bay, Ambrose especially, as his was forbidden. He was full of admiration for the lad, for he coped so easily with the situation, and had even managed to steal some honeycombs from the bees, by lighting a small smoky fire under the tree to make the bees dozy, then had climbed up with ease. The natural sweetness was what they all needed, boosting their energy, as well as tasting wonderful.

Blythe was really enjoying herself. All the times spent with her brother, making small camps after rowing to various destinations, getting the dogs to catch rabbits which they skinned and cooked over campfires had made this adventure really easy for her. She wasn't worried about what was to happen next, for she had such a positive nature and she enjoyed the present time, and made the most of it. By now, her face, arms and lower legs were as brown as berries, but she had kept her shirt and waistcoat on at all times to preserve her disguise, therefore she really was so hot, and envied Billy and Ambrose, who had long ago discarded their shirts in the heat. When she noticed that Ambrose and Juno were sleeping in the shade one afternoon, and Billy was off at the lookout point, she decided to go to the stream and have a really good wash. Her hair was itching like mad—the grease she had applied when on board the ship was really stinking, and she wanted to feel clean and cool. On her rambles around the island, she had found a bush that, when the twigs were snapped, had a soft centre that foamed when wet—she thought it would serve as a soap for her hair. By now, her hair had grown quite a bit but was still tied back in a queue. Billy had found her an old and battered tricorn hat in the skiff, which she had slapped over her hair, which while keeping the sun off, made her hair itch. Right now, she just had to get it clean!

As she strolled down to the stream, Blythe felt really at peace with the world. There might be dangers ahead, but they would cope, she was sure. She smiled to herself as she remembered Nicholas Culpeper's words about her travelling abroad into dangers. Passion too…well, she didn't know about that…

Disrobing, she first of all washed her clothing and spread it in the sun to dry, then stepped into the cool waters and paddled until she found a natural indent in the bed of the stream where she could sit down and let the water flow over her. How blissful it was to just lie there, letting the water cleanse her body. She applied the sappy centre of the twigs and indeed it did foam and made washing the grease from her hair an easy matter. She lay back in the water, closed her eyes, and enjoyed the sun dappling down through the leaves. She smiled as she listened to the gurgle of the waters as it splashed and plopped around stones and boulders, and enjoyed the song of the birds in the branches above her.

Ambrose awoke gradually, then stretched his limbs. His ankle wasn't hurting very much at all, and he thought it would be a good idea to exercise it by walking along to the lookout point to relieve Billy from his duty. He looked up at the sun's position, and realised that there was no rush, so he would take a detour and inspect an area that he hadn't seen yet. He had had enough of inactivity, and the thought that a lad and a small boy had been looking after him really irked. He was so grateful to them, of course, but he was a grown man, and ought to be in charge. It was time to get back to being Captain. They must make plans to get off this island. He was almost ready and his ribs felt a lot better, so long as he was careful in the way he moved.

Juno rose and stretched too, and wagged her long tail. She sniffed in the air, and Ambrose said, "Are you wondering where the others are then, Juno? I expect your master is down with Billy. Go find him." Juno, not used to her mistress being called a master, but understanding the word 'Billy', sniffed the ground and loped off following Billy's scent.

Ambrose, hearing the distant sound of the stream as it meandered along its course, thought it time that he went and had a good wash, not realising of course, that Blythe had already thought of that idea. Picking up his staff to aid his progress, he pushed his way through the woods carefully, not wanting any branches to hit his ribs, or roots to trip him up and injure his ankle again. Therefore, his slow progress was a quiet one, so what with the sounds of the birds and the gurgling waters, Blythe did not hear him coming.

As Ambrose came through the last of the trees, he could not help but see a beautiful woman, her tresses swirling gently around her head in the waters, her long limbs splayed in an abandoned manner, her eyes closed, a sweet smile on her features, her beautiful pert breasts on display and the soft triangle of hair between her legs.

A shot of desire coursed throughout Ambrose's shocked body—who was this woman, was she a nature goddess? a Nadir of the woods? No, of course not, they were just stories, but who could she be? His puzzled mind noted the breeches, shirt and waistcoat drying on a bush in the sun, which he recognised as Barnaby's. Surely this wasn't the lad who had been driving his senses mad since he came on board the *Evening Star*? *Now* it all made sense!

Ambrose turned on his heel and returned to the cave. He could not confront the girl when she was naked. He settled down on his herb filled couch and smiled as the herbs once more filled the air with their wonderful aroma. No wonder 'Brown' had made the cave so homelike, had tended him so well—the woman's touch. Why hadn't he realised? What a fool he had been. He hadn't been hallucinating when he thought he saw a naked woman on the beach…and thank the Lord, he wasn't an unnatural man—his body had recognised a desirable woman, even if he hadn't. He'd like to take the wench over his knee and smack her bottom senseless! He grinned at the thought, but put aside more lascivious thoughts—this was the daughter of his employer and he must treat the girl accordingly.

Blythe came out of her reveries as she heard Juno barking nearby. Not finding her mistress with Billy, she had turned back and picked up Blythe's scent and found her at last. Blythe sat up in the water, feeling deliciously clean and saw the hound wagging her tail at the side of the stream. "Come on in, it's okay Juno—you could do with a nice cool down and a wash too." The dog splashed into the waters and drank her fill, and on Blythe's command to "Lie!" She lay in the water and let the water run over her, which she enjoyed. Blythe rubbed Juno's hair until it was clean, and they both stepped out onto the mossy bank, Juno shaking her body so that droplets of water scattered far and wide. Blythe laughed, and lay herself down in a sunny position until her skin dried, then rose to check if her clothing was dried. It was, so she climbed into them, tied her clean hair back loosely, and wandered back towards the cave.

Ambrose had gathered his wits and decided to prepare the fire for the evening's meal. There had been no point in lighting it other than for cooking, and it would soon be time for that. He didn't know what was on the menu, but was sure the capable girl—what was her name? Was it Bridget? He couldn't remember, it was so long ago when he had joined her family for a meal when she was very young. As he pulled twigs and larger branches into position, he wondered how he was going to broach the subject with the girl—he couldn't admit to having seen her naked in the water, that would embarrass her probably, and he didn't want her to think he had been peeping. He still couldn't get the image out of his mind. How beautiful she was.

Juno came bounding through the bushes with the girl following, her arms full of yet more herbs. The place was full of them, and they did make their meals very tasty.

"Hallo, Ambrose—you are awake, and clearly feeling better. Thank you for preparing the fire. Billy caught some fish earlier, they are in the shade under some stones, so you can light the fire. He will be back soon. How are you feeling?"

"I'm feeling smelly and dirty, and I think I will do as you have clearly done, go and have a wash in the yonder stream. You look more like a girl than ever, Brown. Are you sure you aren't one?"

Blythe went pink, and busied herself with the wood pile.

"I found some twigs whose sap make a lovely foamy soap. Look, here they are, I'll just poke some out for you, and it will make your wash even more enjoyable. You could try lathering your beard—it's getting quite long now. If you would like, I have some scissors in my bag, I could trim it for you. There is a nice hollow in the stream opposite a large tree. It's rather like a bath—just follow the path I made—it's lovely down there, but don't tarry, for the fish won't take long to cook and darkness will fall soon—it seems to come quickly here, doesn't it?"

Ambrose nodded, took the soap the girl offered, and wandered off to bathe. He still didn't know how to broach the subject of the girl's gender, but supposed it didn't matter, really, if he said nothing.

Outside the cave, Blythe got the fire going nicely, and fetched the fish to prepare them. As she gutted and scraped off the scales she threw the bits straight in the fire otherwise flies would descend in their thousands—it was bad enough without inviting more. She pushed some of the herbs she had picked into the fish cavities, and then threaded them onto the stick to be used as a spit, and placed them at the side. She had already prepared some flat bread using ship's flour and some of the fat saved from the meat. She placed three on some even topped stones in the embers and they cooked quickly enough. She wasn't sure what they would taste like, but they would make a nice change. Some water was boiling into which she had thrown some herbs, some wild garlic and carrot-like roots, and some cubes of deer. It smelt wonderful.

Billy soon came skipping up the path from the lookout, whistling a sea-shanty, happy as a pig in clover. Dusk was falling, little red sparks from the fire drifted up into the trees and Billy flung himself down beside Blythe. "Coo, Miss, that smells bluddy wonderful! I've never 'ad such bluddy good food in all me life like wot we've 'ad 'ere. Wouldn't mind staying 'ere for ever!"

"Ha, *Miss,* is it!" cried Ambrose as he reached the cave just in time to hear Billy say the banned word.

"Oh bluddy 'ell, I've gorn and dun it now, ain't I Miss? I'm bluddy sorry, but Capting, if you can't tell she's a bluddy girl by now, your eyes need bluddy changing!"

164

Blythe had leapt up in shock, with her hands over her face, peeping through her fingers at Ambrose who gently smiled back at her, his eyes softening as he did so.

"Oh, that food smells wonderful," Ambrose uttered as he licked his lips, "are we going to eat now?" As he settled down to sit, he turned and said, "I have to say, Billy, that I had thought young Brown was very feminine, and kind of put two and two together, but hearing you give the game away, I think Mistress Brown has a few explanations, don't you?" He smiled gently again at Blythe to reassure her, and proffered his bowl for the meal.

Realising that the situation was not going to be difficult, after all, she dished out the meal and said with a shy smile, "Well, you have found me out now—are you going to make me walk the plank?"

Ambrose inhaled the delicious aroma of the food presented to him, looked at Blythe and said, "I don't think any lad could have looked after me so well, nor cooked such appetising food, and I can only applaud your many abilities to take command of the most distressing circumstances which would have done credit to any man, let alone a woman. I think it is time for you to tell me your story, and why you appeared late at night, dressed as a boy, just as the *Evening Star* was leaving the port at King's Lynn. I want the truth this time."

"Well," replied Blythe, setting her bowl down and breathing in a deep breath to steady her nerves, "I don't really know where to begin, but I suppose the reason why I fled onto the ship that night is where I should start. I was running for my life from Matthew Hopkins, who had come to arrest me. Luckily for me, after I had quickly changed into Barnaby's old clothes, grabbed my bag and climbed out of my window, over the roof and pelted towards the docks, I had a head start. He must have guessed I would try and flee to my father's ships and sent his men after me. I could hear them in the distance. Father had told me to get onto the *Morning Star*, as she was sailing first to France, where I could go ashore and stay with his friends—he gave me a letter, the one I showed you, but it got wet and all the ink ran. As you know, she had already sailed. The gang plank to the *Evening Star* was already being lifted just as I ran on with Juno following me."

Matthew nodded at Blythe's narrative then asked, his eyebrows lifting, "Isn't Matthew Hopkins the Witch Finder General? Did he suspect you of being a witch? I've heard differing stories about him, none of them flattering."

"I'm afraid so. I was with my father, stepsister and stepmother, dining before a ball, and he was sitting opposite me. My stepmother 'laughingly' pointed out the fact that I have a mole over my lip." Blythe touched her mole as she spoke, "And she also told him that Juno must be my familiar, that I dabbled in herbal arts as well as astrology—she was almost handing me to him on a platter—but I'm **not** a witch, though I do sometimes 'know' things—like I told you about the storm." Ambrose nodded, "And Goody Truman," Blythe continued, "told me I had a natural ability that only a few people have, but it is nothing to do with the Devil. That awful man had her hanged as well. She was such a kind and knowledgeable woman"

"So, Hopkins' men chased after you through the docks, did they? You must have been frightened," said Ambrose, his eyes intent.

"Well, I wasn't really frightened, it was quite exciting actually. I'd had a good head start, and they could only guess where I was going. The sea fret had come down and it was only because I knew the way well that I could be fast—they must have been blundering around, falling over barrels, not knowing where they were going. I knew I must get away quickly, though," continued Blythe, "for that man would have had me hanged by the neck in Tuesday Market Place, just like he did all the others."

Ambrose followed Blythe's look as her eyes glazed a bit as her memories became more real. She added,

"Through the fog, I could only see the shape of one ship left in the dock, and the gangplank was just being lifted, so I leapt on, told the sailor who challenged me that you knew I was coming, and then hid in the rowboat until morning. Juno, of course, had followed me, and I couldn't push her off a moving ship into the sea. I'm glad she came with me though. In the morning when you saw me, you automatically thought I was my twin, Barnaby, so it was easy to carry on with the deception, though you weren't pleased to see me!"

A wry smile crossed Ambrose's face before he said, "No, I wasn't, and the more I saw you, the angrier I became." Ambrose noticed how upset Blythe looked at his remark and added, "But probably not for any reason that you can think of!"

Blythe dropped her head and watched her own fingers twiddling in her lap and as she did so, the twine that she had tied around her newly washed hair dropped off, and her hair, now shining and clean fell to her shoulders and curled around her face, and Ambrose thought how beautiful she was and how feminine and how much he would like to caress those long legs and pull off those breeches. He pushed such thoughts away, smiled at her and said, "Well, you don't have to keep up the pretence now whilst we are here, though I think that when we do attempt to leave this island, you should continue with your disguise. It's safer that way."

Blythe nodded. Billy had been watching the pair talking, and to him, even though he was only a nipper, it was clear that these two really fancied each other. He chuckled to himself. He also wondered if the Captain actually remembered her name. Miss had told him what it was, and also that she had first seen the Captain when he was invited to a meal many moons ago when she was only fourteen, when he had barely noticed her, so maybe he didn't know her name. Time, then, for a bit of subterfuge…

"I suppose we o'rter call yew Mistress Blythe now, Miss." said Billy with a sly grin.

"Oh, just call me Blythe," she replied, with a laugh. "It would be nice to hear my name spoken again," she told him. "Anyway, I do like being in boys' clothes, I've worn them so often when adventuring with my twin brother, but much as I like my freedom, as my mother used to remind me, I am still a girl!"

Ambrose, relieved to be prompted by Billy as to Blythe's name, did remember it now. That Billy was astute—he must have realised he had forgotten. "Well, then, Blythe, it's dark now and it's getting late and time for sleep. Maybe I should sleep outside under the stars, as I would be compromising you by sleeping in the same space?"

Blythe blushed, and retorted, "We have been close to each other at night for ages now, so it won't hurt at all. We can concoct a suitable story once we reach habitation again and revert to social niceties."

They all settled down for the night, with Ambrose well away from Blythe, but now the atmosphere was very different and they both felt somewhat awkward, so aware of each other with the charged dynamics. Blythe wasn't frightened that Ambrose would try and seduce her—she was sure he was moral enough, but there was a definite tension in the air that even Billy was aware of.

Ambrose could think of nothing but clasping Blythe in his arms, his hands caressing her all over, while Blythe tried to imagine what it would feel like with Ambrose's lips upon hers.

A long time passed before any of them fell asleep, but the rhythmic chirruping of the crickets outside eventually lulled them into a heavy slumber, so heavy that they slept much longer than normal. They didn't hear the sounds of men's voices shouting on the beach.

It was Juno's low warning growls that eventually woke them, and Blythe immediately sat up and noticed the hair raised on the scruff of her dog's neck, then heard distant drunken shouts and felt real fear that raised the small hairs on her arms.

She called softly across the cave, "Captain, wake up!" Ambrose was awake in a trice, used to trouble and the need to be alert in an instance.

"Ay, I can hear them—I'll go to the lookout point and see what is happening. Keep in the cave and don't move. If the men are as drunk as they sound, they will probably not be friendly." Ambrose left the cave and hobbled away to see what was happening.

Billy had woken by now and was rubbing his eyes and stretching. Hearing the distant noise, he turned to Blythe saying, "Cor, wot a turn up for the books. Dew yew think we're gunna be rescued?"

Shaking her head, Blythe answered, "I don't know Billy—just listen, they all sound blind drunk, and even if they were British, they might be in an evil mood. They are more likely to be foreign and could be our enemy. In case they come this way, we had better disguise any signs of our home here. We've kept the cave entrance clear, but let's just cover the ashes over with earth and leaves and disguise our pile of wood just in case anyone comes this way, otherwise they will search for us."

"Good idea, Miss, said Billy, racing outside to throw earth and greenery over the fire, taking away anything that looked 'residential' and pulled some branches over their log pile."

"All done," said Billy, returning to the cave mouth, "Let's go an 'ave a look shall we?"

Blythe said, "No, Billy, the Captain told us to stay here, didn't he." Billy's face dropped. "But I wanna see," he wailed.

Brushing dirt off her pants, Blythe grinned. "Actually, so do I Billy. It could be that the Captain might need our help don't you think?" Blythe was so used to making her own decisions and following her own instincts that it went against her nature to meekly do as she was told. She slipped on her boots, and thrust her small dagger into the side of one—a relic of her days gutting fish for the fire on her days out in the boat with Barnaby. She quickly tied her hair back in its queue, tying it tightly this time. She certainly didn't want a bunch of drunken sailors to see her as a woman. Billy, noticing her arming herself, looked around for a weapon for himself and found the only kitchen knife and clutched it tightly in his hand. Together they set off for the lookout point, with Juno trotting close to their heels. Blythe had given the hound the signal for silence, and knew that the dog would not make a noise. As their feet trod over the many thyme plants along the path the strong heady aroma hit the air, already heating up from the morning's sun. Overhead the sky was a brilliant blue,

They soon reached the point where the beach could be seen and Blythe absentmindedly noted that the sea was like a mill pond—there had been no breeze for a few days now. Ambrose had moved along further where there was cover, and she could see he was lying looking down at the beach through some bushes. Blythe could hear men's voices more strongly now, and realised the language being bandied around was not English. Ambrose heard a twig snap and quickly turned round, then realising it was them, gesticulated that they get down and stay down, so they both did so and wriggled forwards.

"I told you to stay in the cave" hissed Ambrose once they had reached his side.

"I know, but I felt useless there and I like to know what is going on and take my fate in my own hands!"

Ambrose frowned and whispered, "If that lot down there discover us, *your* fate will be at *their* hands, not yours, and it won't be good. Pirates—and that's what I think they are—capture fit young men and women and sell them as slaves. Anyone old or maimed they consider useless and kill, so for God's sake, keep your head down."

Blythe pulled a face and peeped carefully through the rough grasses and undergrowth and was horrified at what she saw. She was used to rough sailors and had seen many foreign tars on the docks at King's Lynn, but she had never seen such a ferocious bunch as those she could see now on the beach. They were dark skinned, with material wound around their heads that made a sort of hat, their pantaloons were puffed out just around their knees. Some wore no shoes at all, whereas others wore footwear that curled up at the toes. Their noses *were* like beaks on cruel faces and were so different to any seafaring man she had ever seen before. She certainly didn't want to imagine what they might do to a girl like herself. She shuddered.

"What do you think they're doing here?" she asked Ambrose in a whisper.

"My guess is that they probably know this island, and maybe have been becalmed for a while and decided to row ashore to get fresh water supplies and bag some meat, with the added excuse to party and get extremely drunk."

Blythe, peeping through the foliage nodded her agreement—she could indeed see a couple of barrels that were being rolled across the sands towards the small estuary made by the freshwater stream. They only had to go a short way up it to be able to fill the barrels. Patting Juno's head, she commanded her once more to lie still, be quiet and stay, and then jumped as she heard the sound of a gun being fired.

"Hopefully shooting a deer, not a man," she whispered to Ambrose.

"Let's hope so—though I wouldn't put it past them to shoot someone just for the fun of it."

After a while, the barrels were rolled back across the sands and manoeuvred into the boat, then some orders were issued and men scurried across the sands picking up driftwood to make a fire. They could see two men carrying a deer across their shoulders, so clearly they were going to cook it and have a feast.

"I hope they don't find our boat," hissed Blythe to Ambrose, "If they do, they will put two and two together and might send out a search party."

Ambrose nodded, "Let's hope not. They are further along the beach and none of them are coming our way. We can but pray we are not discovered."

Billy up to now had been quiet, but Blythe noticed he looked very worried and had paled under his tan. "Don't worry Billy, we shall be alright—they look as if they are settling down to eat and drink even more, and nobody has come our way. It doesn't look as if they have sent any scouts out."

Billy nodded. "They look a right scary bluddy lot, don't they miss? I wouldn't want to be catched by them!"

Ambrose softly said, "Stop talking you two. It only needs someone with sharp ears to hear us, even though they are making enough noise to waken the dead. Now you have seen what a brutal lot we have invading our beach, I want you both to go back to the cave and see if you can hide the entrance. Pull down creepers and cover it so that if they don't already know about the cave, they won't notice it if they do come this way. I know it's hidden quite well in any event, but I just want to be sure. I'll stay here and keep watch—it's best we are not all here together. Gather up all our belongings and take them to the back of the cave where it is dark and can't be seen—do all you can to make our area look untouched."

170

Blythe realised this was a good plan, so was quite happy to do as Ambrose commanded. However, it wasn't going to stop her from later returning to view the scene once they had finished disguising their cave. She didn't like blindly waiting for bad things to happen—and if they did, well, she wanted to face them straight on.

Billy, Juno and she ran back to the cave and once well away from the beach scene, Billy burst forth with, "Bluddy 'ell miss, them men looked like a load of demons, didn't they? I've never seen men so scary, and me having sailed the seven seas for years an' all. They'se gotta be cut-throat pirates, ain't they? Did you see them cutlasses and things? They are all armed with vicious curved blades an' guns an' everythin…"

Billy tailed off into silence and clearly his imagination was working overtime. As it happened, so was Blythe's—she could see herself being bound and thrown across a pirate's back and taken on board ship. Maybe she wouldn't be raped there and then, because probably virgins got a better price, but ultimately she would be sold into captivity to a 'fate worse than death' if she were discovered. Until she had met Ambrose, she had never bothered to think about love and what came after, but now, she was thinking that her fate could be very nasty indeed. She thought again of Nicholas Culpeper's forecast of travel, passion and danger… well, she had been through one danger with the dreadful storm, and while passion might not have occurred, she had certainly thought about it a great deal and now they were in danger again. Blythe heaved a sigh, thinking that thankfully, they hadn't *yet* been discovered and hopefully nor would they be.

Blythe and Billy dragged their belonging to the back of the cave which, as they had previously discovered, went back a fair way. They had explored with the aid of flaring sticks and been surprised at the depth, but hadn't bothered to utilise it, as there was no need. But now, everything was pulled back and stacked around corners until there was no sign that they had been living there. They used the branch trick to erase the signs of activity and pulled down the creepers to cover the entrance as suggested by Ambrose.

Their work done, Blythe picked up a couple of flagons previously filled with fresh water, and said to Billy, "Come on, let's take this water to the Captain. He will be parched by now, and I want to know what is going on."

"Oh awlright Miss. S'pose it's best to know wot yer enemy is up to."

With Juno following directly at their heels, the pair carefully made their way, checking in all directions at every footstep, to where Ambrose was hidden while he watched the beach revellers below. The pair got down on their stomachs and wriggled their way to lie beside him to see what was going on. By this time, they could see that a huge bonfire was burning, and a makeshift spit was roasting the animal that they had shot. Ferocious men lay or squatted on the sands quaffing their fill, laughing or cursing—body language indicating that some of the pirates were at loggerheads with each other at times, as drunks often are.

Billy tugged at Ambrose's shirt tails, pointing to sea. "Look, Capting, there's another boat being rowed to shore—wot dew fink's goin' on?"

Turning his head to where the lad was indicating, he replied, "I don't know Billy, but luckily my spyglass survived, so let's have a look." Drawing it out of his pocket and putting it to one eye, Ambrose focused on the small boat. "They have got some men tied up!" he said quietly, "Why would they be bringing prisoners here? If they are not worthy of ransom or selling, I would have thought they would have just thrown them overboard. How strange."

"Let me see," said Blythe, grabbing at the spyglass, then noticing Ambrose's quizzical gaze, she added, "Please."

"That's more like it," added Ambrose with a smile.

"Maybe they are crew who have mutinied, or done some kind of wrong?" queried Blythe. "Well, of course we shall never know, but I shall be interested to see what they are going to do."

"Um," said Ambrose in agreement, "And I am sure that it won't be pleasant. I want you all to stop whispering and talking unless it is necessary. No-one has a clue we are here, and that's the way we want it!"

The small boat soon landed and some of the men already on the beach met them and pulled it out of the water. There were four men roped up, presumably prisoners, who looked a sorry lot. From a distance, it looked as if they were bruised and hurt, dressed in tatters and at the end of their tether. They were roughly pushed up the beach then given some shovels and shown an area away from each other, where they were to dig.

As the men dug, they were kicked and hit by various of the pirates, who could barely stand themselves, being so inebriated. Blythe thought maybe the cruel blows were not as hard as they would have been, had the torturers been sober. Eventually, the four pits were dug, with the sand piled up around them. The prisoners were individually pushed upright into their respective holes, with the

172

pirates kicking the sand back into place around the prisoners, until just their heads were left showing, each man about six feet away from the other.

With much jeering and whistling, the buried heads were kicked by their tormenters, who took great glee making sure sand flew into the prisoners' eyes. Blythe held her hands to her face in horror—she could see blood flowing down the men's faces, and already clouds of flies were thickening the air around them, attracted by the blood. She turned to Ambrose, saying, "How sickening. Those poor men. There's nothing we can do to help them at the moment, is there. Maybe those drunken sots will all fall down and lose consciousness, and then we could aid them, but they would probably kill us too if we showed our faces."

The drunks began to return to their places around the feast, until one of them drew his cutlass from out of his waist sash, and took a running leap back towards the nearest head. Blythe didn't know what he was going to do, but with the sun shining on his blade, the cutlass swished down towards the head and cut it off at its neck in one blow. Blythe stifled a shriek and felt bile rise in her mouth.

"Bluddy Hell!" exclaimed Billy quietly, utterly fascinated.

The man crowed with laughter, and kicked the bloody head towards his ship mates and soon a game of 'kick the head' was in progress, though not a lot of prowess was shown, legs unsteady with drink and delayed reactions made a short sport of it. One man leaned over with his hands on his knees and brought up his meal onto the golden sand. Then he collapsed into unconsciousness on top of the severed and bloodied head.

"They are barbarians" whispered Blythe, appalled.

Ambrose agreed, knowing that they were in the most vulnerable of positions. "All we can do is to remain undiscovered until they have gone and in the meantime, keep an eye on them in case any come our way. We must behave with the utmost caution." Both Blythe and Billy nodded their heads in stunned agreement.

Over the course of the day, the pirates ate and drank and ran riot until most of them were unconscious. Just as Blythe was about to leave her post and return to the cave for something to eat, she noticed one of the men unsteadily slipping away from the group, with a box under his arm and a shovel in his hand. He was coming their way, but not directly towards the cave, so she didn't think he would discover them. She thought she had better warn the others, who had gone back to eat and quench their thirst, but then decided to track the man to see what he was up to. Using all her stealth she followed the man through the trees, hiding behind the large ones in case he looked up and saw her, though he seemed to be concentrating on keeping upright with that intent look that drunks have when on a mission. He stopped before the largest pine tree and began to dig. Once the hole was large enough, he popped in his box and covered it loosely with earth. He was too inebriated to make a good job of it, but seeming to be satisfied, he lurched off back to the others on the shore.

Once the man had gone, Blythe ran over to the tree and scrabbled at the loose earth to retrieve the box, pushed the earth back into position, and ran back to the cave. Ambrose and Billy were finishing off some cold meat when she returned, and looked up when she rushed in. "Look what I have found!"

Blythe showed off the box and rattled it. "I followed one of the pirates and watched him bury it under the large pine. I wonder what is in it?"

Ambrose scowled at her. "What on earth were you thinking of? What if he had seen you? What if he returns to check on the box? You have behaved irresponsibly Blythe."

"Yes, I know, but I couldn't help myself. I actually felt I should do it—one of those feelings I get. I am safe, he was too inebriated to notice me, and I doubt he will return. While I was returning, I thought of a plan to escape. It's rather mad, but it might work. Apart from the man I followed, they are all dead to the world and asleep on the beach. He probably is by now. What about we take one of their rowing boats, which already have the barrels of fresh water, take the bungs out of their other boat and also ours, in case they find it, quickly load up our supply of foods and row back to their ship? I have been watching and saw no signs of life on it. As there is some breeze blowing up now, we could surely rig a few of the sails and get it moving?"

Ambrose thought for a moment and pursed his lips. "I suppose we could give it a go—once we get rowing and away from shore we would be alright. He had been watching Billy trying to get the box open." "Knock the lock off with a stone, Billy, that should do the trick."

Blythe grinned and said, "Oh, what an excitement—I can't wait to get going! I'll pack my bag and sort out what we need. We have to be quick before those men wake, and I would like to check on those poor buried souls in case they are still alive."

Billy gave a shout as the lock burst and the top of the box flew open, revealing a mass of twinkling jewels! "Gor bluddy blimey!" cried Billy in excitement, "If these are real, we 'ave a small fortune 'ere."

Ambrose and Blythe leaned over to have a look and Blythe let the stones fall between her fingers. "Well, they certainly look real, don't they Ambrose?" "I wonder if we could keep them? They must be worth a fortune. No wonder that pirate buried them—he didn't want to share them with the other men. We must hurry. When the pirates find out their skiff has gone and the other scuppered, there will be trouble!"

"I think all the more reason we should get a move on. Quickly, let's get cracking. We must move along the coastline in the bushes, to check no-one is awake, and then head down to the boats. Billy, sneak down to our skiff and take out the bung." Billy raced down to attend to that, and when he returned, Ambrose and Blythe had packaged up what they thought they needed, and left the rest at the back of the cave.

Once they reached the group of men, they could see they were all out for the count, so Billy took their belongings down to the boat, then took the bung out of the second one, while Ambrose and Blythe carefully made their way over to the poor men up to their necks in the sand. It was clear the first three were dead, but Blythe detected a small pulse in the fourth man's neck and began to silently paw at the sand around him. She beckoned over to Juno, who soon understood what she had to do, and they both dug away until they had uncovered the man's arms. Ambrose tried to lift him out, and had a job as the sand had by now packed around him quite heavily, but at last, he was drawn out. Ambrose indicated to Blythe to pick up his feet, while he got hold of the wretched man under his arms and they hurried with him to the boat, which Billy had by this time pulled into the water.

Billy took up one of the oars, Juno jumped in, Ambrose and Blythe pulled the man in and laid him in the bottom of the boat, then Blythe, noting the pallor on Ambrose's face, realised that his rib was hurting him, so took up the other oar. She and Billy began to row, the breeze helpfully blowing them in the right direction. Ambrose grimaced at the fact that Blythe was rowing, but could see she was totally competent, and sat back, easing his pain and feeling very unmanly.

It wasn't long before they reached the ship where they found a rope ladder left conveniently dangling over the side.

"Ow are we gunner get the poor bloke and Juno up?" queried Billy.

"There is bound to be a sling up on board we can use, or a net" answered Ambrose. "Go and have a look Billy and see what you can find."

Billy shinned up the side of the vessel, while Blythe looked at Ambrose. "Are you going to manage it?" she asked. "You have lost all your colour, and clearly you're in pain from that unhealed rib."

"I shall be fine—I feel such a weak fool, letting a woman row instead of me. I shall make it up to you soon!" replied Ambrose, who was determined to show himself a better man as soon as possible.

Billy's face appeared over the side with a cheery, "Ere you are. Not a soul on board wot I can see. We're bluddy lucky in't we?" He slung over a hoist and once it was in the boat, Blythe instructed her hound to climb into it and fastened it around her neck so that she couldn't struggle and jump out. "Stay." She commanded, then shouted to Billy, "Hoist her up Billy."

"Cor, she's bluddy heavy, I don't know if I can do it on me own" panted Billy. Just as Blythe was about to jump onto the rope ladder to go up and help Billy, the dog's hoist swung out of the boat and began to move upwards and Billy managed to heave her on board. Once she was free, Juno shook herself thoroughly and began to sniff around her new surroundings. Billy threw down the hoist again and Ambrose and Blythe pulled the unconscious man into a sitting position within the materials of the hoist and tightened it up. Before Billy began to pull, Blythe stood up in the boat and grabbed hold of the ladder. The swell of the sea made it difficult to launch herself on to it, but once she had managed, she began her climb up, holding onto the man with one hand as Billy pulled him up. Blythe climbed on board and helped Billy get the man out of the canvas and laid him gently on the deck. The hoist was sent down again for the water barrels and their own belongings, all of which Ambrose dealt with. Once the skiff was empty, Ambrose attached it to the side of the ship, and then pulled himself up the ladder and on to the deck. Blythe, perceptive enough to realise that while he was in pain, Ambrose did not want to shirk any duties, so she asked him to help her to carry the man out of the hot sunshine and into the shade.

Ambrose, once on board ship again, got into his stride, despite the pains he still suffered in his chest. "We have to draw up the anchor, unfurl some of the sails, let the wind fill them and steer off. Blythe and Billy, you must both help—leave the man for the moment—we don't want those Corsairs to wake up and swim to us before we get her into action. It looks like a fine ship under the filth—I wonder who they plundered it from?"

Billy and Blythe leapt into action and began to unfurl the main sail, no mean feat for just a young boy and a woman—they both scrambled into the rigging until the sails were unfurled, and the wind billowing life into them. Blythe laughed with exhilaration. "We are so lucky the wind has blown up at last and we can sail away from our island!" Billy grinned back, pulling tight the last of the ropes that needed securing. "We've done the work of at least ten men, Miss—I reckon we've done bluddy good!"

Ambrose, now at the wheel, laughed with relief. "You have both earned an upgrade from ships' boys. I'll think on that when we have sailed far enough away and dropped anchor for the night!"

"Those bluddy pirates are going to 'ave sore 'eads when they wake up, in't they?" chuckled Billy. "I wonder 'ow long it'll be before they realise their ship has gorn?"

Ambrose smiled at them from the steerage, and Blythe said, "Let's look around first, Billy. We must make sure that there is no-one on board. We can look in the hold later to see what cargo they have. It's riding quite low, so the hold must be full."

After a quick look around, it was obvious no crew had been left on the ship, so they were safe in that respect. The light by now was beginning to fade, so Blythe asked Billy to go and find some lanterns before it got dark. Then she went back to the dark-skinned man whom they had saved. She hadn't taken a good look at him yet, but his face looked bruised and bloody. Ambrose had cut him free of his rope bindings when they pulled him out of the sand. All he wore was loose material tied around his waist and up through his legs and tucked in at the waist fabric forming baggy trousers. His hair was long and black with speckles of grey, and his beard hung down to his chest. Blythe carefully moved his head, and began to use some of the fresh water from the barrel to carefully wash the blood and sand away from his face. She was surprised to note that despite all the kicking, his face wasn't badly lacerated. He had been furthest away from the other prisoners, so perhaps hadn't been kicked so often, and maybe the pirates had been too drunk to use much strength. She placed her hands gently across the man's face and head and was pleased to feel the familiar surge of heat that happened when healing was taking place.

She turned away for a moment to wring out the rag she had been using, but when she turned back was surprised to see dark brown eyes watching her.

She broke into a smile, and said, "Oh, you are awake! I am so pleased. Are you hurting very much? Oh, you won't understand me, will you?" She picked up a tankard and dipped it in the water and proffered it to the man with a smile and questioning look on her face. The man smiled back and nodded. With her arm propping up his head, Blythe tipped the mug towards his mouth, from which he gulped thankfully. She gently wiped his mouth and laid him back down carefully. She hoped that he wouldn't slit their throats when they were asleep. Just because he had been the pirates' prisoner didn't mean that he would take kindly to them—they were Christians after all, in Infidel waters

Blythe smiled at the man gently, and said, "I'm just going to get some food for you and a hot drink, once I have found somewhere to heat up water. I have some herbs to aid your recovery, and soon you will be feeling much better. I'll be back shortly." As she rose to her feet, she knew the man would not understand her, but hopefully from her actions and tone of voice, he would realise that they meant him no harm. She felt tired now. As she wandered off to find the galley, she noted that the sun was sinking into the sea, lighting up the clouds with reds, yellows and orange and that some large fish were leaping out of the water and back in again with such grace. She smiled to herself and went below to see if she could find what she needed. It wasn't long before she found the galley—a dirty hole to be sure, but with enough kindling to start a fire and a grimy cauldron hung over it on chains.

Blythe jumped when she saw something move in the gloom and realised it was some rats. There was no way she was going to use anything in this place until she had cleaned it up—she didn't want to think that they had all escaped so much, only to die from the filth on the ship. No, they would drink the fresh water, and eat the cooked meat they had brought with them from the island. Tomorrow, when she was rested, she would think about getting the galley into order. She wended her way back to her patient, and pulled a face at him. "I'm sorry. The galley is filthy and I don't want to cook anything in there until I have cleaned up. I'll bring you some meat that we cooked on the island that will break your fast and leave you fresh water to quaff your fill when you need it." The man smiled weakly at her, as if he understood. Blythe was pleased that he was recovering from his ordeal—tomorrow she could sort out things on board that were more to her liking.

Darkness was coming down quickly now. She heard Ambrose yell out to Billy to drop the anchor and place the lanterns in position to warn of their position should any ships sail by in the night. They decided they would sleep on deck—it was warm enough—and they would be able to get more organised with the dawning of a new day.

Ambrose was pleased to be on board once more. His ribs were hurting, as was his head, for although he was much improved he was not yet himself. He lay down and gazed at the stars, automatically gauging their latitude and longitude as he did so. He didn't think they were so very far from their designated port of call. Tomorrow was another day, and it would be a good one. Billy lay down near to Blythe and Juno, who was completely unfazed at being back on board a ship again, and they all fell into a deep and healing sleep.

Chapter Ten
King's Lynn

Resisting wildly, Arabella, her hair tumbled out of its neat styling, her gown torn from her back, was pushed by Hopkin's men down the rank and slippery steps into the damp dungeon and pushed over to the torture table. Her housekeeper and maid were similarly taken, screaming their innocence and attempting to scratch and bite their jailers, into separate chambers and tied down to await their fate.

Upstairs, Matthew curbed his impatience. He knew that leaving his victims alone for a while to wonder what was to happen, gave them that extra edge of fear when he eventually appeared, whip in hand and knife evident in its sheath. Setting his high crowned hat more firmly on his head and checking on the small ruff at his neck, he eventually descended the steps, careful not to slip, and pulled back the bolts to the door of the first chamber, into which the Brown woman had been taken. How he wished it were the wench, Blythe. My God—how he had fantasised about torturing her and squeezing out her confessions.

His reveries were shattered by shrill screeches from the woman Arabella tied up on the table. "You bastard! Untie me at once and release me! I should not be here!" He glared at Arabella and struck her a blow across her mouth. That shut her up, and he watched as a dribble of blood trickled down her chin and onto her shoulder. Remembering that he must have a witness for any confessions, he reopened the door and bellowed up the steps for his assistant, Mary, who scampered down as fast as she could, apologising for her tardiness. She was pleased that she was part of ridding the country of wicked women, happy that she was doing it for God. She prided herself that she was able to present a bland face with so much inner arousal and excitement. She took her place at the side of the room, hands clasped in front of her skirt and remained quiet, as Matthew liked. She noticed the blood on the woman's face and wished she had been present for the start of the interrogation.

Hopkins drew his knife out of its sheath and cut open the first lace of Arabella's bodice. Not taking his gaze from her frightened eyes, he handed the knife to Mary and said, "Keep cutting those laces until her bodice falls. She has a mole in the centre of her breasts that needs to be pricked." Arabella struggled in vain while Mary scurried to her side, taking the knife from Matthew and doing as he asked. She did it slowly, relishing every cut, exposing more and more white skin until the bodice fell away, releasing the woman's breasts and exposing the mole. The very mole that she had assured Matthew at the ball was only a patch.

Matthew gently caressed the mole with a fingertip, and noted she had a lust upon her face. My God! No wonder he must get her hanged. No good woman should be sexually aroused when being interrogated in God's cause! He gestured to Mary for his knife. As she handed it over to him, he felt her hands quiver, and felt pleased he had such a diligent and religious woman at his side.

He led the blade across Arabella's chest and releasing the secret mechanism, thrust the blade deep into the mole. Not a sign of blood. "You see, Mistress, your mole does not bleed, which is proof in our eyes that you are indeed a witch."

"No, I am not!" screamed Arabella, "it is Blythe, my stepdaughter who should be here in my place. Instead of falsely accusing me, you should be seeking her instead. Let me loose, I beg you!"

Composing himself, Matthew ordered Mary to tighten Arabella's bonds so she couldn't get away, and the pair left the cell, bolted the door and left Arabella lying in the darkness. She thought of the mild-mannered Peter and wondered if he were dead yet. Pox on the man. Pox on all men—though that Hopkins pervert was a different thing altogether. She lay, bound and aching, awaiting her fate, listening to the scratching and gnawing of rodents in the stinking straw.

Matthew preceded Mary into the other two cells, eventually gaining confessions from the two women. Conferring with Mary, he said to her, "We know that Arabella woman is a witch, despite her not confessing. To save time, we will say that she did confess to witchcraft and many other sins, which we will concoct before her trial." Mary nodded her agreement—it was the way things were done and ultimately saved time.

Chapter Eleven

Blythe woke to the aroma of herbs. She opened her eyes to see wafts of steamy heat coming from a silver jug that had been placed on the deck beside her.

She quickly sat up and noticed her 'patient' squatting at her side, dressed in resplendent clothing: a silk turban rolled around his head with his hair tucked up inside it, exquisite billowing pantaloons down to his ankles, his feet encased in slippers with turned up toes, and an embroidered waistcoat buttoned across his chest. Over this clothing he wore a loose silk garment of blended colours made from the most wonderful material. His eyes twinkled amongst the various bruising, and he had a gentle smile on his face. His beard was now neatly clipped and combed and smelt of aromatic oils. "Good morning," he said politely, though with a heavy foreign accent.

"Oh, you speak English? And you have prepared some mint tea? And you are dressed in splendid clothing? How can this be?" Blythe was astonished at the transformation of the man, and the fact that he spoke some English. She poured the hot tea into a small brass handle-less cup with a glass container and inhaled the glorious aroma before sipping the liquid.

Their voices had awoken Ambrose and Billy, whose faces showed astonishment as they noticed the transformation of the wounded prisoner.

The man rose to his feet and bowed to them all. "I have to thank you for saving my life. I am forever indebted to you. My name is Koprulu Mehmed Pasha and I have recovered my clothing that was taken from me. I am the Grand Vizier to the Sultan Murad IV of Constantinople, charged with a mission for him across the seas, but the pirates plundered and sank our ship. I was thrown into the hold here together with my officials—those who were buried at the same time as myself on the beach. Some of the crew from our original ship were also bound and thrown in the hold. They would have been sold by the pirates as slaves. I have now released them, and they are now willing to act as your crew."

"No, do not be alarmed, no harm will come to you from any of us. This is now your ship. You are now in a position where you can return to your own country." The Vizier made a short bow to Blythe and Ambrose, then clapped his hands, and a bunch of grinning dark-skinned men ran onto the deck, immediately falling to their knees in front of Ambrose, their hands outstretched in front of them in supplication. "You see," said the Vizier, "they are yours to command. These men have already cleaned out the galley and are ready to get on with further work. I have told them that you will be a fair master, as will be your young healer here. We are all indebted to you." He eyed Blythe up and down, saying, "Madam, I do not know why you dress as a boy, but before we get into port, I advise that you either make your disguise more believable, or dress properly as a woman."

Blythe blushed and pulled her shirt away from her body and tried a manly cough. "But, sir, how have you become so quickly well again? You looked close to death last night."

"I am a Yogi, madam, as well as Grand Vizier. When I was cast into the sands, I immediately put myself into a trance that slowed my breathing and metabolism. This kept me alive while the other men unfortunately died. Apart from some discolouration and scratches on my face, I feel perfectly fine this morning. However, your gentle ministrations brought me back from my trance state. I could feel that you have healing hands, and I suspect a connection with other worlds. It is in your eyes. You see into the future in dreams and have 'the knowing'?"

Blythe blushed and dipped her head in acknowledgement. "Yes, at times, sir."

The Grand Vizier continued, "Quite. As I thought. I will speak to you about this later, but in the meantime, I will translate any commands from the Captain to the men, as well as any duties that you would like attended to, madam. We shall be at your disposal. As to that lad, he has the makings of a fine man, is he your brother?"

Billy grinned at this question, and Blythe replied, "No, he was the ship's boy on my father's ship, The *Evening Star.*, He quickly became my very dear friend and actually saved my life, as well as the Captain's when a sudden storm swept us over board. We don't know what became of our ship. The Captain's name is Ambrose Bonnesby, and mine is Blythe Brown. And, by the way, just Brown, when I am dressed as a lad—but mine, too, is a long story." The Grand Vizier nodded.

Ambrose by now was on his feet, if gingerly, though a good night's sleep had restored his strength and he was ready to begin the day and sail for Constantinople. He gave the Grand Vizier a bow, and asked the gentleman to cross the deck with him, so that he could give the translated orders to the men for the morning. Apart from continuing their journey, he wanted the decks swabbed, everything cleaned up and order made below decks. That they had already made a start in the galley was a pleasant surprise.

The two men walked away, heads together, while Blythe asked Billy to come with her to see what their new crew had achieved. She guessed they must all be very hungry, having been held prisoners in the hold, so asking Billy to bring down their own supplies of food to the galley, she made her way down the ladder and was completely surprised by the amount of work that had been done in the cooking area. Everything was gleaming and clean, not a sign of rats, and even the fire had been started, ready for the pans. She looked in various containers and found some rice and other food she had not seen before, and noted some spices too. There was plenty of fruit—again, nothing she was used to, but which made her mouth water. She was just considering what she could prepare, when a large man dressed in outlandish clothing entered with a big smile. He wore large hooped earrings in his lobes and a turban with peacock feathers displayed in its folds of material. Blythe could not help but utter an "Oh" of alarm, but quickly realised by his smile he was not dangerous.

"Me do cook." He grinned, taking hold of a large knife. Blythe pointed to some of the meat they had brought with them from the island. "You can use that," she uttered with an uncertain smile.

"Good, very good. You, out now!" The man made shooing noises and fluttered his big podgy hands at her, indicating her to leave the galley, so she backed up, knocking into Billy, who had his mouth open.

"Bluddy hell, Miss, I fort 'e was gunna knife you for a minnit, but he looks like he knows what to do in the kitchin' department. We can go and explore now, can't we?"

Once out of the door, Blythe grinned at Billy and said, "Let's go and see the Captain's cabin. I wonder if there are any treasures in there!" They raced along the narrow passage and up the ladder and towards the area where the Captain's cabin was traditionally positioned.

"Pooh, wotta pong!" cried Billy when they wrenched open the door. Blythe wrinkled her nose in disgust saying, "We'll get those men to muck out this place and give it a good scouring. It smells like a midden!" Billy was pulling open drawers to see what was in them. Charts and other papers, found in any Captain's room, were in total disarray, but when Blythe opened a closet door, she exclaimed in delight. "Look at this Billy, he might have lived like a pig, but look at these clothes! He must have plundered them from other ships!" Billy opened another locker door and said, "He must of bin saving these for you, Miss!" Blythe wandered over and was amazed to see some beautiful gowns hanging untidily on hooks. "They look as if they would fit me!" she said in delight. Much as she enjoyed wearing her brother's clothing as they were so comfortable, now that Ambrose knew she was a woman, she would like to present herself to him as one.

Billy had tracked down that the worst of the smell came from behind a screen, which revealed a built-in ornate commode, the lid of which was left up with its vile contents slopping around near to the top. Pulling a face of disgust, Billy gingerly pulled the lid down and said to Blythe, "Once this lot has been cleaned out, it'll smell a bit sweeter in 'ere. Dirty bastward!"

Blythe said, "Let's go and find the Vizier and ask him to get a couple of the men to clean this cabin for the Captain. I think I'd better ask him what he thinks about me wearing one of the beautiful gowns. I know that some sailors believe women bring bad luck to a ship, and maybe the same applies to those of a different religion. We don't want to offend them, do we?"

Billy nodded, and said, "Right-o, Miss" and preceded Blythe to find the Grand Vizier, who was with Ambrose, pouring over some charts, both talking like old friends.

"Excuse me," interrupted Blythe. "When it is convenient, perhaps I could have a private word with the Grand Vizier, please sir?"

Ambrose nodded his head and smiled, gesturing with his hand "Please do," so Blythe drew the Vizier away to the ship's rail and begged him the question.

"First of all, sir, I wondered if you would ask some of the men to clean out the Captain's cabin. It's in a filthy mess and not fit for anyone." The Grand Vizier nodded and said, "Of course." Realising Blythe had more to ask, he leaned towards her with his eyebrows raised questioningly. Blythe continued, "I've found some beautiful gowns in the Captain's cabin, and would love to surprise the Captain by donning one of them. However, I was wondering if it would be prudent to do so? I have heard that women on board are sometimes deemed to bring disaster to the ship. Would the men be worried if I came on the deck with all the frills and furbelows that I have found in the cabin?"

The Vizier frowned. "I'm glad you asked young lady. I think maybe it best for the moment that you continue your disguise as a lad because in our country, women are kept locked away from the eyes of men other than those of their families. If they are accompanied from the home, they are covered from head to toe. The men might be shocked to see you 'uncovered'. But, if you want to surprise your man, why don't you dress in one of the gowns this evening in the Captain's cabin? You could have your food served there—Billy could be your attendant—and you could share your meal together. Once you have finished, return on deck in your lad's clothing and nobody else is the wiser."

"Yes, I think I would like to do that," said Blythe with a blush—"I haven't been a woman for a long time now!"

The Vizier bowed his head, and then clapped his hands to the men as he walked towards them. He uttered some commands in what sounded like gibberish to Billy and Blythe.

"Cor," said Billy, "'e don't 'arf jibber-jabber, don' 'e!" Blythe nodded as she stifled a giggle.

Just then, the banging of a gong could be heard, and the crew downed tools and rushed to get their breakfast, laughing and joking amongst themselves in their strange language. A tray of fruit and bread was brought out for Ambrose, Blythe and Billy, and they tucked in with relish. Already the decks were scrubbed and even some of the brass work had lost its tarnish and was gleaming. There was still a lot of work for the ship to be as ship-shape as Ambrose required, but work was well on its way.

Once everyone had broken their fast, Ambrose stood up and addressed the crew, giving them his thanks for their good work, which was translated by Koprulu, after which the crew grinned back at Ambrose. They were so thankful that the ship's captain was not going to flog them or throw them to the sharks, that already they would do anything for him and his friends, even if they were peculiar white-faced foreigners from afar. The crew returned to their work in a happy mood, while the ship cut through the gentle waves towards their destination.

After a while, the Vizier returned to tell Blythe that the cabin was ready for her inspection, and went with her to make sure it was to her liking. Blythe could not believe the transformation. The smell had gone, the woodwork was shining, the recessed bed had been stripped of the filthy bedding and remade with clean linen that had been discovered amongst the plunder, and an incense burner was releasing sweet aromatic smoke into the air. Sweet smelling beeswax candles had been placed around the room ready to light when darkness fell.

Clapping her hands and smiling in delight at the Vizier, Blythe said, "Oh, thank you so much! It looks wonderful, doesn't it? The Captain will sleep well tonight. Which reminds me—Billy and I must find cabins for us all before the night falls. But, first, will you ask the cook to arrange a meal for the captain and myself tonight at seven bells, at which Billy will serve?"

The Grand Vizier bowed and said, "Of course. And while we are on this voyage, Madam, you may call me Koprulu."

"Thank you, Koprulu, and you may call me Blythe when I am dressed in women's clothes, but when in male attire, please call me Brown!"

The Vizier bowed once more and left the cabin. Blythe flitted around, checking on everything, pleased with how sumptuous the cabin now looked, and then went to the cupboard to view the gowns. They were very splendid. Up until this time in her life, she had never been interested in 'being a woman', but she wanted very much to be feminine now for Ambrose, and to look her very best. She pulled out each gown, deciding finally on a rose-pink gown embroidered with silver thread and decorated with tiny seed pearls. The sleeves were made from a wonderful silk of shot colours in muted greys and pale mauves. As she inspected it, she thought of her dear Papa, and how he would love to see rich material such as this. She even found some slippers to match that actually fitted, and also a string of pearls that would complete the ensemble. She laid everything out on the bed, ready to don later, and left the cabin, thinking, with a little smile, that there could be something to piracy after all, if she could pick and choose from such abundance!

Blythe looked for Billy, who was already trying to figure out the language of one of the men, pointing to various things and saying the word in English, until the grinning man spoke it in his own language, which Billy then copied. He smiled when he saw Blythe approaching him, and said, "Oh bluddy hell, Miss, don't stop me now. I'm jist gettin' the 'ang of the lingo!"

Blythe laughed, and said, "Come with me Billy, you can catch up with that man and his language later. I want to explore some more and find cabins for us, or if there aren't any, a quiet corner where we won't be disturbed."

"Oh awlright, Miss. I 'aven't seen anything up 'ere, so we'd better go below decks. I'll go first darn the ladder and ketch you if you fall." Billy grinned at Blythe and nimbly slid down. Blythe followed somewhat more sedately, and they walked along the corridor, opening various doors to see what lay within, turning their noses up at the rank odours everywhere. Eventually they came across two small cabins—untidy but not so smelly as the Captain's cabin had been, and each containing a reasonably comfortable bunk bed. Each cabin had a porthole that could be opened to let in air. "You can 'ave the biggest, Miss, said Billy kindly."

Blythe smiled and said, "Thank you my friend. You have the cabin next door to me." It was smaller, but Billy was thrilled with it. He had never had a cabin to himself, curling up in corners wherever there was a space. The third cabin they discovered was bigger than theirs and they felt it was more fitting for the Grand Vizier.

Sniffing at the musty odours, Blythe said, "Let's go and ask Koprulu to get the men to clean these cabins out, Billy and let's also look to see if we can find some clean bedding somewhere. I doubt the men bothered to keep the bedding washed and I don't fancy sleeping in it. Maybe we can find some decent linen in the 'plunder lockers'."

"Awlright, Miss. Let's go an' look." They made a thorough search and did find what they wanted, though nothing as fine as the bed linen in the Captain's Cabin. They left the bedding hanging over some chairs in the respective quarters so the bunks could be made up when the rooms were cleaned, and went to find the Grand Vizier to ask him to relate their requests to some of the crew.

As Billy and Blythe went about exploration of the ship, they bumped into Ambrose, and told him not to go near to the Captain's cabin, because they were getting it ready for him, and it was to be a surprise, but to expect a meal there in the evening. Ambrose smiled, his eyes glowing when he looked at Blythe. He wanted so badly to have time to sit and speak with her, but he had a ship to sail to Constantinople, so had little time to talk with her. He would do that later when he had got through his duties. He longed to hold her in his arms, but didn't want to compromise her, after all, she was in his care. Not that he had done much looking after, more the other way around.

Once the cabins had been prepared, Blythe invited the Grand Vizier to view his. As she showed him into the cabin, Blythe smiled and said, "I am sure this is not nearly grand enough for you, Sir, but it is the best we can do for you under the circumstances. At least, it is clean now and while basic, at least you will be able to sleep well. Did you lose a lot of your belongings when you were wrest from your other ship?"

"Yes, I had many trunks containing my belongings. Many books, many clothes, my jewellery, and even worse, I had a box of jewels from the Sultan, intended as a gift I was carrying in my position as Envoy. Nothing is left."

"Oh!" said Blythe with a wide smile. "I think we can help you with one of your lost items. When we were shipwrecked on that island, I followed one of the men who had a box under his arm. He buried it under a tree, and after he left, I dug it up and we opened it up in our cave. The jewels are beautiful. They must be yours—I have them in my room. I'll go and get them."

Blythe ran back into her own cabin, picked up her duff bag, and returned with it to the Grand Vizier. She pulled the box out and showed it to him.

"Yes, that is the box." He said and nodded his head for Blythe to open it. As she lifted the lid, the jewels twinkled and she pushed the box towards the Grand Vizier, who then pushed them back towards her with a smile on his face.

"Yes, they are the jewels, and you are very honest to give them back to me. You didn't have to tell me you had them, for I would never have known. Take them child, they are yours. They are valuable and if you sell them, the money gained will help you return home, and you will also be able to purchase good cargos to fill the hold and make yourselves a fortune!" Blythe's eyes opened wide at the thought of what the jewels could do to enhance the lives of herself, Ambrose and Billy too. He continued, "To the Sultan, their value is nothing—he has plenty more—and to me they were lost in any event—so therefore the finder is the keeper."

Blythe was not so sure about that, but the Vizier insisted she keep them as a gift, so she begrudgingly agreed, thanking him profusely, although she intended to discuss this with Ambrose later on. It was one thing keeping the jewels after finding them, but she wasn't so sure when she now knew that they belonged to the Sultan.

***

Evening time had arrived, and Blythe scurried off to the Captain's cabin where she quickly took off her boy's clothing. Billy had previously filled up the basin with washing water, so she took her time cleansing herself. There were some sweet-smelling oils on the table, which she worked thoroughly into her skin, then wriggled her way into the pretty shift, liking the feel of the soft material next to her skin. Next were the padded shapes to tie around her hips, after which there were some lacy under-skirts to climb into and then finally the beautiful gown to go over the top. Blythe had to call for Billy, who had been waiting outside, to assist her in tying the pretty sleeves into place, which she couldn't manage on her own.

Billy's fingers were rather clumsy as he tried to tie the fine material into bows. "Cor," he complained, "There's one thing tying ships knots, but this is a right tricky business!" They both giggled at his ineptness as a lady's maid.

Last of all, Blythe wriggled into the bodice that had copious lacing at the back, and Billy had to pull and tug until the bodice was laced tightly, giving Blythe an incredible shape.

"Bluddy 'ell, Miss, you look right beautiful!" "The Capting won't recognise you. Wot you gunna do abart yer 'air?" He passed a brush over to her and some pins and hair combs.

"I don't know Billy—I've never bothered with my hair, and it isn't really long enough to fashion properly. I think I will just have to brush and leave it hanging."

When she was finished, Billy looked at her from head to toe and whistled. "If 'e dun't ask yer to marry 'im, then my father is a Dutchman—which I don't think 'e is, 'cos I never 'ad no clogs on me feet!"

Blythe laughed. "Oh, I don't know about that, but I have to say it does feel very good to be a woman for a change! Oh, Billy, perhaps you can clasp these pearls around my neck. They should finish off the ensemble very nicely."

Once Blythe was ready, Billy lit the candles, shut the shutters on the large window, tweaked at the tablecloth on the desk that doubled as a table, rearranged the wine glasses, fiddled with the cutlery, and when all was to his satisfaction, he said, "Right then, Miss. I shall go and tell the Capting that dinner is served, then I shall give you five minutes for 'im to settle at the table after admiring you, an' then bring in your food."

"Alright then Billy," said Blythe, smoothing down the front of her bodice and wondering if she should have quite so much of her bosom on display. She was feeling nervous now, and queried if she should have been so bold with her plans for the evening. She didn't have long to wait, for there was a tap on the door, and Ambrose walked in.

The sun was setting as Ambrose set foot into what was now his cabin, though, coming from sunlight into the gloom of the candlelit cabin, his eyes didn't adjust at first, so he only saw the outline of what looked like a most beautiful woman. His shocked wits were a bit slow, but he soon realised, of course, that it was Blythe, standing there in front of him, dressed in a most exquisite gown and looking the epitome of loveliness.

Stepping forward with a smile of awe on his face, he clasped Blythe's hands, saying softly, "You take my breath away!" Then he leaned forward and kissed her gently on the lips. Blythe sighed and leaned into Ambrose, who, letting go of her hands, swept his arms around her body and the gentle kiss became more urgent. Blythe, who had never been kissed before, felt her body become on fire. So much emotion, so much feeling surging, so much passion rising. Her kisses became as urgent as Ambrose's. Her mouth parted under his, and his tongue entered and thrust at hers, and she found herself responding instinctively. Ambrose was now holding her tightly in a lover's embrace and she just could not help thrusting her hips forward, her back arched, to feel his quick response—she had never felt like this before, and the excitement was astonishing.

There was a knock on the door and a loud cough, as Billy backed into the room with a tray laden with a sumptuous meal that smelt wonderful.

Ambrose and Blythe broke apart while Billy, eyes averted but with a grin on his face, laid the food on the table. "Enjoy yer meal." He said with a grin. "I'll be back with yer pudding, which looks bluddy brilliant, by the way." Directing a saucy wink at Blythe, who had composed herself and was standing by her chair that Ambrose, all courtier airs and manners about him now, pulled out for her to sit down. He just could not resist the temptation to kiss her gently just behind her ear, at the same time noticing the delightful skin aroma that was Blythe's and Blythe's alone.

At the touch of Ambrose's lips, Blythe felt tingles that travelled down her body, right to her knees and beyond. "Oooooh" she breathed.

"Oooooh, indeed," said Ambrose smiling, as he crossed to his side of the table.

They both exclaimed at the delicious spicy smells that wafted from the platters. Blythe had never seen food like this before. While Ambrose poured wine into their glasses, Blythe dished the outlandish food onto their plates, and with glowing eyes, smiled at Ambrose, who raised his glass to her. She picked up her own, and they clinked their glasses together, eyes locked, then both sipped at the delicious wine.

"Ummm," said Ambrose, with relish. "Nectar of the Gods."

Blythe smiled, feeling ridiculously shy and feminine. *"How silly of me,"* she thought. *"I have been close to Ambrose these last few days, talking with him like I would my brother, but now in this lovely gown I feel so girlishly tongue-tied."*

Ambrose had sampled meals such as this on his previous travels so was able to tell Blythe the spices that were contained in this one. "It's delicious," said Blythe, at the same time noticing that Ambrose couldn't seem to take his eyes off her lips. She found herself mesmerised by his too, and hoped he would kiss her again later.

The pair leisurely ate their way through the delicious meal, making small talk while they did so.

After they had finished and put their cutlery aside on the plates, Ambrose, looked deep into Blythe's eyes, then said earnestly, "Blythe, I have a terrible confession to make." Blythe lifted her eyebrows questioningly. "You have got under my skin from the moment you stepped onto this ship. All the time, I wanted to hold you, to kiss you, to make love to you, but felt disgusted with myself, because I believed you to be a boy. That is why I kept away from you, or was short with you when we spoke. You must have thought me utterly boorish." Blythe smiled at him. "But now I have seen you as the woman you are, I am totally in love with you. Dare I ask if I have the slightest chance that those feelings might be reciprocated?"

Blythe just nodded her head, then dipped her chin a little in shyness. Ambrose lifted her hand across the table, and kissed it, looking into her eyes as he did so.

Loud banging on the door stopped their discourse. There was a great deal of pointed coughing as Billy entered to collect the plates. As he took them out, he remarked, "Pudding'll be 'ere in a coupla ticks. Keep yer 'ands to yerselfs until I've served ya." Blythe and Ambrose both laughed and waited until Billy was back with a most delicious fruity dessert, all fluffed up and absolutely mouth-watering, which he placed in front of them.

With an exaggerated wink, Billy announced, "I won't be coming back now, so enjoy yerselfs, but keep the noise darn." He grinned and exited, making a great noisy fuss and to-do making sure the door was shut, which made Ambrose bark with laughter and Blythe to giggle.

Eventually, Blythe finished her meal and pushed back her chair to stand. "That was delicious, wasn't it—I can't believe that the cook produced such a wonderful meal out of next to nothing. We must certainly keep him on as crew, don't you think?" She had felt a little shy at first with Ambrose, because of the different circumstances. She was feeling all woman now and having felt the frisson of passion at Ambrose's gentle kissing, wanted to experience more.

Ambrose rose from the table knowing that while he was filled with passion for this wonderful woman in front of him, he should not seduce her as he wanted to, or to take things too fast. Before he could think what to do next, Blythe said, "Ambrose, I had never been kissed before, so yours was my first, and I liked it very much. Do you think you could do it again please?"

Ambrose laughed, and in a couple of paces was by her side, swooping her up into his arms, kissing her behind her ear again, which tickled and made her squeal.

Without any more to-do, he strode over to the bed and tumbled them both on to the luxurious covers, and laid his lips on hers. This time, the kiss was not gentle, but urgent, and Blythe met his passion with her own. Ambrose's tongue found its way into her mouth again and she loved the feeling, and experimented with her own, entwining and probing. Ambrose's hands then coursed over her back, which she could not stop from arching. She was groaning with desire now, passion completely unleashed, especially when she felt Ambrose's hands moving round to her breasts, bringing sensations she had never felt before. By now, she felt completely smothered with the copious materials of her gown and cried,

"Oh, undo my laces, please, Ambrose, I can't bear this dress any longer!"

He smiled at her, gazing into her eyes, brown to vivid blue, and said, "Are you sure? I should not be seducing you Blythe, but truly, I cannot help myself. Tell me now to stop, and I will, but you are so beautiful, so wonderful, I cannot cease unless you tell me!"

"Just undo my laces!" she responded urgently, "I don't want you to stop either, and I want you to do whatever you will! I want to find out what I have been missing. We might die tomorrow for all I know, and I don't want death without this first, and I want much more of it too!"

The bodice laces were soon undone and Ambrose gently released Blythe's breasts and ran a finger down one beautiful globe to the other, then teased her nipples until Blythe was wriggling in frustration. He then bent over and licked one pert nipple until it stood out, then turned his attention onto the other. Blythe wanted to feel Ambrose's skin too, so began to pull at his clothing. He ceased his ministrations of Blythe's bosom while he took off his jacket and waistcoat, while Blythe pulled at his shirt. She had seen his body before, of course, but this was very different and she wanted to see him naked as a full-blooded man, instead of a wounded unconscious one. She wanted to feel her skin on his. "Help me with my skirts, Ambrose—I want them off!"

Ambrose laughed at Blythe's impatient passion as skirts, underskirts, pantaloons, stockings, garters, shift, all went flying across the cabin, as did the rest of Ambrose's clothing too.

The flickering candles shone their mellow light on the gleaming woodwork in the cabin. The beeswax smelt delicious, and the many little flames flickered and danced enhancing the bodies of the couple entwined upon the bed. The aroma of the incense added eroticism to the atmosphere. The swell of the sea and gentle lapping against the side of the cabin sounded sensual and other worldly as Ambrose led Blythe into the gentle passions of her first lovemaking. He sensed that her desire would be far greater after this first time, but as it was, her fingernails were raking his back, and her groans and cries as she reached fulfilment were music to his ears.

"Oh, Ambrose! I never thought it would be like that! It's so wonderful!"

Ambrose kissed her gently and said, "And, it will get better. What an amazing woman you are, and I am totally in love with you!"

"And I with you, Ambrose, and I have been since I was fourteen years and you came to dine. I know you barely noticed me—but thank goodness, I think you have noticed me now!" She smiled at him, her eyes hooded with satiation and he smiled back at her with the smouldering look of love.

"Oh yes!" he growled. "And how I have wanted you. You are mine now. All of you." Brushing Blythe's hair gently away from her face with his fingers, he kissed her once more and they settled down, spooned together and were soon fast asleep, lulled by the slapping waves, the distant sound of gently rattling rigging and the satisfying aftermath of their deliciously eventful lovemaking.

***

Blythe woke to find Ambrose's arms wrapped around her. She shifted her position, and his grip tightened. She kissed the muscles of his forearm and

194

inhaled his heady, masculine aroma. She hadn't realised how wonderful a person could smell before. She turned and wrapped her legs around his body, and he groaned, and sleepily exclaimed, "Witch! That Hopkins man is right. You *are* a witch and you have completely entrapped me in your powers!"

Ambrose ran his hands down Blythe's back, sending shivers down her spine, until he reached her buttocks, which he gently slapped. Blythe liked that and wriggled her bottom for more. Ambrose turned her onto her back and began to trawl her body with his gentle hands, tweaking, tickling, probing. Blythe gasped with pleasure at every new sensation. "Goodness!" she murmured with a gurgle, "I felt so good from your ministrations last night, but you are surprising me even more now. Is there any end to your surprises?"

Nibbling her ear, Ambrose whispered, "Oh, I have so much more for you, and long may I continue to do so."

Blythe was then introduced to further initiation into the wonders of intimacy, but this time tried to stifle her cries, as she realised that if any of the crew were awake and about, they would think the Captain was bedding a fellow!

When they both had reached a shattering climax, Blythe giggled and told Ambrose her thoughts on what the crew might think was going on in the cabin.

Ambrose grinned lazily, "Oh, don't worry about it. While we think it unnatural for a man to have relations with another, in some of these Mediterranean countries, you see men openly walking hand in hand—it is quite common for some of them to be intimate."

"Don't they have wives then?" queried Blythe.

"Yes, they do, but the women folk are confined to the house, to cook and bear children. They are not considered an equal, more a chattel. Their ways are very different to ours. But, my darling, we must cease for the while. I must get out of bed and get to work. We are not so far from Constantinople, and once we reach the port, I have to decide what to do. If you want to lie a-bed, please do so, but I must leave you now."

Blythe watched Ambrose with pleasure as he slid from beneath the sheets and stood and stretched, showing all his manly glory. How she loved to see the muscles ripple in his limbs, to notice how beautiful his body was, to admire the chest hair that filtered down into a single line until it reached his manhood. She gazed with pleasure as he stepped into his clothes then combed his hair and completed his ablutions for his day ahead. He was soon attired, and came over to the bed and kissed Blythe. "Will you stay with me tonight, my beautiful woman?" he asked with a saucy raise of his eyebrows.

"Oh yes please!" she replied with a theatrical pout of allure.

As Ambrose went out of the door, he backtracked and just poking his head around the portal, grinned, and said, "Hussy!"

Blythe laughed, and then laughed again, as Juno had hurtled through the door to greet her mistress. She had spent the night with Billy, and was keen to ensure Blythe was alright. She could then hear Billy coughing pertinently outside and then knock on the door and say, "'ot drink, Miss?" He came in bearing a tray with a steaming jug and small drinking cup. Already Blythe could smell the aroma of delicious mint. "Cook said you'd like it. Mint tea, 'e said. Looks like you 'ad a good time!" Billy pointedly looked at the tumbled sheets and Blythe's clothes still scattered around the floor.

"Oh dear. Ambrose said I was a Hussy. I suppose I am. But yes, Billy, I did have a good time, not that I should really be telling you."

"Well," replied Billy, "As I'm now yer lady's maid, I'd better pick up all your cloves, and get yer clobber ready to wear, 'adn't I?" Blythe grinned and sipped at her mint tea. It really was delicious. She felt absolutely wonderful. She was a real woman now, and it didn't matter now what happened to her, she had tasted love and life was good! She noticed Billy was rooting around in one of the cupboards.

"What are you doing?" she asked.

"Just looking to see if there are some clothing a bit better than them rags you've been wearing all this time." Billy replied, pulling clothing hither and thither, then coming up triumphant with a pair of striped pants and a fine linen shirt. "'Ere yew are, these will be better for yew, and 'ide all yer curves. There's a 'broidered waistcoat too, if you want it?"

Blythe looked at the proffered garment, but decided she would prefer to keep her brother's waistcoat. Billy lay the garments over the back of the chair, and said, "Right, I'll be off then. See yew later on."

"Thank you Billy—you've got the job as my lady's maid! Close the door behind you, and I will get dressed."

Billy blew a raspberry as he left and Juno settled herself down beside her.

Rising from the bed, Blythe pulled on the new breeches, bound her breasts, then put on her shirt and the covering waistcoat but left off her boots. She liked to feel the smooth grain of the deck under her toes. As she came out of the cabin and into the sunlight, the crew nodded her a greeting, and acted as if everything was quite normal. "*Gracious,*" she thought, "*if this had happened in King's Lynn, heads would roll!*" Then she thought of that head being kicked about on the beach by the Corsairs, and a shiver went through her—not of the delight that she had enjoyed last night, but a shiver of foreboding.

Chapter Twelve
King's Lynn

The morning dawned for the hanging of the coven of witches—Arabella Brown, her daughter Dimity, Madame Extier and the housekeeper. The people of the town were astir early and keen to see the hangings. This was an unusual state of affairs, for up until now witches had not been hanged in a group.

At The Old Exorcist's House, in his chilly room, Matthew Hopkins donned freshly washed clothing, newly polished and buffed up boots, and his beaver hat brushed to a shine. He had even had a bath and trimmed his beard. He felt this was an important day for him and he was very proud of his achievements. However, he felt very tired. He had not slept well last night. His cough had been bad but when he had eventually fallen into a fitful sleep, the damned bear immediately reared its ugly head again. It had chased him through pine forests, through arid sands, its breath fetid, its paws padding ever nearer to his own pounding, leaded limbs. The sun beat down on them both and he could see Mistress Blythe hiding behind a tree with a smile on her wicked face, watching as he tried to escape. Eventually, the bear caught up with him and grabbed him fast, clasping its hairy arms tightly around him, picking him up like a piece of rag. He could feel the creature's fur on his bare arms and he screamed in terror. The bear, on his hind legs, actually turned him round to look Matthew in the eye. This time the bear's eyes were not red, nor was his breath stinking, but Matthew was too frightened to do anything but scream and kick with his legs that dangled in the air. The bear seemed to be trying to say something to him, but Matthew blocked his ears. His mind was a blur of fear and loathing. He was hot with fright and began to cough, clots of blood spewing out of his mouth, onto the bear's fur.

As he woke, Matthew still screamed, the sweat pouring from his every frightened pore. His heart pounded in his chest; he gasped for breath. What was the bear trying to say, that it was going to kill and eat him? Panting, he sat up in bed and wiped ineffectively at the blood that was dribbling down his face and congealing over his bedding.

Shaking his head, Matthew brought himself back to the present time. He was ready to step out to the Market Place. He had broken his fast, and waited for Mary Phillips and John Stearne who should join him at any moment. Soon, there was a knock at the door, and there stood Mary, poker faced on the doorstep. She looked neat and tidy, her hair tucked into her bonnet, her clothing spotless and clean. *A good woman, she,* Matthew thought, approving of her demeanour. There, too, was John Sterne, his Second in Command, neatly dressed in the usual Puritan black, a gleam in his eyes, his hat set square on his head, a good man of God, like himself. Together the three stepped out, walking through the graveyard of St Nicholas's Church, to be greeted by the parson at the Church door, who joined them as they walked through the wrought iron gates and along the narrow lane to the Market Place.

The square was already packed with onlookers, their breaths billowing in the cold, while others were walking with purpose via the many little lanes that spilled them out into the square. In the centre stood a large platform with four looming hanging posts with fresh ropes looped and knotted, swinging slightly. Ranks of seagulls sat on rooftops, where drifts of smoke lost themselves in the air from the many chimneys. An unkindness of noisy ravens, black and shining in the wintery sunshine, chattered and cawed at each other on various high posts and inn signs. There had been a frost overnight, so the cobbles gleamed with rime and ice had formed partially over the odorous Fleet as it sluggishly wended its way towards the river.

Some young boys, with cold bare feet, nipped through the throng of people, cutting purses neatly and stuffing the contents into their well-sewn pockets. Soldiers stood at every corner, some cavalry men sat on their steeds looking out for trouble, while inn keepers brought out tankards of ale, followed by their maids bringing trays piled high with pies—ever keen for business. A man with a brazier full of hot embers was cooking chestnuts that he popped into cones of paper for people who warmed their icy fingers before cracking open the nuts with their teeth. People hung out of windows, knowing they had a better view than those on the ground. Some of them waved flags or pieces of bright material. There was a tremendous hum and buzz of excitement, despite the cold weather, for at this hanging the people of Lynn believed the women about to be hanged *were* true witches, and a coven at that!

Matthew, John Stearne and Mary Phillips were led by officials to a special place cordoned off at the side of the hanging trees, where they stood importantly, nodding their heads to anyone who caught their eyes.

The square was filled to bursting, a few flakes of snow fluttered and fell, the ravens cawed loudly and the seagulls from the docks flew high overhead, buffeted by the icy wind as they screamed discordantly. Some dogs raced through jostling legs, yapping and barking, until there was a sudden hush from the crowd who had intuited that Something Was About To Happen. The atmosphere felt eerie and even the dogs stopped their noise.

A loud drum roll was heard as a young drummer boy appeared, walking in front of some marching soldiers, their bayonets fixed to their guns. Behind them walked the hangman—a huge giant of a man with greasy black hair held in place with a dirty scarf. He wore a leather jerkin over his shirt and knee length britches, from which his grubby knitted stockings furled in creases down to his buckled and scuffed shoes. The hangman climbed up to the platform and a cheer rose from the crowd. The man smirked, showing yellowed teeth, and bowed.

Once again a silence of anticipation hung in the air, until the rumble and clatter of wooden wheels on cobbles could be heard. The prisoners' tumbrel was approaching. With a collective bated breath, the crowd waited on tiptoe with their mouths agape until the tumbrel was sighted, when the silence was then broken by a roar of unkind cheers and jeers. A weary donkey dragged itself along in the shafts of the tumbrel, with soldiers marching at the side. The four humiliated women, their hands bound to the sides of the cart, stood, dirty and unkempt, their clothing torn and gaping. Arabella, despite her bosoms being partially on display, held her head high and proud with her back straight and eyes a-blazing. Dimity stood with stooped shoulders, her eyes red from weeping, tears and snot still dripping down her face, her whole body trembling with fear. Madame Extier stood erect but with a dull look in her eyes, while the housekeeper was a complete jibbering wreck, which pleased the crowd enormously.

As the donkey pulled the tumbrel into the Market Place, the soldiers at the side of the cart dropped a little way behind. They knew that soon enough missiles would be flying, and didn't want to get in the way of any of them. They were just in time, for soon old eggs and tomatoes and other objectionable items were thrown at the hapless women, who were soon covered in rotting vegetation and stinking filth. The crowd went happily berserk, shouting, jeering and mocking the witches.

Matthew stared greedily at the women as the cart neared the platform. He was responsible for this. He, and he alone. God would be proud. Mary Phillips looked up at him, acknowledging his prowess with a small nod. The donkey stopped, exhausted, while the women's bonds were cut and they were rudely pushed out of the cart and up the steps to their final destination. Arabella remained proud, though there was a mad look in her eyes, but the other three wept and wailed, which pleased the crowd, who threw further rubbish and stones at them.

The Parson, holding a Bible, stood at the side of the gibbets, and asked if the women had any last confessions to make. Three shook their heads, but Arabella shouted out in ringing tones that could be heard as far as every corner of the square, "Yes!" she cried, "I curse every one of you here today. I curse you and your families, your stock and your livelihoods, and most of all, I curse you"— she turned to blaze furious eyes at Matthew—"I curse you, Matthew Hopkins, and may your bear devour you!" Matthew felt prickles of fear course throughout his body. How on earth did she know about the bear?

Arabella faced the crowd again, "Yes, I saw his bear familiar down in the dungeons when he was torturing me. You should ask yourselves why this should be! He is a warlock, I tell you, beware!" There was a gasp of horror that spread through the crowd, while the crowd turned from the prisoners to gawp at the Witch Finder General, who felt the blood drain from his face. He managed to retain his dignity and gestured to the hangman and his aides to carry on with the hanging. This took the crowd's attention back to the witches as each noose was thrown and tightened around the necks of the woman.

Arabella managed to spit out a venomous cry before her rope was pulled tight—"Watch that Hopkins—it's he should be hanged as the warlock!" Another collective gasp came from the crowds, who simultaneously turned again to stare at Matthew, until, at a nod, the drummer boys began a drum roll, the steps were simultaneously kicked from beneath the women, the trap doors opened, and their bodies dropped, necks snapping. The crowd gasped, their attention now riveted to the hangings, cheered as the bodies began to slowly revolve. A few more rotten eggs were thrown for good measure and the ravens flew down to sit on the top of the gibbets and wait to take their pickings.

The sky got darker. Flurries of snow now swirled down in earnest. A colder wind blew throughout the square, biting through the worn and ragged clothing of the poor, while the wealthier folk drew their fur collars tighter and made their way through the crowds towards home.

Those nearest to the corpses waited for the water and excrements to drip from beneath the dead witches' skirts, but all were crossing themselves after the dreadful curses had been heaped upon everyone who had been present. People were very frightened and whispered amongst themselves with dismay. The witch's curses had taken all the fun out of the day and the square was soon emptied of spectators.

Matthew, his face devoid of colour, bar two bright red spots high on his cheeks, felt shocked to the core at the curses meted out to him, as well as the woman's last and awful denouncement. He gave the nod to the hangman to cut down the bodies, which was accomplished quickly, the bodies thumping to the ground and bundled unceremoniously into the waiting cart, that was now to deliver its messy cargo to unsanctified and unmarked graves that had been previously dug outside the town walls and where all the rubbish of the town was discarded. An ignominious end to the ambitious Arabella Brown and her coterie.

The ravens followed the cart, while the seagulls followed the ravens, their cawing and crying echoing around the chilly lanes of King's Lynn, while the snow, now coming down steadily, soon covered the town in a thick, white blanket that muffled all sounds.

**

A brisk wind filled the sails of the new ship jointly owned by Ambrose and Blythe. He, feeling almost his old self, leaned back as he set the ship to a steady course towards Constantinople. He calculated it wouldn't take very long to reach their destination. Blythe leant against the main mast watching his beautiful firm hands on the wheel. She was enjoying listening to the thud of the sails, with one leg bent up and her foot against the timbers. Her battered tricorn was thrust tight over her brow, her tied hair blowing with the warm wind, her smile bright and cheery, as she leant forward to listen to what her lover had to say.

"It won't be long before we reach our port. See, we are sailing along the Turkish coastline at the moment. We need to keep a weather eye out for war ships and pirates, as there is always something occurring in these waters, but why don't I get someone to take over here, and you and I go to my cabin and discuss certain matters? I have a lot to say to you, my girl!" Ambrose lifted his eyebrows and wiggled them in a suggestive manner, while Blythe's grin almost met her ears. In such a short time, she had gotten very used to being with Ambrose and couldn't get enough of him. Her bare feet took purchase of the deck as she scampered away, laughing over her shoulder. If any of the crew noticed, they carried on with what they were doing, other than those to whom Ambrose called out a few commands.

They reached the sanctuary of their cabin and Blythe flung herself straight onto the bed to lie sprawled across it, her arms and legs outstretched, while Ambrose walked in at a leisurely pace, shut and bolted the door, peeling off his jacket and shirt as he strode towards her. Blythe, not to be outdone, wriggled out of her own jacket and shirt, quickly unbinding her breasts, and lay back once more against the covers, her lower body still covered. Ambrose gazed at her with smoky eyes, a sensual half-smile lurking, while he kicked off his boots and pulled off his britches.

Blythe gazed in admiration at the lean, tall, handsome man with wide shoulders and rippling muscles who was looking at her with so much love and desire in his eyes as he approached her. She lowered her lashes, pouted her lips coquettishly, and wriggling her hips, pulled off her pants, then reached out her arms to the man she loved. Ambrose fell onto the bed beside her and pulled her into his arms to embrace and kiss her. Their mouths locked together in a wild kiss that became more torrid as they became feverish with their need. This was not the time for slow and gentle lovemaking—that would come later on—but now, they let their passion take them to urgent and dizzying heights punctuated with groans of bliss and cries of delight, that led to a mutual crashing crescendo.

Panting after their delicious exertions, they turned to each other and laughed joyously. Blythe couldn't believe how wonderful it was to make love to her man, and Ambrose found it difficult to understand how quickly Blythe had become such an ardent and willing participant in the game of love.

Once they had regained their breath, and lay supine and lethargic, Ambrose gently lifted some tresses of hair away from Blythe's face, damp now, from the rigours of love, then let his fingers trail gently down her neck and onto her breast.

"Blythe, I have fallen completely in love with you, and nothing would please me more than if you agreed to become my wife."

Blythe twinkled languorously back up at him, reaching up and twirling her fingers in his hair. "Of course I will agree, Ambrose, my lovely man. But only on two conditions."

"Oh, you come with conditions, do you, woman?" Ambrose licked her neck gently and trailed his tongue towards her breasts then softly placed his lips around her nipple. She gasped with new sensations. "And what might your conditions be, you saucy hussy you?" her handsome hero asked, raising himself up so that they were face to smiling face.

Blythe reached down between their bodies and boldly reached for her lover's manhood. It was his turn to groan a little. While she teased and manipulated, Blythe explained, "I don't want to be a stay-at-home wife. I want to be with you at all times, on the ship, adventuring, going to new places. And, I don't want children. I've watched my mother's health deteriorate with pregnancies and she died in front of my eyes birthing a dead baby."

Ambrose, completely besotted with this brave and fearless woman, let his mouth wend its way down her body, nipping and kissing as he went. In between such ministrations, he murmured, "I wouldn't want it any other way. You are not a woman to be confined in a house with children at your apron strings. But, my lovely lady, in future, we must be more careful. Let us hope that we have not already begun an infant. Blythe, we shall sail the seas together and you can have as many adventures as you wish!"

"Oh good," said Blythe, "I didn't expect you to agree so easily!" Arching her back she let Ambrose do to her exactly what he wanted—she knew it would be wonderful—and it was.

Some while later the pair, with smiles on their faces, lay back amongst the pillows with the lassitude of lovers, loose limbed and happily spent but with a shocking thirst. Blythe picked up a little bell that Billy and she had agreed she would use whenever she needed him for anything. Covering them both modestly with the sheets, she rang the bell and waited for the pounding of Billy's bare feet as he raced to her bidding. It wasn't long before he was hammering on the locked door, and with a curse, Ambrose had to get up and unbolt it. "Wait a moment," he called out, as he sprang back under the sheets. Billy waited to the count of four, then breezed in, "You rang, Ma'am?" stifling his laughter as he spoke.

"Yes, Billy, we would like some hot mint tea please, flavoured with a little honey."

"Cummin' right up, Missus. You look as hif you need to get yer strength back!" He nipped out of the door laughing, as Ambrose picked up his boot and flung it at his retreating back, and missed.

Later on, after Billy had delivered their tea, with much innuendo and grins, the pair sat up in bed to discuss what they would like to do with their new lives, sipping at the delicious tea as they did so.

"Well, my lady, first things first. When do you wish to be married?"

"As soon as possible," replied Blythe.

"Good. Onto the next point. We now are co-owners to an unnamed vessel. What should we call her?"

Blythe thought for a moment, and said, "I don't know. I think that as you will be her Captain, you should name her. I leave it to you."

Ambrose looked into Blythe's twinkling eyes, and said, "It's got to be *Sea Witch* after you, my darling. You belong to the sea, and you are my little witch, and have totally bewitched me with your charms!"

Her eyes lighting with mischief, she clapped her hands saying delightedly, "Oh, I love it, that's just right—The *Sea Witch* it is then! What is worrying me however, is, that much as I wish to return to King's Lynn to see my father, I am loath to go if that dreadful Matthew Hopkins still resides in town, because he would sniff me out in no time. We wouldn't be able to be married there either, for the same reasons."

Matthew thought for a while, and said, "I know what we can do. We can dock at Yarmouth instead, then travel to my parent's home at Barsham and get married there in our own chapel, which is set in the grounds. We can send word to your father, and hopefully Barnaby and any of your close friends will be able to journey along for the service and celebrations. My mother will be so pleased to see you and if Father is sober, he will too, no doubt."

Blythe agreed, it all sounded an excellent idea. "In the meantime, what shall we do in Constantinople?" asked Blythe.

"Well, first, I want to find out if there are any reports on The *Evening Star*. I don't know if she perished in the storm; if she remained afloat, she would have limped into port for repairs, and no doubt some searches will have been made for us, though I don't expect anyone will believe that we survived. If she is in port, then I will need to make the repairs, fill up the hold with silk fabrics for your father and of course, whatever happens, we sell some of the jewels and purchase cargo for the *Sea Witch*. It will be the beginning of our own empire—you do realise that, don't you, my sweet one?"

Blythe nodded her head. Life seemed so full of promise now. She had gone through grave dangers and rough waters and come out now in clear sunshine. She felt deliriously happy, stretched like a cat, smiled at her beloved and curled up on the sheets, promptly falling into a deep slumber. Ambrose, after gazing at her with eyes full of love, carefully left the bed, dressed and went out into the bright sunlight with ultra-blue skies above, to attend to his duties and his destination ahead.

Blythe woke slowly and lay on her back, eyes still closed, satiated and happy, in a dreamy state of half-wake. She became aware of soft fur held over her hands and wondered sleepily how the bear had got in the cabin. She could feel the paddy paws of the great creature; soft and gentle over her own hands. She didn't feel in the slightest bit frightened, as it seemed a very natural feeling. She somehow felt protected and soothed. Then, she felt the bear's head take the place of her own. How strange! She felt the huge teeth in her mouth and wondered how she could possibly have changed into a bear. Sleepily, she knew it wasn't possible, but had to bite down onto the large teeth to see if they really were in her mouth. They weren't, thank goodness! The feeling of the bear gently drifted away, leaving Blythe feeling safe and protected as if she had the ghost of a bear as her friend. But, she 'knew' the bear wasn't a ghost. It had been real enough. What had it been trying to tell her?

She woke properly and sat up and stretched. The bear was still with her in her mind. Surely it wasn't one of Matthew Hopkins's 'familiars' that the man kept accusing people of owning? Her senses told her that the bear was indeed a protector from the World of Spirit, one that she could call on for help at any time, so in a way Hopkins may be correct and she did have a 'familiar' but one that had nothing to do with devils or evil. *How marvellous!* she thought to herself. But she didn't want to tell anyone about it, as she didn't think they would believe her.

Still drowsy from love and sleep, she pulled on her breeches and began to get clothed. She was nearly finished when she heard the cry of "Land ho!" from the crow's nest. Not bothering to tie up her hair, she raced out of the door and over to the rails to search for signs of land, and there, in the distance, she could see the Ottoman Empire with its protective battlemented wall stretching around it as far as the eye could see. Constantinople. At last. She couldn't wait to land.

She waved at Ambrose at the helm and he waved back. All the crew were busy now, reefing sails, doing all the tasks necessary, as they readied their craft to sail into the harbour. Before long, Blythe could make out many buildings huddled together and could see foothills behind the town stretching in the far distance to mountains. Lifting her nose, she could even smell strange exotic aromas on the breeze and felt stirrings of excitement at the adventure ahead. She could make out the shapes of people, looking like swarming ants from the distance and couldn't wait to be ashore to mingle with mixed races and explore. Many ships were anchored in the bay, rising up and down with the swell of the water. She saw some galleons, tall ships such as schooners, barques and brigs, smaller pinnace, pinques and also craft she didn't recognise that were probably local, all jostling for position in the busy harbour.

As they neared the port, many small craft containing dark-skinned, shouting men in turbans and loincloths, with fruits piled high to sell, rowed around their ship, grinning, gesticulating and occasionally spitting into the water. The crew had to gesture for them to keep clear lest they might crush them.

Blythe could see that the dockside was teeming with colour. Then she could see men, donkeys, strange humped animals—that Ambrose informed her were called camels—men with copious bundles or baskets piled high on their heads, weaving their way between the crowds. Many ships were docked, each swarming with men loading or unloading and the nearer their own ship progressed to the docks, the stronger became the odorous yet spicy aromas of Constantinople. The sky above was brilliant blue and the hot sun beat down constantly. Blythe could barely contain her excitement. Everything looked so exotic and totally different from what she had known in her home town of King's Lynn. Ambrose beckoned her over.

"Go and put on your jerkin and your boots. Tie back your hair and pull your hat well down over your face. Make yourself as manly as possible—though that's going to be difficult the way you look right now!" Ambrose smiled and kissed a tendril of her hair, and smiling her love, she turned around and padded to their cabin, doing as her man had said. She understood why she should continue with her disguise. The dock was chock-full with really tough looking men, most with knives stuck in their belts or boots and all appeared quite dangerous. She didn't want to go amongst them as a woman—that would have been madness.

Once Blythe was ready—her own knife sheathed inside one of her boots— and had re-emerged on deck, she found that the Grand Vizier was already standing at the prow, waiting to disembark once the ship had docked. He was eager to get back and report to the Sultan, but first he beckoned Blythe over to him.

"I've already told you how grateful I am to you, but I want to emphasise how much I am indebted to you. Here is my address. If you need any help, whatever it is, please come to me. I also have written instructions here," he pointed to some words in his language, "for you to obtain any assistance, no matter what. Those who read it will bow to your command."

Blythe hugged the man and gave his wrinkled cheek a kiss. "Well, we didn't do anything out of the ordinary, other than dig you out of the sand. We certainly couldn't have left you there!"

"That's as maybe. By the way, I have spoken to your Ambrose about this, for not all of the crew will want to stay with you. I have already had words with the men, and about half of them still wish to serve you. The others have homes here and don't wish to sail far from their families. Once you have landed, there will be plenty of fellows looking for work—some might be from your shores—but care should be taken with your choices. Difficult, I know, when there is a language barrier, but always watch men's eyes, and note their hands."

Blythe nodded. "Yes, I know about hands. I have always been drawn to them, for they can denote a good or bad character. My beloved Goody Truman taught me how to read palms and told me that if all else failed, I could earn my living by telling people their fortunes! However, now the witch finders are roaming England, they would proclaim that anyone reading hands was a witch—so I suppose that is something I shouldn't do anymore!"

The Grand Vizier smiled and took Blythe's hands in his. "Well, it is different here, as are many things. I do hope you enjoy your time in my country. Before you leave, I would like you to come and take tea with me in my house, and if you would like the names and locations of any merchants, please let me know."

Blythe smiled her thanks but their conversation was interrupted by a bump as the ship gently hit the side of the quay. They both clutched onto the rails to save themselves from falling, realising that they had indeed touched land. One of the crew leapt down and grabbed the mooring rope, cast it around a post, while the other crew members hurried at Ambrose's direction, until the ship was tied fast and they were ready to land.

Blythe couldn't wait to run down the gangplank with Juno at her heels. Billy was holding on to Juno's collar, with a smiling Ambrose at the rear, assisting a very dignified Grand Vizier down the slope. Blythe waited for them all to assemble, while the Grand Vizier told them that he required a palanquin to take him to his home. They accompanied him through the dockside crowds that teemed with men from many countries. Blythe saw yellow men with slanting eyes and single waist-long pigtails snaking down their backs, who bore canes across their shoulders from which dangled baskets filled to the brim. There were beggars in rags holding out alms bowls, lepers tolling small bells, hoping for charity, men from Africa with ebony skin, even an Indian playing a flute while a snake uncoiled itself from its basket and swayed to the music. There were stalls bearing spices whose aromas made Blythe sneeze, rubbish underfoot and flies buzzing at every pile. Asses toiled, as did some camels, all laden high while their handlers lashed them to move them along faster. Bleating goats scavenged at rubbish and thin cats with slitty eyes stared from high places, waiting to pounce on birds or rodents—there was so much colour and confusion dazzling Blythe's eyes as she tried to take in all the extraordinary new sights and sounds.

When they had squeezed through the jostling crowds away from the dockside, the Grand Vizier managed to catch the attention of some bearers waiting with a palanquin—whose eyes widened when they recognised their renowned passenger. Blythe was astonished to see the two men prostrate themselves on the floor in humble supplication while Ambrose helped the Vizier into the padded box, covered and made attractive with coloured fabrics. Blythe bent in to kiss his cheek, and told him they would visit him soon. They waved as the litter was born through the crowded streets towards his home.

Blythe was completely overawed at all the seething bustle and hive of activity, noticing the lack of women on the streets and was thankful for the Vizier's advice to continue with her disguise. She found the bright colours, the smells, the multitude of stalls and foreign, glittering eyed people overwhelming. Everything that caught her eye was alien yet so exciting to her. She kept one arm locked into Ambrose's on one side and Billy's on the other. She was glad that Ambrose and Billy had visited here before, for they knew the area and which direction to take, and Ambrose was even greeted by some who recognised him.

Juno was causing a stir as she walked calmly beside them. It seemed that a hound of her size had not been seen before and she seemed a source of amazement to many of the seamen, porters, stall vendors and onlookers, making them cautious and stand back away from them, which Blythe thought was probably a good thing—for many of them looked ferocious to her, with their hawk noses and outlandish turbans. She understood, now she was seeing at first hand, the sailors' descriptions in their evening yarns on board the *Evening Star*.

As they walked along the busy harbour-side, Blythe clutched Ambrose's arm a little tighter. "Look!" she cried, "Isn't that our pennant on the top of that mast over yonder?" Unhooking her arm from Ambrose she left his side to break into a run. Ambrose, clicking his tongue at her impetuosity, chased after her, with Billy skipping alongside. Juno barked and followed in her easy lope, while dark-skinned men with unscrupulous eyes leapt out of her way.

As they came closer, they could see it was indeed the familiar lines of the *Evening Star* that had clearly been undergoing reparation. As they neared the ship, one of the men aboard spied them and called out with amazement, "God's hounds, it's the Capt'n!" The crew stopped their work as Ambrose, Blythe and Billy, followed by Juno, hurried up the gangplank, and much hand-shaking and queries took place, with congratulatory slaps on the back and plenty of laughter and merriment.

It transpired that after the storm, which had apparently died down as suddenly as it had started, there was enough wind to fill the remaining tattered sails and they had managed to limp into port. They had lost four men and the main and mizzen masts, but they had now been replaced, the sails repaired and they were now just about ship-shape and ready to sail home.

Because Ambrose had kept all his papers in good order, it had been comparatively easy for Ambrose's quartermaster, Barnes, to take command. The hold had been emptied and he had negotiated the sale of the contents for good money, with everything neatly documented. Barnes informed Ambrose that silk merchants had been keen to ply their wares, but that he had held back on purchasing anything while the necessary repair work was being attended to on the ship, which was, to Blythe's mind a good thing, for she wished to delve into the area of purchase herself.

Once all their respective adventure tales were exchanged and excitements died down a little, Ambrose deemed it time to accompany Blythe to the various silk merchants, written on Peter's list of instructions, where she was able to choose in vast warehouses, from shelf upon shelf, roll upon roll, of the most luxurious of fabrics for her father. Peter had an eye for good quality, and specified what he wanted, but Blythe was also keeping a keen eye for more glamourous fabrics that she had decided to purchase for wealthy women's tastes, opting for glamour as well as quality. Once the buying spree and payments for

Peter's cargo was accomplished, there were agreements with the vendors to wrap the precious fabrics in waxed linens and then crate them up soundly before delivery to the *Evening Star*. During the course of negotiations, the silk merchants made many low bows, with the palm of their hands to their foreheads—which Ambrose told Blythe was called a salaam—and which she learned to respond to in kind.

After completion, she and Ambrose went to an address given by the Grand Vizier to exchange a few of their jewels for money. This was for their own cargo this time, then Blythe returned to the silk warehouses to purchase the more opulent fabric for her own cargo, after which she scoured the huge covered Grand Bazaar for other items that she thought would sell well in her own country. She loved and purchased carpets that had been woven by desert women, and dyed with the juice of plants—each one with a calculated mistake somewhere in the design, the reason behind this custom being that only Allah could make perfection.

There were many beautiful brass items, such as flagons, table tops, jugs, lamps and incense burners that Blythe purchased, as well as intricately carved bone and ivory objects, especially beautifully fashioned fans that Blythe felt would be extremely popular back home—all so delicate and very beautiful. Ambrose left all the purchases to Blythe, who thoroughly enjoyed the task and became very adept at bargaining with the smiling merchants. Similar arrangements as before were agreed upon for the purchases to be delivered into the holds of the *Sea Witch*. This name had already been painted on the prow, much to Blythe's delight. Ambrose, as a surprise for Blythe, had commissioned a painted carving of a woman with flowing hair, in Blythe's image, to be fixed to the prow of the ship before they sailed.

Neither Ambrose nor Blythe knew what lay in the crates resident in the *Sea Witch's* hold, when it belonged to the pirates. They looked forward to opening them when they eventually reached their warehouses in England, but Blythe had made an exciting discovery on a trip to the hold to see how much space there was for their own goods, and had discovered a crate with crude drawings of flowers on the outside. Searching in the untidy documentation that had been in the Captain's cabin, she found some papers relating to tulips.

"Tulips!" she had breathed to Ambrose, who had been leaning over her shoulder. "But a single bulb sells for a fortune! I wonder if we have a crate full of them? If so, Ambrose, we are going to be very rich indeed, even without all the goods we have just purchased!"

Ambrose smiled at Blythe's enthusiasm. "We shall have to wait and see, my sweet one. They might have perished, or been eaten by rats. Time will tell, but it does seem to be a rich and unexpected haul!"

The holds of both ships were duly battened down and lying quite low in the water. Ambrose and Blythe decided the two ships were now ready to set sail, but first they must go and visit the Grand Vizier at his home. He had explained where his house was located, so together with Billy and Juno, they set out to eventually find the house behind a very ordinary door in a narrow street wall, where they discovered on entry, the most exquisite dwelling that Blythe could ever have imagined.

They were ushered through cool, large rooms with high ceilings, under domed doorways with filigree carvings, stepped upon colourful woven mats that were lain across polished stone floors and noted low furniture of the most exquisite taste. Blythe gasped at rich and sumptuous velvet curtaining draped and hung with silken tasselled cords and felt a little disconcerted by richly dressed servants who bowed from every corner. The building was wrapped around a large central paved area planted with palm trees for shade and with tinkling fountains spraying cooling waters where Koprulu greeted them. Birds in ornate cages that hung from branches sang prettily, while arrogant peacocks wandered, with long dragging tail feathers of the most delightful hues. A mass of colourful blooms were planted in raised stone beds and bright climbers were tied up and along the walls to cascade down in a variety of vivid shades.

They were made extremely welcome, plied with food and drink as well as delicious and delightful pale pink sweetmeats dusted with fine sugar that Blythe thought delicious and wanted to know where she could obtain some for sale in England. Koprulu suggested a merchant supplier from whom she could obtain some.

Blythe was then presented with a wedding gift of a most wonderful outfit suitable for, as the Grand Vizier said with a twinkle in his eyes, the most favourite of all the Sultan's concubines! Blythe peeped in the package and saw diaphanous silks sewn with beads and tiny mirrors, noticed anklets of bells and a headdress of fluttering colourful silks. Ambrose would enjoy seeing her wearing all these in private! She thanked the Vizier prettily, and promised him that when they next came to port, they would visit him again.

After the visit, they walked back through the massive covered Grand Bazaar for the last time, Blythe was still totally stimulated by the colourful mass of diverse people and many, many goods for sale, until eventually they arrived to the lesser chaos of the docks where, amongst the other many vessels bobbing on the water, they could see a ship making its way through the vast throng to find mooring.

"That fluyt looks just like the *Morning Star*," said Blythe, eyes huge, to Ambrose. "Do you think it could be?"

"It certainly does look like it." Ambrose retorted, screwing his eyes against the bright sunlight to see clearer. "How wonderful! Let's get down and see. Do you think your brother might be on board?"

"Oh, I hadn't thought of that!" cried Blythe in excitement. "Oh, I do hope so!"

It was Juno who made the first connection. She had spied Jupiter on board the oncoming vessel and began to bark her recognition. Jupiter heard her and rushed to the side of the ship, and barked back with his tail lashing with excitement. Barnaby leapt from the prow to grab hold of the hound's collar, and Ambrose had that strange feeling of Deja vu, as he saw the tall figure of his lady's twin, taller, but so similar, wearing a tricorn hat, just like Blythe's.

Blythe whipped the tricorn off her head and waved it in the air to gain Barnaby's attention, and she could see the bewilderment on his face at first, which soon broke into delighted smiles as he recognised her. Taking off his own hat, he waved it back at her, while the two dogs had to be forcefully restrained as they seemed intent on jumping in the turquoise briny to swim to each other.

Blythe also recognised the figure of her friend Simon, busy shouting directions to their crew, but when Barnaby called him over and pointed towards Blythe, he could not at first locate her, so carefully scrutinised the crowd on the dock, until he pinpointed Blythe excitedly waving her hat. Simon vigorously returned salutations, his wide grin displaying his happiness at seeing Blythe safe and well on the quayside.

Eventually the gangplank was down and the twins were happily reunited, while the excited dogs sniffed each other, wagging tails and standing on their back legs, front paws scrabbling each other's, causing them to tower over many of the men busy on the dockside. A few made the sign of the cross over their chests, thinking the dogs were some kind of evil entities, but most just grinned, taking in the happy scene.

Barnaby caught Blythe up and swung her round in a circle. He had grown so tall since she had last seen him—he was well above her height now, and his shoulders had broadened tremendously. Blythe could see her brother's muscles rippling under his tanned skin, showing his strength. Simon had similarly changed, and the two young men made fine specimens as they stood, legs apart, their sea legs still with them as they tried out their unsteady balance.

Ambrose drew the party away to a place under an olive tree where they could be seated and drink some herbal tea in the welcome shade. The dogs had by now calmed down, but lay together, sides touching, so glad to be reunited. Blythe excitedly told Barnaby about all their adventures, every now and again asking Barnaby what had happened to him, and eventually told her brother that she and Ambrose were going to get married as soon as they landed on British soil. She told him of their plans, and Barnaby agreed to let their father know, and journey with him to Ambrose's family seat.

"You know Blythe, you are quite right, you mustn't go back to King's Lynn while Hopkins is still there. He has had hanged Arabella, Dimity and the two women as a coven of witches, and has had notices pasted all over the town, with details of you. He has put a large price on your head—as he has on both Simon's and mine too."

"When I returned from France, I crept back home under the blanket of darkness to visit father. That terrible woman had poisoned him and he nearly died, but he's recovered now, thank the Lord. Father gave me captaincy of the *Morning Star*, and asked me to seek out any word of you. I didn't expect to sail into harbour and immediately see you standing there! But isn't it wonderful? Apart from searching for you, I'm to fill the holds of the *Morning Star* with fabrics for Father—I presume you have already filled the *Evening Star*?"

Blythe nodded, and getting a word in edgeways, said, "And, guess what—Ambrose and I have a ship of our own now—we stole it from pirates and claimed ownership—it's that one over there," as she pointed out her craft, "and we have filled it with all sorts of wonderful treasures, which should bring us a fortune! And," she continued, almost all in one breath, "we think we have a crate of tulip bulbs in the hold, that was already there when we took the ship over. They should bring us a king's ransom!"

Barnaby whistled, and noticing a very quiet Billy, who was shuffling his feet forlornly in the dust, asked, "Who's this young man?" Billy looked up, and

Blythe, instantly remorseful for not including Billy in the conversation, said, "why, this is my best friend and helpmate in the whole world, Billy Whoever!"

Billy, who had been feeling very neglected and had been wondering what was going to happen to him now, grinned at Barnaby, feeling the same tug of love as he did with Blythe, for the man he was looking at was so like her. He pulled his forelock as a sign of respect and said, "I all'us wondered if I 'ad anuvver name, and now I knows what it is! Pleased ter meet yer, sir."

***

The following days were spent eating, drinking, exchanging adventure stories as well as purchasing goods for the *Morning Star*, until the holds of all three ships were full to overflowing, all roped down, and decks swabbed and clean. New crew was appointed to replace those who had left the *Sea Witch*, with a few English-speaking men interchanged with crew on the other crafts. Blythe had had a say in the choosing of the crew, and felt they would be good men.

There had been a few discussions upon which ship they were going to sail homeward bound. Blythe wanted to be on the *Sea Witch* as she was already very attached to it, but Ambrose said his duty was to be on the *Evening Star*, and as his betrothed, he would like her to sail with him. Blythe agreed she wanted to be with him too. Barnaby remained on the *Morning Star* while Simon, inordinately proud, was assigned to captain the *Sea Witch*. The two dogs would not be parted, so they stayed with their mistress.

Blythe was feeling inordinately joyful. So much had happened since she fled from the Witch Finder General to escape onto her father's ship—she'd experienced more adventures than she thought possible. The man she had seen in a dream when she was a girl had asked her to marry him and actually agreed that he would take her with him on his journeying in future when she was his wife. And she would be his wife very soon. Blythe let out a happy sigh

All they had to do now was to wait for the tide.

Find out what happens next to Blythe in

The Slink of Unease
Sequel to *The Prowl of Unrest*

CPSIA information can be obtained
at www.ICGtesting.com
Printed in the USA
BVHW052119210323
660854BV00007B/108